the SOUL *of* a SEAL

WITHDRAWN FROM COLLECTION

ANNE ELIZABETH

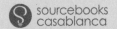

sourcebooks
casablanca

Published by Sourcebooks Casablanca, an imprint of Sourcebooks, Inc.
P.O. Box 4410, Naperville, Illinois 60567-4410
(630) 961-3900
Fax: (630) 961-2168
www.sourcebooks.com

Printed and bound in Canada.
MBP 10 9 8 7 6 5 4 3 2 1

Chapter 1

BEING THE MAN BEHIND THE OP WAS TOUGHER THAN taking point.

In two situation rooms—one in Coronado, California, and the other in Washington, DC—all eyes were glued to their screens, watching as U.S. Navy SEALs tracked their targets. The hostiles were Number Two and Number Three of a recently identified terrorist cell. Less than sixteen hours ago, the Team had captured the head of the cell, and no one needed the runners-up picking up the fight where their leader had left off.

Christ! Navy SEAL Captain Bennett Oscar Sheraton, nicknamed Boss, tensed as the men on the screen moved. *Holding a gun was better than sitting in a chair and watching the action unfold on a fucking monitor.*

Four SEALS, loaded down with weapons and packs, moved through the thick brush. As they penetrated deeper into the forest, the small helmet cams relayed images back to the brass who were avidly watching this mission unfold in real time. Two of the operators held high-power rifles and two held 9 mm SIG Sauers. Their camos were matted to their bodies, and in the intense jungle heat, their heavily toned muscles dripped perspiration.

The faint rustle of branches moving in the breeze and the men's breathing were the only sounds. Even the wildlife had gone silent and the SEALs communicated strictly by hand gestures. As they inched forward, lush foliage, sodden from a recent downpour, dripped water onto their heads and wet the barrels of their weapons.

Snap!

The action was almost too fast to see. A tripped booby trap, probably placed along the trail by the local drug lord, sprang from the underbrush.

One of the SEALs was pinned, his body pierced like a frog to the body of a tree trunk by a sharpened stick. The tail of it was back-cut and stuffed with something foul-smelling.

The range of facial expressions on the wounded SEAL's face was intense, but he never uttered a word.

Silently, one of his Teammates released the rope that held a thin stick in place and sliced the stick in half with his knife. He removed the protrusions and lowered the injured man to the ground while the other two stood on alert. Shots of morphine and antibiotics were administered into the upper thigh. Luckily, the stick had only pierced a small amount of muscle on the far side of the quad, missing vital arteries. Antiseptic was liberally poured and pressure bandages applied to both sides. The leg was braced with splints and wraps, and then the warrior was pulled onto his feet.

The wounded SEAL tested his leg, grimaced, but found it sturdy enough. He nodded at his Teammates and moved into formation to take up the hunt again.

Dark clouds above them threatened to dump yet another deluge on the already overly soaked region. A rising wind blew debris against their faces, dislodging hair from their sweat-soaked heads. The SEAL on point sniffed to the north and then gestured.

The Team had the scent.

In the distance, smoke from an unsecured campfire was visible. Good news for the SEALS; bad news for the sloppy terrorists.

The warriors melted into the forest, spreading out in a fan pattern to encircle their quarry. Slowly and steadily, they moved. There would usually be more of them—at least six—but there hadn't been time to replenish their ranks. Two of the Teammates had been wounded at a previous location and been medevacked out. From the desert region of Libya to the jungles of South America, this SEAL Team had been on the move tracking these terrorists for far too long to let go now. They would see the mission through to its conclusion.

It wasn't luck that had brought them to this place or onto their current path; rather, it was Sheraton's leads. He was the man in charge of Intel at home, and he'd directed this Team to this moment in time. The men were good with that. They'd all worked with him before on other missions and knew he was solid when it came to his facts.

The SEALs were prepared, moving as one, as silently as deer. They appeared from the foliage and stood at the edge of the clearing, watching as the two hostiles shared their last meal in front of the fire.

With guns at the ready, the SEALs fired, and the targets were eliminated with multiple shots to their heads and hearts. It was over in a second: a burst of noise and then a hush.

The forest was like that, a witness to the extremes of predatory violence and sudden harmony. Perhaps all life was like that, but Americans had grown used to subtle shades of gray.

The SEALs took fingerprints, blood, and pictures to confirm identities, and then wrapped and hoisted the bodies to bring them back to civilization. These operators performed their tasks quickly and avoided the locals to reach the extraction point for a safe exit. The helo arrived and lifted the four SEALs with their packages into the air.

The entire room in Coronado sighed with relief. The Team was on their way home. The main screen went dark as the small square in the lower right-hand corner enlarged.

The Commander-in-Chief spoke quickly. "Well done." The President was surrounded by his Chief of Staff, Secretary of State, Secretary of the Navy, and his entire war-room staff of advisers. It was an intimidating group. "I look forward to the full report."

The screen went black, and the lights sprang on in the secure room at Special Warfare Command in Coronado.

Sheraton resisted the urge to rub his eyes against the glaring light. He had sat quietly during the Op. Bennett was the one who would have taken the heat if the Op had gone sideways.

To his left was two-star Admiral Buck Worthington, the highest rank in the room and the Admiral in charge of Special Warfare Command in Coronado, and on the other side of him, the Commanding Officer of SEAL Team SEVEN, Captain Richard Chen. These SEAL operators were his. Albeit in private, Chen would be acknowledging these warriors and their success would be listed on their permanent records. The public would be unaware of the men's pain and sacrifices. The selfless warrior did not require an accolade; rather, survival and success were the greatest gifts of all.

Bennett watched Admiral Worthington's support staff move around the room, gathering papers and filing them. This Op had so many different components. It had been a difficult process, and he was sure of his facts, having spent the past two months wading through emails and an extensive communication trail at Cyber Command. He had translated and retranslated these and additional documents, following the entire cell until the Team eliminated the leader and now the two subordinate terrorists. Bennett had been certain they could nail this mission, and he was relieved to wrap it up.

Seeing two SEALs wounded while capturing the leader and another hurt while acquiring the Number Two and Three guys had caused him physical pain. His brethren would be okay, but all of them had long recoveries ahead of them. He was responsible for that in the same way he was responsible for the ultimate securing of the mission. It was enough to give him an ulcer.

Rotations in Intel were tricky. As a SEAL, he could be called upon to rotate into countless roles, and this one was *not* a favorite. He'd rather have put his own life in the line of fire than send others into action. In his mind, it would be a valiant death, if it were his—and the worst outcome, if he had caused someone else's.

"Sheraton, bravo zulu," said Worthington as he stood and shook Bennett's hand. The Admiral was eager to celebrate and always appreciated opportunities to score a win on the Spec Op's success list.

"Thank you, Admiral." Bennett was pleased to be on the receiving end of a positive response.

"I'm having a few souls to my place, if you'd like to attend."

This wasn't an invitation. It was a request that bordered on an order. Bennett would be an idiot to turn it down. Honestly, though, he needed a breather and didn't feel like celebrating. He started a new rotation as an instructor tomorrow, and he craved a night off. "Another time, Admiral?"

"Yes, of course." Worthington nodded at him, and the rest of the men in the room followed him out.

The one exception to the mass exodus was the beaming Captain Chen, who crossed the room to Bennett and leaned on the table. "You're an idiot, Bennett. You know that, right?"

Bennett chuckled and then shrugged. "Yeah, I know, Richard. I just…need to catch my breath." What else could he say? That he was going to lose his mind if he didn't get a little R & R? The stress was searing his gut, and he needed a cold beer and to not think for a few hours. Being a SEAL could swallow you whole if you didn't open the hatches and get some fresh air now and then. His mind and body needed time.

"I get it. Really, I do. You've been eating, sleeping, and dreaming this mission for months as you put the puzzle together. I get it. Seriously, I've been there. But, if you want to advance to the prime assignments, you need to play the game. Spending a few hours getting to know the brass does that. Trust me. I'm saying this as a friend." Chen stood and rubbed his hands together. "Now, game face on. I'm off to play my role." At the door, he paused. "Whatever you're up to tonight, Sheraton, make it count."

Bennett watched Chen leave, knowing in his gut that he'd made the right move personally, though professionally it probably would tank him. He wasn't politically minded enough to sit around hand-hamming a situation to get a promotion. Either he would rise on the merit of his performance and dedication or not at all. Honestly, he trusted his gut above anything else and knew when to dial out to preserve his sanity. This was one of those times.

He gathered his notes, shoved them in the shredder, hit the Power button, and then headed out of the room. He walked down to the Navy Exchange, or NEX, bought a six-pack of Longboard beer, and headed for the beach. He longed to strip the clothes from his body and feel the warm water on his skin and the sand between his toes. He'd been on the shelf too long; being out of combat was like an extremely slow death by paper cuts.

He loosened his collar and popped a bottle cap, drawing the cold beer into his mouth and feeling it rush down his throat. He took a few more sips, watching the sunset as he stretched out on the sand and communed with the elements. "This is relaxation," he murmured. *Yes, this is exactly what I need to recharge my battery.*

Closing his eyes, he savored the fresh air. The sand tickled the back of his neck as his mind drifted.

Buzz. Buzz. His phone vibrated.

Bennett groaned and jerked awake. *Damn, I fell asleep.*

He rubbed his hands over his face and then reached for his drink. The beer was warm. *Yuck.* He thrust it aside. Five-and-a-half bottles of discarded beer—what a sacrilege!

Bennett sat up. He knew he couldn't spend the whole night ignoring the world, as much as he wanted to. He was an operational SEAL and he was still on call. Sitting

on the beach, staring at the sky like some teenage boy—
he had to own up and end this mini break.

Bennett rolled to his feet. When he checked his
phone, his eyes widened.

Crap! I missed a call from an Admiral. Damn it!

Before he could return the message, his cell phone
sprang to life again. He answered quickly and succinctly. No one dillydallied when Command was ringing
through. "Sheraton."

"Been having a good night." This was a statement
of annoyance. SEALs were meant to be reachable 24-7
when they were on active duty. The only time they could
take off was official leave time, and sometimes they
could get away with what they affectionately called a
UNO Dear—Unless Otherwise Directed, I'm going to go
do X, Y, Z. But, they still had to be reachable. Admiral
Ouster's tone was tense, and his comment on the fact that
Bennett should have answered his phone only empha-
sized that. What could he say? Subtext: it happened.

"Yes, Admiral Ouster. What can I do for you?"

"How long would it take you to meet me at my
office?" The Admiral's tone was curt.

*Huh, it has to be a priority, if I'm being tapped this
late at night.*

Bennett was already moving in the direction of the
Amphibious Base. He could hop the fence at a high-
speed run and be there in less than ten minutes. "Less
than fifteen." It was better to be early than to keep
brass waiting. Maybe it was the fact that Bennett had
started his career as an enlisted man and made his way
to officer that he stayed on his toes and responded with
extra hustle.

Being a captain was not a small thing in the Navy, but the duty could be somewhat limited, depending on what was available, especially for someone who was going to be up for a new rank in a few months. He hoped that whatever this phone call was about…it would be interesting and could change his current duty assignment.

"See you then." The phone went dead.

Bennett pocketed his device and ran to the far fence. He climbed the barrier, dropped down on the other side, and ran as though he was taking fire. Passing the Coronado Cays, the Silver Strand State Beach, and the Obstacle Course attached to the Amphibious Base, he dashed across the street—from the ocean side to Bay Side—flashed his ID at the gate, and headed straight for Admiral Ouster's office. No one stopped him. They knew him around here, and seeing him come in hot brought everyone to attention.

He checked his watch as he neared the building at a full-out run. He was at his destination in under seven and a half minutes. Not bad. Not great. It would do. When he was a trainee, he could have made the run in five and a half.

Was he getting old? Nah!

The door to the building was ajar, and he closed it securely behind him and took the stairs three at a time. On the main floor, he stopped and showed his ID again. Guards were stationed in this spot 24-7. They studied it and him. Ouster wasn't an ordinary Admiral. He ran special programs for Spec Ops in a way that even Spec War and the Special Operations Command, or SOCOM, couldn't touch. Ouster reported directly to the President and often tackled projects that brought all branches of the military together for missions. Some individuals called him the Pied Piper, because he could charm practically anybody in any situation.

Taking long strides down the hallway, Bennett maintained his pace, but his curiosity was piqued. He had met Ouster several times before, in Officer's Country at required-attendance officer events, but this was his first one-on-one. He knew it meant he was being called for a mission.

At the door, Bennett knocked. The crisp sound echoed around him.

"Enter," barked a voice from the other side.

Bennett let himself in and closed the door behind him. He stood at attention. Though SEALs didn't normally stand on ceremony, this was an unusual circumstance. "Admiral."

"Captain Sheraton, at ease. Take a seat at the table." Ouster gestured with his hand as he searched through a pile of folders. Locating the one he sought, he picked it up and joined Bennett at the large marble table. The chair, one of those old leather ones that had an indentation from overuse, protested as he sat. "The reason I called you over here was we recently had two failures on a priority project. We're at a crucial juncture, one where errors are no longer an option; too much is at stake." He handed Bennett a piece of paper and a thick manila folder. The label simply said "WS." "I'd like you to drive out to this location, assess what's going on, and move forward with the required work assignment."

Bennett accepted the piece of paper and the folder and scanned them. "I know this place, the Lester Facility." His eyes widened as he read the notes inside the folder.

"Space?" He hid his excitement. This assignment beat teaching or working on the new base and organizing vehicles or staff. Not only was traveling to space on his bucket list, it was one of the reasons he'd wanted to be a SEAL in the first place.

It was no secret that part of SEAL training had requirements that crossed over into astronaut training. The Underwater Demolition Team men had been used to test a lot of the equipment and apparatus before those golden-boy astronauts used them. The UDT men had also met many of the capsules that splashed down in the ocean. Water was, of course, a Frogman/SEAL element.

As a hobby, Bennett had studied every bit of Intel he could uncover on the latest space vehicles. Being a private-plane pilot and doing test-pilot runs now and then didn't hurt his résumé either. Bennett was pretty sure these factors had added to the reasons he'd been chosen. Quite frankly, though, he didn't care about the why. He was psyched about the prospect of going into space, but he couldn't stop himself from asking, "Admiral, if I may inquire, why isn't the United States Strategic Command (Stratcom) in charge of this project? Last year, they handpicked forty SEALs for their program and forty soldiers from other branches. I know, because I asked to be considered for the program."

The Admiral picked up his pen and tapped it briefly on the surface of the table. "I asked the selection committee to skip over you." Ouster's lips thinned. "I need you, Sheraton."

Bennett couldn't keep the shock from registering on his face. The muscle in his jaw tightened as he gritted his teeth to regain control of his emotions. He'd been sabotaged, and now they wanted him.

"I can see your frustration. Hear me out," Ouster said. Holding his free hand in a fist, a "stop" command, the Admiral dropped the pen on the table and laced his fingers. "I know there's limited duty for Captains. Sheraton, you're one of those souls who easily can handle anything, especially assignments that require sacrifice and go beyond ordinary duty. The work you did on the Hydro Annex Op, where the plans for a new type of submersible plane had to be vetted for feasibility and then brought all the way to testing and implementation, proved that my decision was right. The stages you put the Hydro Annex through produced superior results. The maneuvering system for the Hydro—you reconstructed that tech, right? Brilliant! I couldn't afford to let you go. There's only a handful of SEALs like you. We're balancing too many projects right now, and we needed your expertise right here. Now I need outside-the-box thinking. Everything is FUBAR on this space mission."

Bennett was flattered, but there was something the Admiral wasn't sharing. It sat behind that steely gaze. "I reconstructed a few valves and motherboards, but it doesn't make me an engineer," Bennett said.

"You think on your feet, Sheraton. You are one of a handful of senior guys who I can trust with this, and you're my first choice to fix this mess. We have a communications array about to go down, a bunch more knocked out, and space garbage threatening the space station, as well as a new array that needs to be placed in orbit to protect us from an upcoming meteor shower." His lips tightened. "We don't have military vehicles available to us and the government has had to fish in the corporate pool to locate a shuttle capable of doing what we need and in the time frame we require. So, you're walking into a situation that's a mix of civilian and military."

"Understood." Bennett gave the superior officer a brief nod. "What's the other problem?"

"You're astute," Admiral Ouster continued grimly. "This current mission…has some rather delicate problems, namely murder of our personnel and sabotage. We lost two SEALs, and we want you to investigate, but unfortunately that needs to be a secondary purpose, as there's the pressing priority of the safety of the planet. The Secretary of the Navy has requested I send two SEALs to complete a mission that will take one of you into space. You see, SECNAV has invited six countries that are sending us their best to help fix the current issues and then help us launch, deploy, and reposition certain hardware. I cannot overstress the importance of this mission on both a national-security level, as well as a planetary one. You'll be there to find information on the Warren Shuttle. This is a new space vehicle, so you will be expected to get up to speed quickly. There's a lot at stake here."

Bennett pursed his lips. He considered his words carefully. "Who do you suspect are the hostiles?"

Ouster's hands scrubbed over his scalp. "Tough to tell. The groups at the Lester Facility are from many of our top rivals. If Joe Public knew we were collaborating on programming, software, technology such as lasers, etc., well, there would be hell to pay. The Russians and the Chinese are blaming extremist groups in the USA, while the Middle East coalition is blaming the United Kingdom and the rest of the Eastern bloc. The South American and African blocs are the only ones not fighting. Sheraton, there's a lot on the line. Our technology is proprietary, and we have to play to our lowest common denominator of information. Everything from world peace to national economies is at stake. Worldwide, all nations have signed the Outer Space Treaty, which agrees on the peaceful use of space, and the Secure World Foundation is attempting to hold everyone to their word, but the latest threats have everyone on edge."

"And the threat is…" Bennett knew he should just open the file and read through it quickly. He had a photographic memory and could absorb data very quickly.

"It's twofold. The first threat is getting the mission in gear and the shuttle into space, and the second is the debris. I'm sure you'll remember the articles about Donald Kessler and the associated Kessler Syndrome, which highlight the dangers of litter, a debris field, in low orbit around the Earth. Can you believe space junk could wipe out not only our early-detection systems, but also communication arrays, GPS systems, and do immeasurable damage to the Space Station and everything we have out there?" Admiral Ouster stretched his arms over his head and then placed his hands in his lap. He took a slow, deep breath. "You're going to be independent of Command on this. You'll need to act quickly and effectively, and you are being given full authority to do so."

It was a lot to take in. Space…and lasers too. Fascinating. "Who's the other SEAL?"

"I'm sending Jonah Melo. With his engineering

background and the work he did over at NASA a few years back, he'll be an asset. I have his file…"

Bennett waved it off. "I know him. Didn't he just get married?" Sending that particular SEAL seemed unusual as newly married sailors were often distracted. His Sea Daddy, Gich, called it the "moonstruck effect"—the first time a mate saw his honey's hind end, he was so blinded that he couldn't get enough of it until the shine wore off. That was usually sometime around the birth of their first baby or a year or so after back-to-back deployments.

"Melo assures me that his being married isn't a problem."

"Understood." Bennett noticed a notation at the bottom of one of the pages. "Admiral, I acknowledge that the investigation into the death of the SEALs is secondary, given the circumstances, but what happened to the men who died? What about NCIS?"

Ouster sighed heavily. He shook his head, pain filling his features. "Our men…"

Bennett glanced down. He didn't like the look of the report on the next page of the file. It showed pictures and brief descriptions of the events surrounding the fatalities. There was a lot of information missing, such as primary interviews, and there was no mention of any personal effects, weapons, and phones. The holes were evident and screaming *Investigate me*.

"I'm responsible for their deaths." Ouster leaned forward, resting his weight on his elbows. His gaze was steady. "I handpicked those young men, both engineers. I hate to think they were…perhaps too inexperienced for the job or, what's most likely, that someone got the drop on them. Within two weeks of arriving, they were dead.

We don't know all the details. An investigation with NCIS is on hold until the launch is complete. Sheraton, I need someone capable and seasoned enough to handle this, and that's you. You'll go through accelerated training, testing, and then launch. As a SEAL, you're already seasoned in many of the areas, so I'm sure you'll fly through the requirements. If you find additional data on the reason these men died, contact me—or better yet, handle it. Do I have the right man? Will you accept the mission?"

"Aye, aye, Admiral. Here I am." He could read the subtext. Bennett would do his best to keep things on the down low as much as possible. "Is Melo up to speed?"

"As much as you are, though he's probably already at the Lester Facility. *He* answered my call on the first ring."

Bennett smiled briefly. It was a sign of respect to rib each other in the military. "Well, we can't all be wallflowers, Admiral."

"Your contact, and I mean your point person, is Dr. Kimberly Warren." The Admiral cleared his throat. "I believe you were in one of the classes that did some training there. Not all of them did."

"Yes, I did training there. Test flying and impact studies," said Bennett. "I look forward to seeing what's on the docket for me now."

"Good stuff. Ah, to be young again." Nodding his head briefly, Ouster smiled. He held out his hand for the file. "Have a good trip. Keep in mind Melo's going to give you a run for your money. He has stars on the brain, and he's going to test your mettle."

"I would expect nothing less." Bennett handed over the documents and stood. "When do I leave?"

"Tonight. Now. Is that a problem?" No one ever denied a request from Ouster. Bennett wasn't going to be the first either.

"I'll muster and be on the road within the hour."

The Admiral gave him a curt nod and headed back to his desk. "Sheraton, use Alpha Protocol on this. My eyes and ears only."

"Understood, Admiral." Bennett's eyes tracked the portly man. He wasn't a SEAL, yet he could send any Special Operator anywhere, even to space, on a second's notice. He wondered how this man had made it to where he was today—not that Bennett envied him. Everyone had a different path in life. To be an admiral, it would be a tough row to hoe, but he couldn't stop himself from mulling the role and its responsibilities over in his mind.

"That will be all." Admiral Ouster seated himself behind his desk. He inserted the folder back into the stack, then picked up the whole pile and turned aside.

Bennett didn't see where that pile had gone as he pulled yet another door closed, but he had to assume it was to some kind of safe or vault. Brass didn't go old-school, using paperwork, unless it was off the books. There were usually only a few copies, and burn bags were not far away.

Bennet thanked God his memory was sharp. If he had been out drinking with his Teammates, he would have been well screwed. But he wasn't a kid anymore. At forty, Bennett knew what he loved, and that was being a SEAL. He'd go the full thirty years before he retired, if he could. This was his life—serving his country—and nothing was going to get in the way of that.

He nodded at the guards before he made his way

downstairs. Did people ever wonder what else was in this building? There was no way it held only one office. Sometimes it was better not to look too closely. There were things it was impossible to "un-know," and knowing things you weren't asked to be a part of was a swift way to get the boot out of the Navy.

Commitment. A lot was implied when you signed on the dotted line with the military forces. Duty wasn't just a job; it was a dedication to responsibility, a way of life that consumed everything else until it was one's entire world, and that was fine by him…for now.

Bennett shrugged. He made his way past the Discovery Bridge and down the Strand to his condo in the Coronado Cays. He didn't have time to indulge in idle thinking. Right now, he had a mission to prep for. Getting a move on was at the top of his list. Packing a bag was second. Beating out Melo, well, that was going to take some work.

Patience, perseverance, courage, and fortitude were values his father had instilled in him from birth. Thus far they had served him well, and for this challenge, they would again. A SEAL never quit. With that thought blazing through his brain, he broke into a run, adrenaline pumping through his system as if it would never ease up.

Dr. Kimberly Warren lay on her back on the flat roof of the Lester Facility, located due east of San Diego and north of the Mexican border. Its location wasn't on any publicly accessible map. It was a covert place with high-security clearance and enough guards to rival Area 51 or the Pentagon. Only certain private contractors were allowed access, though the military was often in and out, doing training and testing.

There were four airstrips, with the only camouflage-painted runways in the region. Night-time running lights could be accessed only from within the facility and were used for approved planes only. Enormous amounts of red tape dwelled here.

Honestly, it was sort of a miracle she had ended up here. Her buddy Ouster had arranged it, recommended that she be first in line to have her creation, the Warren Shuttle, developed and built at the facility.

Staring up at the night sky, she fantasized about soaring among the planets in her own shuttle, discovering new galaxies or perhaps just seeing the places she had dreamed of up close and personal. *Moon, what mysteries do you hold? Sun, if I studied you more thoroughly, could I harness your power better?*

The sound of Kimberly's voice broke the eerie night's silence. "Star light, star bright, first star I see tonight. I wish I may, I wish I might, have the wish I wish tonight." The nursery rhyme her mother had taught her still bounced around in her head. What would she wish for? Success. The fulfillment of her lifelong dreams and ambitions. Oh, how she wanted those wishes to come true.

Sirius, a brilliantly shining star, blinked at her, and she knew that it would take over three thousand one hundred forty days for the light to reach her here on Earth. If she were out there among the stars, out by Sirius…what would life hold? Would she be happy? Would the shuttle mission have been a success? Would she still be alone?

Crossing her arms over her chest, she sighed and

lowered her gaze back to Earth. Traveling in space was the sole aim she'd had since she was a little girl, and it had brought her to this moment, when a vehicle of her design was housed in the hanger right below her. Had she ever imagined she would get this far when she'd conceived the idea?

The obstinate side of her personality screamed yes, and the more reserved side said maybe. Regardless of the internal war that ate away her confidence at times, she had done it.

The shuttle would travel to space, perform a number of tasks, and return intact and ready for use again. Hopefully, in a few short weeks, they would be launching it. The big question was…who was going to pilot it?

Her eyes brimmed with tears. She'd thought she would be the one taking the shuttle into space. With a bum ticker that was unfortunately inoperable, she wasn't going anywhere.

She swiped at the tears that flowed freely down her cheeks and stood. Pacing the considerable length of the Lester Facility—ten football fields—would take her a long time. Her phone buzzed. She ignored it. Being up here was the only way to get away from the people inside this building. All of them wanted something from her, and she didn't have any answers for them at the moment.

Lifting her head back to the heavens, she thought about Clarence Leonard "Kelly" Johnson, the Lockheed genius whose designs had been so far ahead of their time. He inspired her. She'd gotten her pilot's license at age twelve and fallen head over heels in love with the Lockheed Model 10 Electra. Kelly's creation of the H tail and experiments with the wind tunnel had motivated her so much that she'd drawn her first plane design that summer. And, when she was working on her graduate degree, she'd been granted access to those actual plane designs, and she'd remember that intense excitement forever.

Now, with so many roadblocks ahead of her, she was losing hope that her greatest dream was not achievable. "Have I wasted my whole life?" she said. "Am I a fool to reach for the stars?"

Her words fell flat. There was no one to answer her.

A computerized voice sounded from her pocket. "Kimberly, warning. Kess is heading for the roof."

A chill raced up her spine. Kimberly ran in the opposite direction of the two roof access doors and headed for the side of the building. Lowering herself over the edge, she jumped down onto the large garbage bin and scrambled to the ground.

She ran around the building and let herself in through the front door of the Lester Facility. Pausing in the white room to be decontaminated, she slipped through another side door and ran down the hall toward her suite of rooms.

A shadow fell across her face. She stopped abruptly, her heart thudding her chest.

"Where do you think you're going?" asked Kess, the man in charge of the shuttle project and the person she'd sold her soul to when she accepted his money to aid in the building of her dream.

"My—my office," she stammered. Her mouth went dry as he loomed over her.

"I think we should have a few words first." The veiled

threat was there, in Kess's stance. He started to reach for her, to grab her arm and stop her from leaving.

The look she gave him was icy and full of determination. With that glance she communicated she'd have his ass in a sling if he so much as touched her.

Kess dropped his arm. His voice pattern slowed. "Another time. Perhaps."

She didn't answer. The statement didn't require her acknowledgment.

"You will need to work closely with me." He appeared to regain his usual arrogance and leaned toward her as if nothing had happened. "I hear we are going to have a few more pilots vying for our shuttle launch. While I'm pleased the government is on board with our project, I don't feel we need anyone else to, uh, get in the line of fire."

She gritted her teeth. "Is that a threat?" As far as she was concerned, she would never choose to be alone with him. For a woman who liked to get along with her coworkers, this was an instance where she didn't give a crap if this jerk knew she didn't like him. She knew instinctively that malice—or, at the very least, indifference—would keep this guy away.

"No. Of course not! It's just that we have skilled people here already. Let's use them." He held both hands open, flat and empty. What was this man attempting to communicate…that he was harmless? *My ass!* He was an enemy, and she knew it as surely as she drew breath. She just couldn't prove it to anyone else yet.

"Too late. The Secretary of the Navy has spoken. We have new arrivals on their way. I expect you to give them their due. Now, if you'll excuse me." She stepped around him, slipped inside her suite, and locked the door behind her.

The look on Kess's face as the door closed was priceless, a combination of frustration and outrage. What was she going to do with him? Whom could she trust?

"Kimberly, are you okay?" The sound of the computer's voice was a comfort to her.

"Yes, Sally," said Kimberly flatly.

Staring at herself in the mirror, she said, "I should have punched Kess in the face. If only it were that easy to solve all the difficulties Kess is creating in my life. Ideally, I'd love to fix his wagon permanently and get him out of here." But that feat, she knew, would take an act of God, or some force with the kind of power necessary to separate him from the project.

Please, she prayed. *Please give me the strength to make that wish come true.*

Chapter 2

IT WAS A NICE ADRENALINE RUSH FOR BENNETT, RACING down a dirt road off Highway 8 at ninety miles an hour on a dark Friday night in his 1969 white Mustang, nicknamed Justice, a cloud of dust in its wake. This back road had been abandoned by the military for years, and once he got past the mountains, he could let Justice have her head even more. He'd restored this baby with his father, before he had passed. The memory of that time together was pretty significant. Being raised by a single father made him bond swiftly with his SEAL brethren, but with women…it took longer.

Before it was Boho-chic to recycle and reuse, times had been tough, but his dad had always made stuff fun and cool. His dad was his hero, and aside from him, the only link Bennett had to humanity was through the Navy.

A flash of light ahead caught his attention, and he slowed the car to a crawl. Turning onto the main road, which was well traveled, and then immediately taking a series of dirt roads…something didn't feel right. He flipped off his headlights on the last dirt road and drove slowly. The moon was bright enough to light his way, and having grown up in this area, he was pretty familiar with the terrain.

A rock pelted his bumper as he turned the corner. Flipping on the lights as he saw the gate and guardhouse, Bennett didn't know what to make of the sight.

A giant gated structure was blocking the old road as though something had plopped it down in the center of the oddest place on Earth. That was definitely new.

The last time he was out here had been right after Hell Week. His class had rotated out for some astronaut training, and he hadn't been back since. He wondered if the Lester Facility had changed.

He slowly engaged the brakes. Giving the guards at the gate his warmest old-buddy smile, Bennett waited for their routine set of questions. As a SEAL, he'd learned never to offer information unless necessary and then to give only the bare minimum. Funny how once you had a Trident, that glory mostly stayed under wraps. He kept the tension out of his body as he covertly watched the other men.

"Can I help you?" A tall guard with a .45 strapped to his hip leaned down.

Four other guards surrounded the car. In their hands were semiautomatics, which seemed a bit dramatic, given that this location was in the middle of nowhere. It was a dead giveaway that something precious was inside.

The tall guard stepped closer to the vehicle, making it impossible to drawn his sidearm if Bennett were a bad guy. "What's your purpose?"

"I have an appointment." Bennett kept his hands in view, though he could have had a 9 mm in his hands in seconds. It was stashed in a holster hidden between the edge of the seat and the back, right behind his hip. It wasn't a common place for a weapon, but it was ideal if he needed it in a pinch.

"Let's see your ID." The guard held out his hand. Now, that was something Bennett could snap off. The man didn't seem like he was on a power trip, but he didn't look competent either. Nobody looked in his trunk or under the car; he could have a bomb strapped underneath, drive inside, and *kaboom*.

Bennett's whole life had been centered on weapons and volatile situations, and it was hard not to be critical. He raised an eyebrow.

Another guard was sitting comfortably with his ass on a stool, and if that dude had to pull his sidearm, his partner was in the line of fire. It was very sloppy, not to mention deadly. Six men to guard a gate, and none of them was really thinking about lines, angles, or firing safely.

He sighed.

"A little late for a visit, don't you think?" The guard was stalling.

Bennett located at least four cameras, and then he saw two red dots reflected in his windshield. He moved slightly to the side so that the snipers didn't have a clean shot. "I can come back in the morning," he offered.

The sound of a phone ringing reached his ears. The guy in the guardhouse answered as the main gate sprang to life, opening smoothly and quickly.

"Guess that won't be necessary, Mr...."

Bennett didn't give his name. Instead, he put his Mustang in gear and went through the gate. Seeing the expression on the guard's face was priceless. Not that he enjoyed being a dick, but that guy was clueless. Sometimes that happened with private security.

Of course, the camera system seemed to work. Judging from the swift response, their cameras had gotten a good lock on his face and run his ID. But damn, those snipers were slow. He'd recommend that those guys take up optimal sniper positions for a wider field of vision and cleaner line of fire. Tree cover would provide blinds for them and give them better positioning. Where they were now, they gave themselves away to anyone who had training in antiterrorism.

"Guess there are always improvements to be made in offense and defense," he muttered to himself.

The road changed from dirt to blacktop almost instantly. The trees thinned out.

He eased off the accelerator to get the lay of the land. Even in the dark, he could make out several vehicles and guards tucked behind outcrops of rocks and stationed in blinds within the trees. It seemed, for lack of a better word, amateur.

Going through a second set of gates where he was heavily scrutinized made him feel better.

Inside this second fence was a different story. These folks appeared well trained *and* on high alert. It took him longer to find the guards; some of them were snipers in ghillie suits.

The Mustang ran over bumps in the road, definitely triggering alarms, and there were three tire-piercing apparatuses spaced through the road. As he drove through a bottleneck suitable only for one vehicle at a time, he decided the narrowing of the road was very clever. Whoever had put in the road had created a maze of defensive measures. The question was...did the precautions take place before or after the death of his fellow SEALs?

His gut tightened. He hated thinking of that, brothers dying without answers. He would get to the bottom of the mystery and complete the mission. No way was he going to die trying. He was more of a Yoda than a Skywalker—he "did" rather than "tried."

Finally the road opened to a parking lot. A spot was lit and his name flashed briefly over it.

Things had definitely changed at the Lester Facility and on the grounds since the last time he was here. What else waited for him inside that place?

Bennett pulled his car in, put the stick in Neutral, set the brake, and got out of the vehicle. He could feel at least ten eyes on him. Crazy red lights were lighting up the ground, guiding him into the facility. He rolled his eyes. This seemed unnecessary.

A voice beckoned to him. "Mr. Sheraton. Please enter through this door."

Walking toward the light was pretty uneventful. He stepped inside and the smell of a sterile, hospital-like facility assaulted his nose.

A tall, thin woman wearing a white jumpsuit pointed at a room. "You need to step through there before you can head inside directly. There's a locker, if you need to store a firearm. They aren't allowed in the Lester Facility itself."

Bennett considered telling her that he wasn't carrying one. Over the years, he had worn some serious tech and enjoyed having it to blow away the targets, but in the USA he was overcautious about an everyday carry. Command insisted that SEALs be careful. A sidearm in his hands—or any SEAL's, actually—meant someone was going to die. No one got out of training without being a dead shot, and as everyone knew, in death (unlike in life) there were no second chances. So he preferred to challenge himself with other ways to provide protection or deal with a situation. It gave him a bit of a Jason Bourne feeling sometimes.

That's what he got for being a movie buff. When he was off duty, he rarely slept a whole night through, so he watched a *lot* of late-night television.

He entered the room and waited. It was a white room that appeared clean, empty, and quite uninteresting. Something sprayed at him, and he immediately moved away from the mist.

"Please hold still, Mr. Sheraton. The fine-mist atomizer is simply killing any microbes that might be tagging along for the ride. It will feel like water, and there aren't any long-lasting effects." The voice was that of the woman who had greeted him. She sounded impatient. The flat tone wasn't doing anything for him either. Maybe she should hum a few bars of "When the Saints Go Marching In." That song always stuck in his brain once he started thinking about it.

Effects, huh? Not that you're aware of yet. How do you think they came up with Agent Orange? Originally, it was developed as a delousing solution. Let's hope this stuff doesn't do what that horrific stuff did. Taking his former position, Bennett stood still while a bright white light scrolled over his form from head to toe and a mist bathed him. There was no odor, and it seemed innocuous, but if he were an enemy, he supposed they could put knockout gas in here to slow someone down or stop them completely.

The light and spray stopped abruptly, and an automatic door opened.

He stepped through.

Waiting on the other side of the door were Jonah

Melo and a rather pissed-off-looking tall woman with jet-black hair and very pale skin. She was wearing the ugliest-looking lab coat. "You're late," she said. "Let's get going." She took off down the hall at a quick clip, her long legs making her coat swish as she moved.

His nostrils flared. He recognized the scent. Was she wearing lavender?

Bennett cut a glance at his Teammate. He raised an eyebrow as if to say, *So, what's the info on this lady?*

Melo shrugged in return. The tip of his thumb touched his forehead, which translated into watch and see.

Bennett nodded and then cleared his throat. "So, you're *Miss* Warren."

"That's Dr. Warren, gentlemen. I know you're signaling to each other back there, so you can cut it out." Her tone was crisp and no-nonsense.

He liked that; it reminded him of a schoolmarm—a hot one. Brainy. Beautiful. And ballsy. Dr. Warren was going to be a tough cookie to get Intel from. Since Melo was married, it was up to him to be…stealthy. Unfortunately, she was also the type of woman he longed to fall for, but not on this mission and not with murders to solve on top of a race to space. The goal was to solve the mystery and save the day. "My apology, Dr. Warren. We meant no disrespect. We're honored to be here."

Melo stifled his smile and rubbed one finger on top of another, shaming Bennett for his thoughts, as if the man could read his mind. Maybe he could.

"Space has been a lifetime interest of mine." said Bennett. "I'm…excited for this opportunity." He was backpedaling, trying too hard to make a good impression. Oh, well, humility was good for the soul.

"Excited. I'll bet." She smiled slightly, just the corners of her mouth turning upward, as she pointed them
in a new direction. Her stride was long and her pace
sped up, and Bennett had to lengthen his stride to keep
up. Usually, he was the one having to wait for people to
keep up with him.

It took twenty minutes to reach the room she sought.
Dr. Warren leaned down, holding her ID over a black
glass rectangle. A red light scanned her ID, and the
door opened. When it closed behind them, she said,
"Everything requires a key card. It logs in every individual and tracks their movements throughout the Lester
Facility. There are several places that are off-limits."

"That's not going to work for us. We need access to
everything," Melo said flatly. "If there's an emergency,
we need to be able to get in wherever it's necessary."

Her lips thinned. "I thought you'd say that. The other
men, Wallace and James, said that. I'm sorry for your
loss, gentlemen."

Nobody said anything for several seconds.

Bennett broke the silence. He nodded to the folders on her desk with their names on them. "Are those
our IDs?"

"Yes." She walked around the desk and sat down
in an ergonomic chair. It was one of those ball-like
contraptions that were supposed to be good for your
back. Seemed like a lot of work just to sit down, in
Bennett's opinion. "Let me just replace your IDs
with a full-access version. I had both made, in case
it came up."

"You like to be prepared, don't you?" asked Bennett
as he watched her chop the two cards in a small desktop

⟨ shredder. It was always strange to see your face cut into tiny, unidentifiable pieces.

"Of course, don't you?" she asked defensively. She placed the new IDs inside the folders and handed them to the men. "Can I have your phones?"

The men looked at each other.

Finally, Melo asked, "May we ask why?"

She pulled her phone—a large, sparkly purple iPhone—from her pocket and pointed to a round metal disk on the outside. "This device keeps your calls private and allows me to send you data without worry that it's being transmitted outside of the Lester Facility. When you leave for the day, the proprietary information disappears, then reappears when you return. Everyone inside this building is required to have one. It allows us to track who is accessing which files, and it can be used like a walkie-talkie in a pinch."

Leaning forward, Bennett asked softly, "You keep saying 'we,' and I'd like to know who that represents."

"Phones first." She held out her hand. Obviously, Dr. Warren was a woman who demanded to have things her way and got it. Were they going to butt heads?

The men exchanged a silent conversation before giving her their phones. She snapped the circular magnets into place. An icon appeared on their screens. With the tip of her index finger, she tapped each icon and said, "Access on. Access on."

A voice issued from the phone, "Yes, Dr. Warren. Access granted."

"Please give them full and complete use of all files, except my personal ones." Dr. Warren handed back the phones. "Thank you, gentlemen." She tapped a button on her desk. "Now even Sally cannot hear us. I'm sure Ouster briefed you on your mission. We need a pilot for the Warren Shuttle. Both of you are in the running for this position, though there are eight other men on this base vying for the role. Given the advance training you've had, we can slot you in anywhere. If it weren't for that, neither of you would have even been considered as candidates, nor would you be standing here right now."

She laced her fingers together and stared over the bridge they formed, looking first at Melo and then at Bennett. "When you break through the atmosphere and reach the designated altitude, you will be asked to deploy a new communications satellite, which will be a global hub for all countries in our space agreement. If developing nations reach the stage that they too would like to join us, they will be given the codes to access it." Dropping her hands to the desk, she looked down briefly and said, "The next part of the mission will be to continue upward until you reach geostationary orbit, where you will deploy a laser array. You will fire the array to eliminate the bulk of space-garbage debris that has collected around the planet."

Shaking her head, Kimberly's lips thinned briefly. "The tragedies that you haven't read about in the news involve astronauts in private vehicles that had inadequate navigation systems and onboard radars that slammed into this mess, creating more issues. This is a loss of life that didn't need to happen." She took a deep breath and exhaled slowly. "When the laser is finished clearing away—rather, blasting away—the debris, you will then turn the system outward to deal with any incoming threats. Our biggest issue is developing an effective locking system. We don't want another power gaining control of the array. Everyone is working madly on the locking-system issue right now, as well as a few technical bugs between our hardware and software. Like most software and hardware designers, the two technical specialists would rather not work together. In this instance, we are breaking tradition and doing just that. So, differences aside, let's fix this stuff."

Melo leaned forward. "The dangers are…"

"Meteors, comets, space junk, the unknown, or any issue that could arise. We need pilots who can think on their feet. This mission might be a one-way flight." The sadness in her eyes was real. She hated that idea.

"Can the shuttle return? Is it capable?" Bennett studied her face and body, watching for any telltale signs of lying.

"Yes!" She lifted her phone and pushed a button that sent a load of information to him and Melo.

Bennett stared at his device for a second or two, watching the data fly across the screen. At first glance, the shuttle looked impressive. There were personnel files, Lester Facility layouts, and best of all, tons of data on the weather, launch specifics, and the space shuttle itself. He pocketed the phone and studied her, this lady whose hair was as tightly wound as her personality. Did she ever let her hair down, or loosen up? He needed to break the tension, put her at ease. How else was she going to trust him? He was going to need her help; she undoubtedly had the inside scoop.

She raised both of her eyebrows in his direction. "Question, Mr. Sheraton?"

"Bennett," he replied. "That's my name. I prefer it, Dr. Warren, for my close friends and working buddies, and this informality will be especially useful if Melo and I are going to keep a low profile."

"I'm Jonah, but I prefer my last name, Melo. Just don't call me Mellow Yellow," said his Teammate. "In case you want to add that to your information bank too."

"Right." She made a derisive noise. "I *do* prefer formality, but I will attempt to accommodate your request. For the record, I *don't* mix pleasure with business or make friends in the workplace. But for the success of this mission, I will attempt to relax the formality and call you by the names you prefer." She cleared her throat. "Bennett. Melo."

"Wow," said Melo, staring at his phone. "This data stream is awesome."

Two bodies collided as they attempted to look over Melo's shoulder.

Hands still clutching each other, Dr. Warren and Bennett Sheraton locked gazes.

Her mouth dropped open. She made a choking noise before she regained her composure and pulled away. Her cheeks flamed red as she cleared her throat.

Bennett felt a rush of heat as well from their skin-to-skin contact. He scratched the tip of his nose, hiding his expression. The unexpected chemistry caught him off guard. "Sorry, Doctor."

She waved her hand between them. "No problem. Um, where was I?"

"You were going to tell us who the royal *we* was," reminded Melo, breaking the tension in the room, which had suddenly increased.

"Yes, right." She stood up and ignored Bennett as she scooted past without touching him again and walked to her bookcase. "Sally, please adjust the air temperature—lower by two degrees." She pushed on the corner with a flat palm, and the bookcase opened like a revolving door, as if sourced from Mel Brooks's *Young Frankenstein*. Bennett was on his feet, psyched to follow her. He loved that movie. Gene Wilder was a riot! The humor was golden.

The room he entered was filled with banks of computers, a main desk and operating console, and one chair. This was obviously the sanctuary of one person who had a fondness for beige and gold.

Dr. Warren gestured to the computer banks. "I had these rooms modified to accommodate all of my equipment and needs when I moved in here. I like the additional security: you have to access my room to speak with this gorgeous creature. This…is Sally. She's the brains behind most of our systems here, and parts were copied for the main computer elements and placed in the shuttle, a computer system we call Sully." She smiled broadly; evidently she was very proud of her creation. "I've spent the last five years perfecting the operating systems, and I've recently synced Sally and Sully to help me monitor the shuttle more closely."

"Interesting." Melo studied the console. He put his fingers on the keyboard, and it shocked him. Rubbing the abused digits together, he eased the snaps of pain.

"Now, now, Jonah. Oh, right, Melo," said Dr. Warren. "Aren't you married? Don't you ask a lady for her permission before you lay hands on her keys?" She looked directly at Bennett. "It's just good manners."

Bennett laughed at the pointed barb. This lady had a sense of humor. Good, it was going to make working with her significantly better. "Touché. Dr. Warren, how about a tour of the Lester Facility? It's been a while since I was here."

"Right. I read about your Basic Underwater Demolition/SEAL training here in the early days of the Lester Facility's development. I'm sure things have changed a lot since then."

Another point for the doc—she did her research. Of course, he wasn't *that* old.

Melo joined in the conversation. "My class didn't stop here. We went straight to physical conditioning, combat diving, and then land warfare. They were pushing the limits on the phases during my time. We were a really small class."

"Of course." She turned quickly and almost fell into Bennett. "You're, uh, you're standing too close." Her nostrils flared as she breathed in quickly. Her hands were braced on his chest. He almost reached out and touched the tender skin of her hand, but thought better of it. Working relationship. Right, that's what he needed to focus on.

"Just getting a bird's-eye view," Bennett said, staring into her hazel eyes with glints of chocolate and green. He pointed at the computer, just over her shoulder. It was a small room; this was a valid point. He really was attempting to get a better visual, and he hadn't planned the action.

"Ohhh, I see. As long as you behave yourself, Captain."

He gave her his best military salute. "Aye, aye, ma'am."

She couldn't hide her amusement. Her arms crossed over her chest, which vibrated with a few contained chuckles, and then she rubbed an invisible spot between her breasts until he could make out the outline of a small, circular pendant under the button-up lab coat. Her face was flushed as she said, "Work, Captain. Let's get to it."

Had she been a stutterer when she was younger? He found that sort of adorable, if she had been. His best friend in grade school had stuttered, and Bennett had bloodied the nose of the bully who teased him. A wave of protectiveness washed over him.

Crap, he told himself, *don't get soft on her. She's part of the job. It's a mission. Focus is imperative.* "Lead the way, Dr. Warren."

Seriousness took over, and he took a step back and gestured with his hand. He'd have to keep his distance from her. "After you, ma'am."

—◦◦◦—

Kimberly slipped back into her room to freshen up before they went on a tour. She shook off the feeling that she had met Bennett Sheraton before. Something about his manner, his demeanor, was familiar, and it tugged at her. She hated feeling as if she knew someone but didn't know why.

She washed her hands and splashed water on her face. After patting her face with a towel and drying her hands, she was ready to take on the world again.

Her phone beeped. It was another text from Kess. Her stomach clenched.

Why did she hate Kess so much? Mainly because he was an ass whose presence on the shuttle project had usurped her power and position. He had demoted her to the role of "creator and technical adviser." Kess was also a condescending jerk who wanted to get way too friendly with her.

She ignored the message and tucked the phone back into her pocket.

Kess couldn't change one fact: the U.S. Government had made her the point person in charge of choosing the best pilot for the mission. One of these guys, Melo or Bennett, had better fit the bill. Kimberly was going to put these SEALs through their paces and figure out the best one to pilot her shuttle. Sure, it was a short timeline, but these were special circumstances, ones that these two Americans could fill with ingenuity and, she hoped, brains.

Bennett, such a tall one, smiled at her. It annoyed her that he was handsome *and* engaging.

She rejoined them, resuming her role as hostess. She knew she could be an amazing tour guide. Facts and history were things with which she was very comfortable. It was emotions she shied away from.

"Dr. Warren, can you brief us on the individuals directly involved in the shuttle project? People with hands-on access." Melo was eager to see it; his face was lit with enthusiasm.

"Of course. First we have the hull designer, that's me. I worked with Victor Chasing on the foam insert that connects the interior frame. We have an enormous list of engineers and hardware designers who created the consoles, but the software adaptation—its framework is a smaller version of the facility computer. We'll go over that." Kimberly noticed a few of the secretaries walking by. Had she noticed they were pretty before these SEALs arrived? Probably not. She watched the men's eyes scan over them. It was hard to tell if this was part of their "protective" behavior or if they were just being extremely male.

Frowning at them, she wondered if perhaps she was biting off more than she could chew. Hadn't that been her usual habit? As she advanced from her bachelor's to her master's to her doctorate, everyone had told her she couldn't do things, and she had notably defied the odds. Her beautiful space shuttle was an innovative design using materials that had never been considered before, and it functioned. So if she applied that logic to her current situation, if these men weren't right, she would spit them out and chew on something new.

"You're lagging behind, gentlemen. We have a lot of work to do. Let's move."

～∿∿～

Dr. Warren chattered on. She was as an animated lecturer. Still, it was hard not to let one's mind drift with all the amazing things they were viewing. Information floated in the air around them, and truthfully, Bennett digested only about half of it.

He had to admit, this place was pretty impressive. It had changed significantly in the decades since he'd been here with his BUD/S class.

The Lester Facility, roughly the size of ten football fields, according to the information on Bennett's phone, was not visible from the air. The foliage folded back to reveal the runway for test flights, and they were able to climb to forty-five thousand feet, avoiding commercial traffic in less than a minute without any ill effects to the pilot or crew.

They walked the entire building as Kimberly not only gave them a tour, but also pointed out what areas required their input. It was no surprise to either of them when she said, "I'd like you both to start work in the morning. The day begins with an 0600 shift. Melo, you can tackle the engineering bugs that keep cropping up between Sully, the shuttle computer, and Sally, the Lester Facility computer. Bennett, I'm afraid I need you to submit to a few tests before I can put you behind the test version of our shuttle controls, unless you'd rather do something more related to your degree in astrophysics."

"I'll fly," stated Bennett, grinning like a Cheshire cat because he was getting the assignment his buddy wanted. In truth, this was his dream job, besides being a SEAL. Pretty cool that he got to do both.

"Wait, I'd like to be considered for the pilot role. I'm better qualified in terms of mechanics and electrics, if there's trouble up there." Melo wasn't going to let the conversation go. He wanted in on the race to space.

"Yes, of course." Dr. Warren shifted her weight from one foot to the other. "Happy to consider it. But first, eliminate the ghosts in the system—the problems and bugs—and then you can take the tests. Agreed, Melo?"

"Hot dog!" shouted Melo as he slapped Bennett on the back. "I'm going to kick your ass, brother. Teammate or not, I'm going to the moon."

"Check the mission statement. We're orbiting." Bennett spoke flatly. He was tired and needed time to review the specs of this place, the shuttle, and...well, her. There had to be information on the good doctor in the computer.

"Fine. Watch out, John Glenn, here I come." Melo whooped quietly and then went back to studying the control panel. His smile was almost as bright as the sun.

Bennett wanted to give Melo crap, but he was stoked, too. What they needed now was a place to settle in. "Is there somewhere we can bunk, work, and eat? I'd like to spend some time going over the information you've provided for us without losing it every time I drive off the lot."

She pursed her lips, considering her options. "Good point. If you're going to get up to speed in time, you should probably stay here as much as possible." They headed toward her office.

She tapped a no-smoking sign next to her office door and a keypad slid out. "This is, uh, my private apartment. I use it occasionally, but the two of you can bunk here, and I'll stay in my office on the couch if I need to be here overnight."

The door pushed back and then pocketed itself into the wall, leaving an adequate doorway. All three of them stepped inside, and the lights turned on.

"Sally, please set the entrance, use, and exit access to Melo's and Sheraton's badges or voices." Dr. Warren spoke clearly as she rushed toward a chair where a discarded skirt, blouse, bra, and panties were draped. She dumped them into a bin and pushed the bin into a standing wardrobe on the far wall.

"Where will you be staying, Kimberly?" asked the computer.

"Uh…in my office." Dr. Warren straightened up, grabbing the lapels of her lab coat.

"We can bunk in there," said Bennett quickly. "No sense kicking you out of your home. Or if there's an empty room, we can make do there. We've slept in worse."

"So true," confirmed Melo. "We would like use of a shower now and then. Sheraton might not mind smelling like hellfire, but I'm not fond of his stench."

"If you're sure…"

Bennett placed his hand on her arm. "We are."

She stared at his hand.

He could feel the heat rising from her fair skin. A strange urge to learn the texture overwhelmed him suddenly. Was it as soft as it looked? She was younger than he was, maybe by ten years, and she was brilliant. Could she be a prodigy, have tons of education and experience, and be running this place at her age? Guess so.

It was obvious her mind was going in ten directions at once. She wasn't easy to read.

"Point the way." He gestured and caught her staring at him.

Her eyes were locked with his. Oddly, it felt as if she was looking into that quiet, secret space where no one entered. Not his soul necessarily, just the dark spot he kept hidden from the world.

She nodded. "Yes, of course. There's an empty room on the other side of this one. I'd meant to use it for a library. I helped design this wing of Lester Facility, but I never got around to bringing all my books in." She paused as if contemplating what they might need. "Uh, there's furniture, though."

Walking to the far side of the room, she pushed a red button and a door opened. The light illuminated the large space. There were two old-fashioned "shrink" couches covered in worn brown leather with bald patches in places, and two wall-sized white bulletin boards that stretched from floor to ceiling. The rest of the wall space had empty bookshelves waiting for some attention and a large table with chairs.

Her hand lifted, and she pointed to the two red buttons. "The one on the left goes out to the hallway, and the one on the right goes to my—um, the bathroom. Sally, reset Melo and Sheraton for the library. I'm going to stay in my apartment."

"Yes, Kimberly," said the female computerized voice.

"Uh, I'm going to let you both get settled. I have some work to do." She paused at the doorway. "There are extra toothbrushes, toothpaste, shampoo, et cetera in the closet next to the sink. I have an extra stock of pretty much anything you can imagine. I...I d-don't get out much." She blushed, her cheeks brightening to a pretty pink, and then she turned and left. The door slid into place, closing behind her.

"I feel like I need to watch *2001: A Space Odyssey* and brush up on the best way to handle Hal. If I remember correctly, the answer was to pull the plug," said Melo as he punched buttons on his phone. "I already feel like neither computer likes me. They keep asking me why I need access to every file on their systems," he grumbled.

"We don't have feelings," replied Sally. The sound of her computerized voice coming out of the blue like that was pretty eerie.

"Please don't listen to our conversation. Tune out until I ask you a direct question. Confirm command," Melo stated flatly.

"As you wish," said Sally. "Good night, gentlemen."

There was a popping sound, which must have meant she'd logged off.

"Damn Hal look-alikes. Space: that's where I want to be. Not grounded with this crap." Melo sat down on the couch closest to the door. "Give me your keys and I'll get your bag."

Bennett was already at the door. "Let me get yours. You might piss the computer off so much that she won't let you back in."

Melo tossed his keys into the air.

Catching them with one hand, Bennett said, "You still driving the truck?"

"Yep. In the parking lot next to the door." Melo stretched out on the couch. "Not bad. Beats sitting on an anthill in the bushes, or dangling from a rope." He closed his eyes. "If I'm asleep when you get back, don't wake me. Being married is tiring. I need at least two hours before I can make sense of any of those schematics."

Bennett grinned. Working with Melo was going to be interesting. The man was built like a tank and had the personality of a teddy bear. What would his Teammate think of his habit of internalizing the crap out of everything except the mission? In that respect, he was too verbal for most folks. His personal life, of which there was none, was always off-limits to others. Though he might make an exception for Kimberly Warren.

Man, that thought caught him unaware for the second time.

As he turned the corner, he smacked right into her as if he had conjured her, sending her heading for the floor. He wasn't a small guy. At six feet and 180 pounds, he was all muscle and could have been a decent wide receiver for any NFL team, even in his early forties. He ran every day, worked out, and had serious stamina for whatever task was at hand.

His hand caught hers, and with one tug he had her safely in his arms. He cradled her against him. He murmured in her ear, "Sorry about that." His first instinct was to be polite and distant, but this contact brought a wave of protectiveness with it that made him even more uncomfortable. He needed to keep his perspective. "I always seem to be apologizing to you."

"Must be something about me," she murmured against his chest. Her body changed from pliant to stiff almost instantly. They were locked together for several seconds.

"Guess so."

Realizing that she had to be at least five foot ten was kind of nice. It meant he wouldn't have to bend down when he kissed her. Shit, there went his libido. He *was* attracted to her. Now he was going to have to be careful he didn't compromise the mission.

Bennett righted her, and his hands dropped away from her gorgeous form. "Dr. Warren…"

Kimberly looked up at him. Her hands settled on her hips. Frowning, she said, "Captain, it was me. I wasn't watching where I was going. I needed to consult with you anyway."

"You were…looking for me…"

"I…I have files for you." The way she was groping for words meant he definitely had an effect on her. At least they were both in the same boat. Besides, his gut told him that she was an ally, wanting to get the shuttle off the ground and to find out who had killed the SEALs.

She pushed several files into his hands. "If you'll excuse me." She stepped around him, making a wide arc. Before she rounded the next corner, she stole a glance at him and blushed.

He smiled at her. Damn, he couldn't remember the last time he'd been so drawn to a woman. The scent of lavender still filled his senses, and a hint of something else. Not rosewater. What was it, jasmine? Mmm, intoxicating.

Yes, Dr. Kimberly Warren was intriguing…and he wanted to know what happened when she let her guard—and all that thick, inky black hair—down completely. He tucked the files under his arm and forced his mind away from her alluring qualities and back to work.

Chapter 3

A SOFT LIGHT GREW SUBTLY BRIGHTER UNTIL HER ROOM was fully lit. The sound of chimes brought her the rest of the way out of her slumber. Her computer, Sally, had a pleasant way of rousing her, and it brought a smile to her lips.

Kimberly Warren practically hopped out of bed, ready to start her day at the early hour of 0500. If she were a singer or a person who hummed, she'd have been doing that too. Was it strange that Captain Sheraton was the source of this odd delight? His fingers brushing her skin had sent electricity zipping up her arm. She wondered what would happen if he touched something else.

Heat flooded her cheeks. There was something *unique* about that man. She had instantly felt like she could trust him, and her need to know him better could definitely become a serious distraction. Yes, she had read his file, but she wanted to know more…intimate details. His full story had to be interesting. He had just turned forty with no kids, no wife, and no significant other—not even a dog. Could someone live without attachments?

She supposed she had…though she did have Sally, and all of her inventions. Those counted, didn't they?

If she could have a pet, she would. Animals were an impractical luxury at the Lester Facility; even she could admit that Sally was half pet and half friend. Artificial intelligence could be an enormous comfort, and it was a lifesaver. She'd be pretty lonely without it.

At twenty-nine, thirty years old in a month and half, she'd almost reached one of her greatest life goals: space. With her thumb and forefinger, Kimberly pulled the plastic guard from her teeth and plopped it into the glass of cleaning solution on her nightstand.

Temporomandibular Joint Dysfunction—TMJ—was sooo sexy! They say being a teeth grinder was a "thinking person's malady." If only turning her brain off could be so simple, maybe her joint wouldn't act like a sliding hinge linking her skull and jawbone, causing random pain and clicking. Her dentist told her to meditate. She preferred beating the crap out of a punching bag in the Lester Facility's gym.

Taking several tissues into her hand, she gently dabbed at the night-cream residue clinging to her face. She repeated the action several times before reaching for the astringent.

Graduating high school at eleven and then completing her bachelor's in electrical engineering and dual master's degrees in mechanical engineering and astrophysics by the age of twenty didn't win her many friends. But it did earn her significant grant money and a plethora of jobs. Since she was a little girl, she'd known that her heart was in the stars. Her earliest memories were of her mother, showing her the heavens through a telescope. Traveling around the world with her and listening to the lectures her mother delivered filled the brightest part of her mind and soul. When her mother abruptly passed away at a young age, Kimberly began her race to space.

Nothing would ever get in the way of her quest, not even her attraction to Sheraton. For the past decade, her life had been devoted to the cause, and she had a very strong feeling that with Sheraton on board, they would finally reach their goal.

When she opened the door to the bathroom, a cloud of hot air blasted her in the face. When her vision cleared, her jaw dropped. The man she had been obsessing over all night was standing in front of her, toweling off.

His back was to her, and from her vantage point, he not only had amazing muscles through his shoulders, arms, and back, but he also had a *great* backside. Firm, bitable, rounded cheeks with two dimples above them, as though she could squeeze tight and...

"Dr. Warren?" His voice was a baritone, and the timbre hit spots inside of her that longed to have him whispering in her ear. He cleared his throat.

Her eyes lifted to his. She had no words as a flush that began in her toes rose to the top of her head. If she were to walk four feet to the mirror and look, she knew she would see herself as red as a cherry tomato. "Uh...s-s-sorry..." she finally said. *What a time to stutter!* Rubbing her hands together, she walked to the glass-enclosed shower, opened the door, turned on the water, and then took off her silk teddy and matching silk panties. It was time to be bold.

Glancing over her shoulder, it was her turn to smile. His jaw was practically on the floor.

"Can you hand me my loofah?" She turned toward him and pointed to the shelf next to the sink. "The fluffy pink one."

He nodded his head, but it was several seconds before

he turned and complied with her request. As he closed the distance between, she congratulated herself on being courageous…for changing the rules and making the playing field between them level. She'd seen his, and now he'd seen hers. That was out of the way, and they could move forward.

She put out her hand for the loofah, her smile smug and delighted. What she hadn't prepared for…was him pulling her gently, and oh, so tenderly, against him so the heat of his body seared hers, and then kissing her until she was gasping for air as her hands held on to his biceps for dear life.

Time froze and the kiss lasted forever, or maybe it was only several seconds. It was hard to tell, because all thought had fled from her mind. When he urged her against the shower wall and slowly pulled away, she saw his smile—one of such male satisfaction that anger bloomed inside of her.

"That's why they call me…Boss. Well, one of the reasons." He waited, as if he wanted her to respond.

She couldn't believe the idiot was just standing there. Why did he have to speak? Why doesn't the male species know when to leave well enough alone? That kiss had been amazing! If only he'd chosen to be a gentleman, and mute. She sighed as she gave in to her emotion.

"Out!" she said indignantly. *Men!* She'd get him back in less than half an hour, when his first duty of the morning would be regurgitating his breakfast onto his lap.

Oddly enough, she didn't regret the kiss. His tenderness was memorable and surprising. Even in his rush to kiss her, he had been kind, gentle, and sweet. She'd never felt that mellow sensibility in a man. The heat of him was still there, pressed into her skin, and she…honestly wanted more.

But not right now. There was work to do. So she pushed on his stomach to make him leave faster and slammed the shower door as best she could. Shower doors could be woefully anticlimactic! Then she turned the shower on, setting the dial to a much colder temperature than she was used to. It braced her as she rushed through her routine. There was no sense in dawdling when there was work—and in Boss's case, some mischief—to be performed.

—⁓—

Jogging to the hangar had released some of the tension lacing through his body. He was used to a ten-mile run every day, about two hours of lifting, and additional cardio on top of that to keep in shape. Today it felt like he was slacking, even though he was on a mission.

From the open hangar door, Bennett could see the sky was clear: no clouds, which meant no low ceiling for their flying excursion today. When he received a text on his phone to meet Dr. Warren at Hangar C on the far side of the Lester Facility for a test flight, he'd been thrilled. For one thing, he might be able to pilot a new machine. Any day he was in the air—whether it was a hang glider, parachute, jet, or just a regular plane—was a plus in his opinion.

Besides, Dr. Warren was what men would call a "sleeping hottie": quiet in public, with the promise of a fierce, raw beauty in private. Perhaps he was just the man to inspire her, or perhaps she would draw out the secretive side of his soul.

Focusing on the machine in front of him, he admired those lines instead. Bennett examined the contraption before him, visually cataloging all of the possibilities. It wasn't a car and it wasn't a plane, yet it was both. He scratched his chin as he tried to figure out how they were going to get inside.

The smell of fuel was a welcome distraction as he walked around the object of his fascination, wondering if he would get brownie points for figuring out how to make it function. A voice spoke from directly behind him, and he startled.

Man, she is a quiet one! He knew how to shake things up and break the silence. "I noticed that your file was *not* listed in the personnel records," he said. "I definitely need to know this, for security purposes. Are you currently dating anyone?"

"What? Hardly!" Her face flushed with red splotches. Embarrassment looked adorable on her. "Trust me, you couldn't keep up with me, Captain."

He lifted an eyebrow. That statement was definitely a dare. His inquiry was an icebreaker. Did he really want to date her? Yes, he did. His eyes strayed to her figure; the voluptuous hips and rounded backside drew him like sweet succulent red flowers did a hummingbird. She was tempting. "I've got skills, lady, ones you'd never guess."

Two mechanics entered the hangar. He cleared his throat and motioned with his head toward them.

She gave him a half smile in acknowledgment. "Right. So. Um, glad to see you're, uh, on time. I'd like to introduce you to a versatile vehicle I call the CarP," said Kimberly. She pulled a key fob from her pocket and touched the center button. The contraption beeped, and the wings shifted slowly backward, revealing a door on either side. They lifted out and up, like a DeLorean.

"Impressive."

"Wait until you see the inside." She cleared her throat. "Bennett, you need to blend more. Consider what you're wearing—black cargo pants, gray sweater, and a gray polo shirt?" she asked him. "You scream Spec Ops. Bennett, you need to study how to dress like a geek. Otherwise you're going to stick out like a sore thumb around here."

"There are other military personnel on the project. I'm not changing. The less acting I have to do, the better. Right?"

"Fine." Looking up at him, she added, "Don't blend, Mr. Smarty-Pants. But keep in mind that I'm the boss in this vehicle. Got it?"

He pursed his lips and nodded his head. Who was she to say that he wasn't dressed appropriately? Was she a fashion plate? She looked normal to him. Dr. Warren was wearing a long-sleeved North Face T-shirt that clung to her curves as if she were a marble statue on display. Her jeans were fitted, and her hiking boots were worn. She was ready for a day off, not a flight. Shouldn't she be wearing a flight suit or something?

His mind flew through several compromising images. Nuts! What was he thinking?! He was contemplating their clothes lying in a pile on the floor as he made love to her. Maybe it wasn't such a smooth move to have kissed her in the bathroom. There was no way he could have resisted that moment. It was practically perfect. With a body like a model and a mind to rival any of his SEAL brothers, it was hard not to be attracted to her. And it was seriously impossible to ignore the effect she had on him, even for this shot at a ride into space. He'd have to figure out some other way to deal with the attraction. When he left that bathroom this morning, his cock had been so hard, he could have used it as a construction tool.

Melo had made some pretty humorous remarks, too. "Should I get you some nails? I see the crane, where's the load? How about pointing that jackhammer in someone else's direction?" The best one was, "I didn't realize you felt that way about me. I'm married, you prick," and then Melo had laughed until tears streamed down his face.

The worst part had been pulling on clothes and trying to convince his body that it needed to chill out. If he was being truthful, he still had a pretty decent chub-on for Dr. Warren right at this minute. He shifted his feet, though no movement was going to take away this predicament. "Yes, ma'am."

She frowned at him. "You are welcome to address me as Dr. Warren or Kimberly, but never as ma'am, as I'm not yet a hundred years old. Got it?"

He leaned closer to her, knowing that his scent would envelop her. It was his lavender soap, the one he left in the shower, which he personally enjoyed using when he was in town. On an Op, no one wanted to smell like anything but the environment they were in. Safety first! With "boots on the ground" at home, lavender soap was his favorite scent, and it would smell musky on him. Women had told him in the past that it was heavenly. Did she think so, too?

Her nostrils flared, and instead of being offended, he

watched her breathe in the scent slowly and deeply. He smiled. "Yes, Kimberly."

She swayed slightly, and then seemed to catch herself. "To work, Captain Sheraton. If you will take the right side and be my copilot... I assume you read the manual last night."

"No, Kimberly. I did not realize that today was the day we were going to soar in a flying car. Have you crashed much?" He teased her, but there was a part of him that was annoyed she'd tapped him and he wasn't prepared. That wasn't like him. As a SEAL, he arrived early or on time, and like most Boy Scouts, was overly prepared for any eventuality. Crap—he realized there was this "desire" to please her. He actually wanted to impress her.

She ignored the barb.

He sighed as he walked around the vehicle and got inside. He was a pilot and a very quick study. He could make do.

The controls were similar to a small aircraft, with the exception of a row of panels along the top and down the center. As he strapped himself in, he studied them, attempting to figure out what each one was for.

Her hand touched his arm. "Relax. I'll walk you through everything." She placed a fob onto the dash. It stuck like a magnet, and a computer voice asked, "What is your command?"

He recognized the voice. "Is that Sally?"

"Yes, pretty cool, right?" Kimberly didn't wait for an answer. Instead, she gave a command to start the car and to drive in manual mode, and off they went. As they headed out of the hangar, Bennett enjoyed the ride.

They were silent for a long time as she drove down a dirt road going away from the Lester Facility. Finally, he said, "Impressive."

She smiled.

He watched her whole face bloom with joy. It almost took his breath away, or maybe it was just because in that moment the wings extended and the rotary blades sprang to life and blasted them upwards. "You could warn a guy," he said, swallowing his eggs for the second time that morning.

"There's a puke bag under your seat. I will kill you if you get anything on my controls."

He nodded, not trusting himself to speak for a few more seconds. *Note to self: no eggs on launch day*.

A few breaths later and Bennett's digestive issues were gone. Mind over matter was a necessity in the Teams, and one of the first lessons they taught their tadpoles, a.k.a. trainees, during BUD/S.

As Kimberly pointed out the various panels and their uses, Bennett lost himself in his fascination and appreciation of the vehicle. Lifting straight into the clouds using two mini rotary blades, it could act like a helicopter, and the bird's-eye view of the compound was incredible. *Popular Mechanics* had boasted of such fantasy vehicles for years, but nothing came close to this gorgeous machine. The CarP was extraordinary. How the world would change if such a vehicle were in use! It could be driven like a car, lift straight up in the air, or even glide like a plane. The radar system updated constantly, alerting the pilot and copilot to air traffic, birds, and other flying creatures in the vicinity. It also monitored weather conditions and their effect on its many functions.

"Can I fly?" Bennett was eager to test the vehicle.

She glanced sideways at him. "If you can answer these questions, then…yes."

"Shoot," he said eagerly.

"At what angle and altitude will the CarP stall, and how do you recover from it? Can the rotary blades be used in plane/glider mode? That's a yes or no, just to give you a hint. And what would you do if we suddenly lost all our fuel? I need to hear two options for this question." She raised an eyebrow in his direction. "Answer in any order you'd like."

Studying the controls, he answered slowly and carefully. "Given that I haven't read the manual and am answering somewhat blindly, I'll give these questions my best shot. In terms of the fuel, I see an option for a parachute. I noticed it has a safety light and a set of stages to ensure the rotary blades are off or disengaged before a parachute launches, so that would be one choice, and the other option would be to use the automatic descent function. I doubt there's any steering, so my guess is that we would need to be over a fairly flat area to engage it."

"Impressive," said Kimberly. "Next?"

"From the positioning of the blades at the end of the wings, my guess is that they could be used to propel forward, but the significant drag wouldn't get us anywhere quickly, and if the wind hits the vehicle in a downdraft, we'd be pretty screwed. It'd stall and we'd drop quickly." He leaned forward and studied a few gauges. "But I think if we modified a few things, we could make the plane mode more effective. With the engines off, especially if it could be tucked farther away or inside itself, the glider mode would be very effective for silent descents."

"Not bad," she said, putting the vehicle through several maneuvers, including a stall. "Watch me." She flipped a switch that elevated the wings, dipped the nose, and at the same time lifted the tail. The vehicle moved into a glide, giving them ample time to reset the engines and put them back into running mode. "Now, the last question."

"Ninety-degree angle, it'll stall, and you need a forty-five to correct it. Am I right?"

She grinned at him. "Nearly. Yes, most airplanes will stall at ninety, but not this one. Because of its vertical ascent and descent, it stalls when the nose drops below thirty degrees on the horizontal."

"Wow, you need a steady hand for this thing." His fingers itched to hold the yoke. He needed to feel how she'd respond under his touch. The vehicle, he told his libido, not Kimberly. Well, not right now, at least.

"Yes, and how would you recover?"

"First keep the nose steady, and if it drops, try to recover by lifting up. If you stall completely, follow the landing protocols of the parachute or autorotate to the ground." He scratched his head. "That's the flaw... This vehicle can't be steered in any direction with either of those options. Why would you do that? Don't you want to keep it safe? What about the pilots or this multimillion-dollar craft?"

"Billion dollar," she corrected him. "Yes, the steering is the flaw. The reason we're taking this little jaunt is...this vehicle is part of the prototype for the shuttle. We need options to assist it in handling different parts of the mission."

He shook his head. "I wish I understood how this craft and the shuttle are connected, but I'm willing to learn…fast. May I fly her?"

Kimberly laughed. She took her hand off the yoke. "Fine. I give up. She's all yours."

"You like me, don't you?"

"Only your brain," she mocked. "There's something unique in your thinking. You appear to analyze how something works and then figure out how to break down all the steps, following several trains of thought at once. It's cool, though I hate to admit that fact."

Bennett laughed. "I guess I subscribe to the theory of 'chunking it'—that's a SEAL thing, though I also read it in a great children's book by Amber Stewart called *Little by Little*."

"Do you read a lot of kids' books?"

"Only when I babysit. Empowering kids to try new things is important. We take that skill into our adult lives."

She smiled at him. This was a side of him she hadn't seen coming. "I agree." She was definitely going to find a copy of that book. And was that a hint that he liked kids?

As Bennett took the controls, he made sure he followed the same path Kimberly had taken so that he didn't endanger them or the vehicle. A gentle nudge of his fingers caused CarP to respond. "She flies like an angel."

Suddenly, a light flashed bright red.

"What did I do?"

"Nothing. Something's wrong." Small female hands moved quickly in front of him, pulling all the switches down the center and taking control of the yoke. Relinquishing control was not easy for him, but he didn't relish crashing either.

She pulled a battery from the dash and put another in its place. When she attempted to reengage the engine, it wouldn't start. "Sally, please send out coordinates and inform the control tower of our situation. We'll need a ride for both the vehicle and us."

"What's happening?" he asked.

"A signal has been lost between the control and the engine. Everything checked out perfectly this morning when I preflighted the CarP. This shouldn't happen."

"Tracking is on, Kimberly. The communication of a Mayday has been made." Sally's voice was oddly comforting within the confines of the tiny vehicle as Kimberly fought to keep the nose up. Finally, after consulting the topography on the screen below the radar, she touched the auto-rotate sequence.

Her hand left the controls. Her body shook slightly as if her emotions were attempting to escape and her willpower was holding them in.

They both watched as the vehicle slowly descended. Luckily there were not large boulders or mountains below them. When the CarP was safely on the ground, the doors automatically opened.

Bennett got out of his side and walked around to Kimberly's. He crossed his arms over his chest. "This has happened before…hasn't it?"

She nodded her head. Her eyes were filled with tears. "This is CarP II. One of the SEALs was killed in CarP I. It was a similar type of incident, except their auto-rotate didn't work. He was soloing, and he had been up at least twenty times with another instructor. The instructor survived, but he's still in critical care in an induced coma at the Scripps ICU. It's an excellent hospital…" Her mouth quivered. "I just…I couldn't stop it. I couldn't stop it. I stood in the control room watching CarP I plunge downward and crash."

Bennett felt for her. Powerlessness was not a gentle emotion; it often ripped the ego out along with the heart. He took her arm and pulled her out of the vehicle. Gathering her into his arms, he held her while she cried. His hand stroked her hair as her body shook with sobs. This lady cared. About him, and about his brothers. She'd held in her pain for a long time, and she was taking responsibility for their deaths.

As hiccups jerked her body, Kimberly pulled away. She wiped her face on her long-sleeved shirt, leaving little splotches of wetness on the cuffs.

"Flat out, it's sabotage. The engine quit due to something outside of your control. You cannot blame yourself, Kimberly. Turn that emotion into fuel, and help find out who did this." His eyes were locked to hers. He could see the earnestness in them.

"I-I-I have been t-t-trying to find out, Bennett. That's why I called Ouster." She wrapped her arms around herself. Shock was settling in.

"The other SEAL was killed in the Lester Facility, right? I read that in one of Ouster's reports."

"Yes. It's all so horrible." Her arms shook.

He pulled his sweater over his head and wrapped it around her. There was plenty of time before they needed to worry about the nighttime cold weather. Surely someone would arrive by then. "How do you know Ouster?"

"I've known him for years. He was on the board of the college I went to in Boston. Alum, and all that. He made contact when I was a teenager and kept in touch after…sort of like a father figure. His wife and kids are pretty nice, but I still feel awkward around them." She sniffed and then rubbed her nose. "I'm happiest when I'm buried in my work."

"Me too," he admitted. "I get lost…when I'm idle too long."

"Yeah, if only work, fun, and idle time could be combined. Wait, they can be: stay 24–7 at your place of employment." She laughed at the joke. "Yeah, it's tough when that's your reality."

He smiled at her. The sound of her laugh was intoxicating. "Look, about this morning, I'm sorry I took advantage of the moment. I shouldn't have kissed you that way."

Her cheeks flushed red. "Your kiss *was* pretty devastating."

"Is that good or bad?"

She leaned into him. "Let's find out." Standing on her toes, she reached her lips up to his and kissed him. It was her turn to take control and lead them on the path she wanted. Hadn't she told him earlier that she was the boss?

The kiss turned hot and steamy quickly. She pushed him away long enough to pull a survival pack and blankets from the vehicle, then led him to a sheltered spot that would give them some privacy. The land was private, owned by the Lester Facility, but trespassers happened from time to time. Besides, they had hours to wait before anyone would reach them by vehicle. By her calculations, it would be over three hours.

As she dropped the pack and withdrew the blanket, he asked, "Are you sure? I thought you didn't want to mix business and pleasure."

"I refuse to overanalyze. I do too much of that in my present life." Kimberly pulled her long-sleeve shirt over her head and unlaced her hiking boots. She didn't answer him until she stood naked in front of him. "You have a choice. Either we both let off some steam and get back to the business at hand, or we go into everything, knowing that the sexual tension is too thick to actually get any work done."

"Good point," he said, pulling off his own clothes and shoes. "Who am I to argue with the boss?"

Her hands beat at him playfully as they wrestled each other to the ground. They romped and played like a couple of puppies until their bodies reminded them of what they truly wanted…to make love.

Rolling him onto his back, she grabbed the pack, opened a side pocket, and withdrew a small foil packet. Handing the condom to him, she watched him open it and roll the latex over his engorged cock, and then she lifted herself slowly over it and teased the tip before plunging herself onto him, taking away his breath and her own.

Each time his hands reached for her, she pushed them over his head, reminding him that she was in charge. Setting the pace to her own need, she rode him hard and fast until her body took her over the edge, climaxing with sheer, cascading delight.

With her initial appetite satiated, she relaxed. Placing her hands on his chest, she leaned her head down until her eyes were level with his. She studied him. "Is Bennett a family name?"

He chuckled. "Really? I'm sitting here suffering, and you want to know my life story?"

She licked her lips. "Yes."

"Fine. One question and that's it." His breath shuddered as he said, "My mother was a Jane Austen fan, loved *Pride and Prejudice*—that was her favorite book. She died giving birth to me, and my father thought it would be a way to celebrate her and her favorite book. Supposedly she read it to me while I was in the womb. Of course, he added the extra *T* on Bennett for an extra special touch."

"That's sweet." She sat up. "I'm sorry. I didn't know you lost your mom."

"It's okay, I guess. I didn't know her. My father told me about her every day, kept me connected to her. Now he's gone, and it's just me." His arms slowly moved down, seeking hers, hugging her close. "Can we turn the conversation back to us? I'm at the brink, Kimberly."

"Definitely! Your turn."

Birds chirped above them, sending down a shower of leaves from above. She laughed, brushing them away with her fingertips.

He wanted her, was hungry for her. He knew that kind of observation would make him vulnerable, but he was strangely okay with it.

She rocked him to the side, rolling herself underneath him. "I'm one of those equal-opportunity bosses, Boss."

His eyebrows lifted. The evil smile he gave her made her shudder with excitement. Perhaps she had spoken too soon. Bennett looked like a child set loose in a candy store, and he wasn't leaving until every piece was devoured.

Stretching her arms over her head, she wiggled against him. He might be ready to tease the dickens out of her, but she was going into this experience with a good attitude.

"Uh-uh-uh. You're not going to get out of this that easily." He pulled her arms down, kissing the palm of each hand before he laid it on her stomach. Then he flipped her over on her stomach. Leaning over her, he trailed kissed from the nape of her neck all the way down her back. As he worked his way over her glutes and down between her legs, she found herself pushing against him, giving him greater access to her clit. The angle was extraordinary.

It was difficult for her to catch her breath as his arms locked around her thighs, holding her closer, not allowing her to escape the delight of his ministrations. "B-B-Bennett," she stuttered. "Too…too much."

Just as he loosened his hold and began to pull back, her whole body shook with a climax so intense that tears squeezed out of her eyes. Somehow they'd crossed the line between blowing off steam and lovemaking. Emotion shuddered out of her until her body couldn't express any more. She was spent…and in a state of wonder.

He lapped at her bounty and murmured against her skin, "So sweet. So beautiful." His lips brushed tender caresses along her inner thighs as she shuddered one more time.

He picked her up and turned her toward him, kissing the tears away. "Are you okay?"

She nodded her head, attempting to catch her breath again. When she could speak, she leaned forward and whispered against his mouth, "Amazing." She kissed him, tasting herself on his lips. It was sweet and tangy, and it pleased her that the look on his face was so delighted.

Gently, he pulled her closer. He checked to make sure the condom was still intact—it was—and lowered her onto his cock very, very slowly.

Kimberly's body was sensitive and spent, yet as he filled her, her sheath spasmed with utter delight, shocking her. She smiled at him as they rocked together. The pace was leisurely as they stared into each other's eyes.

Watching his passion build, she gave herself over to his pace. Pleasure filled his eyes, dilating his pupils, changing his breathing until his lips were on hers. The connection was immediate and intense.

Her body responded quickly as it raced up that climactic hill.

Together, they plunged off the cliff, shouting out each other's name as they fell to earth, sated and panting.

An eagle screeched above them and settled into the tallest tree to feed its young. Bennett watched it for a long time as he enjoyed the smell of pine and the clean, fresh air. If he'd had his choice between being indoors in air-conditioning or outside, running in the heat, he'd have chosen the latter. Was the good doc the same, or was she a slave to her technology, like most of society? "Do you mind if I ask you for more details? Remember, I need to fill in the blanks when it comes to your file."

"Go for it," she said, settling closer to him. Her body fit his as if they were cut from the same cloth or interlocking pieces of a puzzle. A shiver made her skin ripple with gooseflesh.

He grabbed for his sweater and tucked it around her. "Here, this should keep you warm."

"Thanks," she said, and he didn't need to see her to know she was smiling. She did that…responded to the smallest gestures as if they were monumental. Kind of endearing, he thought.

"Okay. Uh, why aren't *you* going into space?" he asked. "You have the degrees and the know-how, telling everyone how, where, and when to do everything. It just seems logical."

Her body stilled. She was quiet for a long time, and then she pushed away from him and sat up. After pulling the sweater down over her head, she said, "I could tell you it was none of your business, and I know you'd probably let it go, but you should know. I, uh, like you, Bennett."

His fingers stroked hers. "Ditto."

She rolled her eyes. "Women hate it when men say 'ditto.' Be original. Give me a *real* response."

His lips thinned slightly. "Here's a shocker: I don't like talking about my feelings. But if I'm required to share…yes, I like you too. I wouldn't be here, making love to you otherwise. It's always been a dream of mine to go to space, and I don't want to jeopardize it by screwing the boss."

"Well, it's obvious that this is mutual."

"Yes, and unique. I've never met a woman like you. I'm not good at relationships. They never work for me. With you, I guess what I'm saying is…tell me how and I'll learn." His tone became firmer. "Now, I've been honest, and you are deflecting *my* question. Tell me why…why can't you travel to space?"

With a swift nod of her head, she said very quickly, "Here goes. I have a heart condition, and it makes me black out sometimes. There's no pattern to it, and even if I could be a copilot, my chances of a heart attack are almost 95 percent, according to the cardiologist on my case. So no space travels for me. At least not yet, but I'm still hopeful."

"Specifically—"

"It is called hypertrophic cardiomyopathy, a thickening of the wall of the heart. For me, it's the left ventricle. They found it on my routine flight physical and confirmed it during a stress test. Sally took plenty of pictures of it with her scanner, if you need a snapshot. Basically, the condition can impede blood flow, decrease oxygenation, and in some cases causes an irregular rhythm, or even a heart attack. I've had a heart attack. Once. I manage it pretty well now. I take beta-blockers and carry nitroglycerin. Though it means I'm not technically supposed to do half the things I love to do, such as skydiving, piloting a plane, or mountain climbing, I still do it all. That's why the CarP is a light sport plane—you aren't required to have a valid pilot's license for it. She also has an auto-land, when it's not disconnected, because of my heart issue—in case something happens in flight."

"Auto-land or not, what if you and the CarP fell on someone or something?" His brow was furrowed. "Flying with a heart issue is no joke."

"I know. I take it seriously, Bennett. That's why I only fly it on *this* land. No one is here except our group. No harm, no foul." She sighed. "Bennett, don't look at me like that. If I can't be myself, enjoy what I love, what's the point of being alive?" Her frustration was palpable. He understood it. Being a SEAL meant the world to him; without it he'd be pissed off too.

She pushed her hair out of her face. "When I was

tapped for this project to use my new technology on my shuttle design plans, the frame of which I put my heart and soul into, I could hardly believe it. Granted, other engineers have contributed systems and pieces to my baby, but it's still mine. The Lester Facility Manager, Hubbard, has given me a lot of leeway here. Then all these problems happened over and over again, and the roadblocks to success grew. When the SEALs died, my heart had an arrhythmia that forced the doctors to shock me to restore normal rhythm. It…threw me off my game a little, and I started to lose hope. That is, until now."

"What changed?" he asked, pulling her back into his arms.

"You," she said. "When I met you, my instincts… I just knew we could put our heads together and figure this out. I read your file. I know what you did in the water."

"That mission was classified."

"Ouster showed it to me." She leaned forward. "There's something about you that I trust. It's familiar, and I connect to it. Bennett, I know the sabotage is coming from inside the Lester Facility. It's the only possibility. Don't bench me as a partner because I have a medical issue that's being handled. I'm more than my diagnosis. Please…trust me."

He gave her one swift nod. "I do. Where do you want to start?"

"Let's see who had the opportunity and go from there." She smiled at him. "Hey, it couldn't hurt that I read murder mysteries. I'm hooked on Joanne Fluke, Agatha Christie, and Charlaine Harris's books right now."

He chuckled. "Murder? No kidding. So I, uh, should

be gentle with your heart and brutal with your brain, is that what you're telling me? Or you'll take me out?"

"Yep! And if this is your attempt to cajole me and take the stress out of the situation, it's working." She laughed, trying to evade him.

He wasn't going to let her get away that easily. He had no intention of traipsing all over the countryside naked, chasing her because their discussion had escalated to something that could have been redirected or avoided.

She stopped squirming. "I'm a tough cookie when you back me into a corner."

"I believe it," he said. "Let me take another bite and find out more."

"Bennett!" Her eyes were lit with passion and fire, and if they could generate heat, he would have been seared alive. Nothing was going to get him out of this conversation now.

His voice was quiet, but steely. "What makes you think I'd make myself vulnerable to you, if I didn't demand the same? I didn't get as many details on you as you have on me."

That comment took the playfulness out of her. "Fair point. I just…want the regulations to be different. I want to go to space, reach into the heavens and soar, to finally know what it's like up there."

"Why? What are you looking for? It's got to be something other than this mission." His curiosity was getting the better of him, but once the question was out, he couldn't take it back.

"I promised my mother when I was a little girl that I would reach the stars. She was an astrophysicist as well as a geologist. She discovered a planet and once toured all over the world talking about it." She leaned her head against him. "Sounds pretty silly, since she's gone. How would she know?"

He stroked her back. "Because you know. Listen, you might not be going into space, but something you created is. That fulfills your promise, don't you think? A part of you is going."

She looked up at him. "I like that. It's a good way to think about it. Thanks." Her lips brushed against his.

"Wait. A part..." Bennett grabbed her shoulders tightly. "I got it! The chip. You made a new type of smart chip, and that's what the shuttle is using too, so that it can have multifunctionality and problem-solving capability—in other words, it learns."

"Yes," she said, smiling. "This is the reason the military is involved. We need to protect the Intel, and we keep finding programming issues where we never had them before."

His arms dropped to his side. "Damn, that's important tech. Are the hacks into this system software related, or is it the chip's hardware?"

"I'm not sure. Both, I think. The minute we fix one, the other has issues." She threw her hands up. "I had everything working before we brought in the military and the foreign members of the project." She shook her head. "The problem is coming from inside the Lester Facility, and it's up to you and Melo to get the chip issue solved, find the bad guys, and get the shuttle into orbit before the communications array fails."

"That's a tall order."

The sound of birds chirping died away.

From a distance, they heard the rumble of an old

pickup truck. Bennett knew that sound. Spying through the bushes, he saw Melo in his giant old pickup chugging toward them. Bennett hastily donned his clothes, tossing Kimberly hers. She tossed him his sweater.

Brushing the leaves and pine needles from their hair and clothes, they hustled out of the bushes before Melo accidentally drove right by them. The man could get preoccupied at times, especially when he was thinking about his bride.

The truck screeched to a halt, sending a cloud of dirt and dust into the air. Kimberly coughed. Bennett shook his head and waved it away.

"Well, hello there," said Melo as he waved out the window. He had a shit-eating grin on his face as he pushed open the passenger door with his foot. He pointed his finger at Bennett as if he were holding a gun and pulled the trigger.

Thank God Kimberly was behind Bennett and didn't see it. He didn't want Melo's antics to embarrass her.

He held his hand out to Kimberly. She took it, and he helped her into the center of the large front seat and buckled her seat belt into place before throwing her pack into the truck bed and crawling into the cab.

Bennett sighed heavily as he shut the door and secured his own seat belt. Well, here was another incident he'd never live down. Melo was racking up the points, but Bennett was sinking swiftly into no-man's-land, and that was stuff you didn't do on an Op. It dragged you deeper and deeper into the muck of no return.

Chapter 4

THE RIDE BACK TO THE LESTER FACILITY WAS UNEVENTFUL.

Kimberly assembled a group to rescue the CarP II and then settled in to review her messages.

Bennett headed back to his room. He said it was to talk with Sally and attempt to figure out a new plan of attack, but his ulterior motive was to view the video of the crash tests for the shuttle. His instincts told him there were some clues hidden there.

Melo had some tests to take for his chance to race into space. He waved to Bennett as he left. What a joker!

Fortified with a quick shower and a larger-than-normal black coffee, Bennett sat in front of the computer console inside his space, a.k.a. Kimberly's spare room. Utilizing Sally's brain was probably the smartest way to go for now, and this was the most private place in the Lester Facility.

"Sally, bring up the reports on the crash-test history of the Warren Shuttle."

"Affirmative," responded the computer.

The screen filled with the following:

Testing Results from 2013 January–2014 December for Warren Shuttle

1. Rolling Test, Bolling Air Force Base, to assess taxiing capability and stopping power without

crew aboard/unmanned automated test run by computer. Five tests performed on various terrains and in inclement weather. Passed.

2. Crash Test at Langley Landing and Impact Research Facility near Norfolk, Virginia. Tests are conducted without crew/unmanned. See video results. Passed.

3. Test Flights, Keesler Air Force Base, from 2013 June 1–2013 August 15 to gauge lift and land with ten tests in total: Flap Test, Systems Active Test, Lift Test, Control Test, Orbit Test, Glide Capability, Systems Failure Test, Fuel Failure Test, Free Flight Tests, and Landing Test. Crew #1. Passed.

4. Five Free Flight Tests performed at Edwards Air Force Base, Mojave Desert, California, on concrete runway and/or dry lake-bed runway from 2013 September 1–2013 October 30. Passed. See video. For Crew #1 and Crew #2 files and for maximum speeds and duration of flight time, click the access link: <u>Free Flight File Logs</u>.

Using the mouse, Bennett clicked on the highlighted file link and a screen opened: File Access Denied. "Sally, who locked this file?"

"Kess," the computer reported. "Kimberly has been unable to open this file. She has hard copies of the report in the safe to the left of the last computer panel. Since she has granted you full access, I've opened it for you."

"Thanks, Sally. Before I review it, who were the pilots for the ten test flights and the five free flights? That's number three and number four."

"Searching…"

Names rolled across the screen:

Crew #1

    Kess, Joseph—Pilot
    Pelsin, Yuri—Pilot

Crew #2

    Walker, Turner—Pilot
    Biggs, Max—Pilot

"Can you locate Walker and Biggs for me?" Bennett had a sinking feeling in his gut as he asked the question.

"Unable." Sally stuttered and then spoke very slowly, as though it was fighting through a wall of commands.

Bennett hunched over the screen. "Why?"

"Deceased on 2013 November 20. Deaths occurred in an automobile accident en route to Lester Facility."

"Sally, how many people associated with this project have died or been hospitalized?" Bennett knew he didn't want the answers to these questions, but he had to know what he was getting into here.

"Six are deceased and eight have been hospitalized and have left the program. It is within acceptable parameters for a newly designed craft."

"Did Kimberly tell you this?" He didn't want to suspect her. There was a possibility she was involved in some kind of cover-up. Fooling around with her didn't take her off his list of suspects, did it?

"Kess set the 'acceptable' parameters. Kimberly has attempted to investigate and alter them several times without success."

A wave of relief swept through him. He liked the sexy doc a lot. Thinking of Kimberly made him feel protective... of her and this project. But Kess... He was another story.

"How long has Kess been a part of this project?"

"Un-un-un-unable to..."

"Sally, let me reframe the question. What role does Kess perform in the shuttle project?" His lips pursed as he examined the screen, waiting for an answer.

The screen went blank.

"Sally?"

A happy yellow emoticon filled the screen. The computer voice came from his pocket.

He pulled out his phone. A digital face, presumably Sally's, looked solemnly at him. "You've triggered a safety protocol that Dr. Kimberly Warren has placed in effect for the following information. Please confirm your identity."

Speaking slowly, Bennett gave his full name: "Captain Bennett Sheraton."

"Voice and visual identification are confirmed. Accessing information..."

Video Playing...
Kimberly's eyes sparkle with mirth. She smiles as she shuffles papers, and then her face becomes more serious, her eyes darkened.

"Dr. Warren's log 145. A man named Kess has joined the group as Project Director. Hired by the government to track spending, he's also become an additional benefactor as well as being a pilot. I don't like him. He's pompous and sexist. In meetings, he undermines me with the structural engineers, the men and women I hand-picked for this amazing opportunity. And, he shows up in the strangest places. I found him in my room last night. I swear, if he makes a move, I'm kneeing him in the nuts!"

Speaking with her hands and her voice, Kimberly is clearly upset.

"Dr. Warren's log 249. Why are my instincts scream-ing about Kess? There's something seriously shady about him, and I can't put my finger on it. I've tried to get him out of this group, but he keeps finding new ways to become important. I'm going to avoid him as much as I can and concentrate on the good stuff.

"Big day coming up—the shuttle is being put together. I'm like a giddy kid in a candy store. Finally, the shuttle I dreamed up is being made."

Kimberly is wearing a hat, and her hair sticks out. There are dark shadows on her face and darker circles under her eyes.

"Dr. Warren's log 277. The crash tests have been frustrating. The hull is in good shape, but the inside structure keeps crumbling. Kess keeps telling me to abort the tests. I won't. I need them so I can break through these issues. But if those test dummies had been actual people… I couldn't live with myself if something dire happened."

With a tear-streaked face, Kimberly is holding a tissue as she speaks in a shaky voice. Her back is bowed as she hunches in front of her recorder.

"Dr. Warren's log 280. It's been six weeks since my last log. My assistants, Keisha Kahn and Jerome Xia, were lost in a plane crash. They were flying a Cessna 172 when it disappeared in the mountains of Colorado. I insisted that monies from our project be used to mount search and rescue. Nothing was found."

Kimberly is pale, no color in her face. Her hair is tied tightly in a bun, and her back is ramrod straight. Her voice is low, with a sense of finality and resignation.

"Dr. Warren's log 399. We lost two pilots today. They were killed on impact, driving to the Lester Facility. Fell asleep at the wheel and went over the side of the road into a deep ravine. I don't believe it. These men were professionals. I can't help feeling Kess had something to do with this. He didn't want Walker and Biggs on this program. They were Air Force officers with over forty years of flight experience combined. I trusted them. I...I almost kissed Biggs. I wanted to... I don't meet many awesome guys, and I know I'm not his type, yet Biggs found ways to spend time with me. Not that I let it go any further. Why didn't I? It's too late now. How can I guard my heart—I mean my shuttle program—if there's a saboteur? What do I do now?"

"Pause." Bennett swallowed. The pieces were coming together. That was the reason Kimberly had decided to leap at love, or at the very least, sex. She'd regretted not getting together with Biggs years ago. So she wasn't having sex as a means to distract from the project; rather, she was letting off steam, or maybe he was

just a placeholder for another man. Bennett would have
to ponder which of these ideas had merit.

As for Kess, the man was definitely bad news. But
there was a difference between being a leech and a
murderer. Or was there? Either way, he wanted the man
gone too. There had to be a way to get Kess to show his
hand. Bennett made a mental note to that effect.

He wanted to finish this task before anyone came
back and gave his attention to the logs. "Play."

*The animation in Kimberly's expression and voice
is intriguing.*

"Dr. Warren's log 472. I set a trap today…for Kess.
The man must be spying on me. It's like he knew it
was coming, and he turned the situation back onto me,
tried to squeeze me out of the project. I talked my way
through it, but everyone's different with me. I've lost
control of my entire group."

*Kimberly is winding a rubber band around her index
finger as she speaks.*

"Dr. Warren's log 590. Thank God for Ouster. He
moved us from the east coast to the west and hooked
me up with the Lester Facility. Hubbard is the overseer
of the entire place, and he's unseated Kess from his dic-
tatorship. I'm starting to get control back. It all begins
with Sally being my eyes and ears in this place. I can see
light at the end of this tunnel."

*Holding her head in her hands, Kimberly is clearly
weeping. She hiccups as she speaks.*

"Dr. Warren's log 620. We lost two SEALs today.

There are six people who have died on this project. Is it worth it? No! I can't believe I'm here worrying about a damn shuttle when these amazing men…have…"

Kimberly is pacing in front of the camera. She cannot keep still.

"Dr. Warren's log 621. It's been a week since the death of our latest pilots. I hardly feel that this project can work anymore. The computer system stopped working completely today. Kess had his engineers take over, and they worked on Sally for ten hours. The world is a dark, dark place, and I don't know if I can keep going, especially with the loss of life."

Kimberly is leaning on her hands as she stares into the recorder.

"Dr. Warren's log 622. I met with Ouster, and he's sending two more SEALs. I didn't want him to do that. I cannot bear anything more happening. I read their bios. I'm already in awe of the one named Sheraton, but I can't risk him—rather, I can't risk getting involved with him. I'll do what Ouster asks and give them full access to everything, but if something happens, I'm leaving this project for good. Damn! Kess is knocking on my door again!"

"Pause video logs." His thumb traced the outline of her face on the screen. She was a beautiful woman. He wondered if she'd ever think that about herself. His gut wrenched as he considered how Kess had been pushing her around for the past few years.

He shook off the emotion. Checking the time, he

recalled that Melo and Kimberly would be back soon. There were still a few more things he needed to know, so he could move forward. "Sally, please send a message to Kess requesting maximum speeds and test-flight times for the five flight tests. If possible, please cross-reference any information he gives you with any and all data that will either support or refute his results. This is for my eyes only."

"Affirmative. All info will be sent directly to your mobile device YEO. Anything else?"

"Run the videos of the crash tests."

The screen on his phone went blank, and then *Langley Landing and Impact Research Facility near Norfolk, Virginia, Crash Test of Warren Space Shuttle* scrolled across in big letters. The shuttle was at the top of a large structure, supported by a giant crane. Cables swung it down to the ground, slamming it into the concrete. A few days later, there was footage of the individuals in the control tower. Kess stared at Kimberly as the test commenced for the second time. When then third test occurred about two weeks later, she had moved away from Kess and was standing next to the cameraman. The look she threw Kess was not friendly.

"That's my girl." Bennett said.

The footage from inside the shuttle loaded. The video narrative began.

"The internal structure pulled away from the wall, slicing off the heads of the test dummies. On the second test, a foam material held it in place. It worked well and protected the pilots. The third test was smooth sailing."

Bennett blinked. Using his forefinger on the touch screen, he pushed the video backward. There…on the left hand side, near the pilot's seat, he'd nearly missed it. An additional box was set into the wall on the third test. He hadn't seen that box on any specs. What was in it, and when did it get on board?

It was time for him to inspect the shuttle. How and when could he make that happen? There was a saying that you have to earn the right to step into a car, a plane, or a shuttle, and no one was going to let him near that baby until he finished all of the required testing.

⁓⁓⁓

Warm water pounded Kimberly's body, washing away the dirt and grime of the outdoors. Nothing could clear away the memory of Bennett's arms wrapped around her, the way his body fit hers as they made love. The experience left an indelible mark on her psyche, her body, and her soul.

She slid the soap down her arms, the smell of lavender filling her nostrils, and the action eased her concern about the lovemaking. Was she rushing things, getting involved with a SEAL, a pilot, and possibly the man going into space?

Rinsing her arms under the pelting spray, she knew she didn't want to answer the question. The answer was a resounding yes, but she didn't care anymore. Years ago, she'd had a chance at love and had never taken it. Regret was a draining emotion. Even a fleeting chance at love was worth the risk, and her chemistry with Bennett was off the charts. Wasn't it worth the pain?

She finished her shower in record time and thought it funny how quickly one can act when left alone with annoying thoughts. She turned off the water and stepped out of the glass-encased stall and onto the cotton rug. Her toes wiggled in the supple softness.

Wrapping a towel around her head and another around her body, she entered her bedroom. "Lights, Sally. Play messages."

"There are forty-seven messages," said the computer. "Should I sort them?"

"I don't even like answering email," she grumbled. "Yes, Sally, please start with anything urgent."

"There are ten messages from Kess labeled 'Urgent,' having to do with his access to the shuttle. Shall I play them or ring him back?" asked Sally.

"Delete," said Kimberly flatly. She pulled out a pair of pants, a blouse, socks, a bra, and underwear. After laying them out on the bed, she donned her undergarments and moved on to the clothing. "Okay, I'm ready for any medical reports."

"There is one message. 'Dr. Warren, this is Dr. Franks. The Chinese and Russian pilots have been cleared for flight readiness. Of the two American pilots, only one is eligible to fly, and that's Bennett Sheraton. The other one, Jonah Melo, has several issues that eliminate him. Please check his scans and confirm that you agree.'"

Something gnawed at her mind. *Oh, crap!* Wasn't Melo doing his antigravity test right now? "Sally, locate Jonah Melo."

"Antigravity chamber. The test is in progress," Sally said. Panic lanced Kimberly's body. She grabbed her shoes and ran from the room, carrying them in her hand. The "crap factor" had definitely hit the proverbial fan!

———◦◦◦———

Melo had parked his truck and waved to Dr. Warren and Sheraton with a big smile on his face as he left them to their own devices. He was then escorted to one of the farthest parts of the building: the Tower, a.k.a. the antigravity chamber. Similar to the KC-135 "Vomit Comet," it simulated a weightless environment.

Melo couldn't have been more thrilled. Here was a step toward traveling into space. Answering questions as he went, he couldn't focus on anything the examiner was asking. All he wanted was to get to the test.

"Are you sure you understand?" asked the technician for the third time. "After this will be the neutral buoyancy simulator."

"Yes, yes, let's do this," replied Melo, in a hurry to best Sheraton at this task. If he had a better rating, the higher-ups would have to consider him, even over a man nicknamed Boss. It was tough to compete with a guy who had so many unique missions under his belt—not that SEALs discussed that type of thing off base, but everyone knew what was going on. They were all very good at keeping their mouths shut at the appropriate times.

"After you," said the technician as he pointed the way for Melo, who dressed himself in a harness and additional gear.

"Thanks." Melo barely got the word out when he was unceremoniously shoved inside the chamber. A door slid shut, air hissed at him briefly, and then another door on the other side slid open. Melo knew he probably should have paid closer attention the minute he felt his stomach clench. No one and nothing had prepared him for what happened next. And here he'd thought he was battle ready for anything. Damn, was he wrong!

The platform pulled slowly out from beneath him. His feet left the floor. Weightlessness made him momentarily as giddy as a child. It was hard not to let loose a few laughs.

As he spread his arms and pulled in his feet, his body rolled. No matter how he moved from there, he rolled over and over until his stomach was lifting its contents into his mouth and threatening to spill.

With a deep and nasty swallow, he shouted, "Get me out of here! I can't stop spinning, and I'm going to lose it if you don't get me on the ground or at least tell me how to reach the fucking platform." The more he swore, the harder it was to get control as he plummeted downward.

The loudspeaker sounded. The voice was garbled and then it smoothed out. "We cannot stop your descent with your current height. You're three stories up. Please either grab a safety-stop handrail and work your way down or… Crap, did he just puke in there?" The technician's frustration was evident as his tone continued to rise. "I explained this to you on the walk over here."

"Out. Get me the hell out of here." In the end, he was shrieking, having a tantrum, and then the vomit erupted like Mount Vesuvius.

"Suck it in, sailor!" yelled the technician. "Damn it!"

It took ten more minutes before the safety crew had Melo out of the chamber. His gut roiled, and the bile kept on coming. He leaned over the side of the antigravity chamber, puking his guts out until there was nothing left. His brain berated him, telling him he should have paid better attention.

Lesson learned. He sighed as his body eased.

Leaning his weight on the cold railing reassured him,

and from the look of the staff, they were pissed off. What could he say—life didn't always hand out gentle rides? At certain times, even SEALs got the fuzzy end of the lollipop, or in this case, the bad ride in the antigravity chamber.

A gentle hand tapped his back. Kimberly Warren's voice seeped into his foggy brain. "Middle-ear issue?"

"Might be." He banged his hand on the side of his head, and a wave of nausea surged inside of him. "Seems likely."

"Pretty sure I'm right. Actually, I know I am. I'm surprised they didn't go through their usual checklist before you stepped inside." Kimberly's eyes traveled up and down his body, settling on his face.

Melo sighed as he turned toward her. Rubbing his sleeve over his face to mop an errant drop, he faced her. "They did. I wanted to go to space. So I sort of blew through it. I'm flunking, aren't I?"

She gave him a half smile, a pity smile if he ever saw one. "We don't grade potential astronauts in that manner."

"Great. Give me five minutes and I'll do it again." Melo stretched his arms, glad his gut was finally empty. That was the best way to go for a test that had him doing flips and flops in every direction.

"No!" Both her hands were out flat. "Please, uh, we have other assignments for you."

He gestured toward the chamber. "How much puke did I get in there?"

She took his arm, leading him away from the ripe smell of his offering to the space deities. "Uh, sort of a lot. But don't worry about it. We'll get it cleaned up. Right now, I'd like you to focus on the engineering issues we're facing."

Melo stopped in his tracks, tugging her to a halt beside him. "You've already chosen Sheraton. Damn it, I wanted a chance to pilot this mission."

Her eyes were kind. They said it all.

He nodded his head. "I know. He has more experience as a test pilot, and he's pretty much a rock star at everything."

"Rock star?" She looked puzzled by the term. Her arms crossed over her chest.

"Yeah, that's what we call trainees—tadpoles—when they're going through BUD/S. The ones who ace all the physical stuff. Sheraton was and is one of those. Most candidates try to stay in the middle of the pack and don't draw attention. The ones at the back of the line... Well, they join the Goon Squad, which means extra physical training, etc." Melo scratched his chin.

"No one is perfect. I'm sure Bennett has his share of issues. We all do. You're good at stuff too, or you wouldn't be here. C'mon, let's get moving and do something useful." Dr. Warren practically pushed him out of the room and sealed it behind them, using her ID card.

He stopped her. "There's something you're not saying. My ability to read people, it's sort of a SEAL superpower."

She sighed. "Jonah, you're not going to like this. In the decontamination room, when you first entered the building, do you remember being hit with a mist and a bright light for a second?" She waved a hand in front of her face. "Doesn't matter if you do or you don't. It's just that Sally found that you have narrow Eustachian tubes in both ears—which isn't a big deal, but combine one with a burst eardrum as well as degradation to the canal, and there's no way you'd be able to keep your stability up there without blackouts. I choose the pilot, as you know, but the doctors overseeing the health-and-well-being tests will rule you out. I'm sorry. You're out of the running."

"Wow, that's like looking under a man's kilt before he has time to warn you there are no Skivvies underneath." He wiped the back of his hand over his mouth. "Good device. It would save some doctors exploratory surgeries on their patients."

"Yeah, I'm giving it to the Navy after a few more tests."

"Good call." He straightened his shoulders, ignoring his rolling stomach. It was empty now, and he refused to dry heave on the lady.

"If it makes you feel any better, we have worse tortures on the docket for Captain Sheraton." Dr. Warren pulled out her iPad and found the screen she was looking for. "There are a couple of surgeons I could recommend. They could probably fix some of the damage."

A surge of frustration welled in Melo. "Damn. Hard to hear I'm growing older. The damage…it's combat related. It'd surprise me if it was fixable, but I will look into it. It's been a while since I did high-altitude jumps, but you never know." His emotion released in a burst of enthusiasm. "Damn, I do like the idea of torture for Boss; serves the man right, freaking rock star. Let's focus on that."

"I figured you'd like that," she said with a full-out grin. Her eyes sparkled with mirth. "None of us likes being passed over for space, but we can do our part from the ground to keep it safe and make the mission a success."

He silently agreed. No one liked moving away from their dream, but it could be an opportunity to make new

dreams happen. He did have the woman of his dreams
in his corner now; Alisha was vital to his happiness. She
would soften the blow when he retired from the Teams
next year. "I asked you to give me a chance, and you
did. I appreciate your fairness in sticking to your word."

"Of course." She held his gaze. This was one classy
lady, and a person who kept her promises. He could
appreciate that fact.

"As my beautiful wife, Alisha, would say, 'Onward!'
So, let's go over the engineering—I'm superb at that. I
read the specs, and I see that you're having problems
keeping the laser array stable once it's deployed in
space. Hardware and software aren't speaking. If we put
the designers and engineers in one room, I might have
a few ideas that could address that. As to the hacking
and the sabotage, my mind is working on that too, but I
don't have a solution yet." Melo leaned against the wall
momentarily, regained his balance, and without missing
a beat, continued his commentary on the technology as
they walked down the hall.

Fake it till you make it. He repeated those words until
his body got into the groove. Gravity was more a friend
than he'd ever realized.

Back in Kimberly's quarters, Bennett checked the
clock. He'd been knee deep in the computer data and
equations for too long. He needed to move. He did one
hundred push-ups and one hundred sit-ups and ran in
place for twenty minutes. It was unfortunate that the
air-conditioning pumped cold air constantly. He needed
fresh air and the sound of wildlife to gather his thoughts,

but he didn't have time to get away from the security of the Lester Facility. With his blood pumping at least a little bit faster, he left the room and found a quiet space to rerun the calculations before he talked to Kimberly and Melo.

There was a series of empty rooms several corridors over from their living quarters. Choosing the second one, Bennett made himself at home. Again, the sterile white on white struck him as redundant, as though the person who had designed the Lester Facility was so worried about cleanliness, they omitted personal style, human comfort, and visual calming cues.

Seating himself at a desk in a room full of classroom-style desks, he put aside his phone, with its convenient math application, and decided to go old-school. He used a pencil and ran through his mathematical computations on a college-ruled yellow pad like the kind he'd used in college.

The outcome baffled him. The second and third times showed him his math had been correct. The fourth and last time proved conclusively that his results were indeed accurate. There was a serious problem. The shuttle was going to run out of fuel.

Tossing his pencil on the desk, Bennett could barely wrap his brain around this fact. He scratched his chin and wondered how a Lester Facility full of people couldn't see that the math for the fuel usage didn't add up. "This can't be right," he murmured to himself, looking over the numbers again.

"It might be," said a tall, thin gentleman wearing a white, short-sleeve button-down and a pencil tucked behind his ear. He stood in the door. "I'm Joseph Kess, the man in charge of this project. Dr. Warren told me you'd be in here working on a few basic flight plans. What did you come up with?"

Well, well, here's the devil himself. Bennett didn't know this man from a hole in the wall, though he'd seen his picture, name, and title on the personnel files he'd reviewed last night. "But not the man who designed the shuttle or chooses the pilot, or even the person who runs the Lester Facility itself, right? That's Warren and Hubbard," Bennett said. It didn't hurt to point out that, though Kess had big britches, he was still just visiting this place. Bennett cleared his throat. "You have a PhD in astrobiology and a master's in physics, a master's in statistics, and a bachelor's in psychology."

"You read my bio. That was fast work." Kess smiled, but it didn't reach his eyes. The action was more of a platitude, a way to get what he wanted that had obviously worked for him in the past. Bennett's mind processed the Intel. He also noticed the man was wearing pressed pants and leather loafers. He walked with a slight limp as he moved across the room. The action was slow, so it didn't give away the limp; perhaps the damage was recent and something he was ashamed of. "Did Sally help you?"

"Dr. Warren briefed me," Bennett lied. Of course Sally had given him the information. He could see that Kess was fishing, and he needed to know if the man could read him in return. Also, why did Kess want to know if there was access to Sally? Was there a link there? He made a mental note to follow up on that train of thought.

"Dr. Warren. Really, well, Kimmy can be very... useful." Kess sat down beside him.

Yikes! He couldn't imagine Dr. Kimberly Warren being a Kimmy, and he imagined she balked at it too. Kess was definitely trying to imply that he and the good doctor were on intimate terms. He'd have bet his car that she'd screech over that one as well.

Kess half smiled, and it resembled a snarl. "Show me. I want to see how you compare to the computer's routes and computations."

"Why not?" Pushing the pad toward the man, Bennett studied the project director. For sure, this man had his head somewhere, but Bennett wasn't sure that his focus was on this mission. From the look of him, he was in his late fifties, gray haired, pale, and underweight. His fragility might be a front, because there were distinctive muscles pushing the seams of his clothes. Yep, there were a lot of inconsistencies here. Body language was such a tattletale.

"I'm impressed. I like the slingshot effect to save fuel and push you farther and faster into orbit." Kess pushed the pad in front of Bennett and stared piercingly at him. "When did you realize that you would need to travel above the space station, past the GPS and communications satellites, to geosynchronous orbit? Did someone give you that information?"

Shaking his head, Bennett spoke very softly. Who knew who was close enough to listen in? Though any good astrophysicist with an understanding of what was orbiting the Earth would have figured it all out pretty quickly, he supposed. "Process of elimination," he said. "As you know, the space station orbits between two hundred and three hundred miles above the Earth, and the satellites for communications GPS orbit around

twelve thousand miles. I remembered the latest U.S. Air
Force Fact Sheet where Command boasted about the
need for complete transparency in terms of mistakes that
had been made in space with equipment and launches.
They also have a number of maneuverable equipment
pieces in geostationary orbit at little over eighteen thousand miles."

Kess smiled. "You're a fanboy."

"Who isn't?" Bennett returned his smile. He could
play nice as long as Kess did. Strange thing was, he had
an odd feeling about the man, as if something in his
nature was hidden or duplicitous.

"Now I remember where I heard your name. You
worked at the Joint Space Operations Center for a time,
monitoring and assessing our tech in space." Bennett
leaned forward. "I met you about ten years ago there."

"Yes," said Kess flatly. "You were the one that
unearthed the glitch from mounds of data we had posted
in the troubleshooting room, and you did it within an
hour of arriving." Under his breath he added, "I had
spent months working on that project, just searching for
a solution, any answer I could find."

"Glad I could help," said Bennett, ignoring the
hidden dig as he picked up the pad of paper and placed
it back in front of him. His eyes bored into Kess's. He
knew, from a long history of dealing with people, that
half-swallowed words were a passive-aggressive tool
of the trade; unless, of course, you were fucking someone silly. Then it was just pure embarrassment. Since
that wasn't the case here, Kess revealed his weaknesses. Given the man's apparent insecurity, Bennett
was going to keep an eye on him as well as put him at

the top of the suspect list. Politely, he replied, "Good to see you again."

"Uh-huh," replied Kess, whose eyes were like hot pokers boring into Bennett's back as he got up abruptly and left the room. The image of Kess floating in space with his eyes bulging and his body swollen and bloated danced in Bennett's imagination. Nope, it wouldn't hurt his feelings at all if Kess was the guilty party. Insecure men were dangerous in times of war, and right now, the race to space was definitely a battlefield.

He tapped his fingers on the pad of paper. There was a lot more going on here than was clear to the untrained eye. He wondered what his deceased brethren had found out, and if there had been any way for them to leave a message.

"Sally, can you guide me to the former quarters of the SEALs?"

"Yes. Follow the map on your phone, Captain."

Bennett looked down at the device. Distracted, he said, "Thanks."

Ripping off the pages of paper with the equations on them, plus a few additional ones so no one could read the impressions beneath, he stuffed them into his pocket and abandoned the pad. Using the map as a directional, he made his way to the rooms.

At the door, he said, "Access."

"Not allowed," Sally replied in a stilted voice.

"By whose order?" asked Bennett, though he had an idea who the culprit was.

"Hubbard, the Lester facility manager. It is sealed until the authorities can examine it."

Huh, he would have thought Kess was behind the request. Now, where would he find this Hubbard?

Love comes in all forms. Sometimes an invitation gets you nowhere; you have to grab the bull by the horns and lead him to where the action needs to take place.

Kimberly had seen Bennett standing in front of the former rooms of the SEALs. She tapped her fingers against his back.

He spun on her, a strange expression on his face. "Sorry about that. You startled me."

"I'm flattered," she said. "You must have been deep in thought."

"I was. Do you know where I'd find Hubbard?" Bennett looked over her head at the different directions that were offered. The hallway split in four directions.

"In his office. It's near the main entrance, the first doorway on the left."

"Okay." He turned to leave.

"Wait. I…I'd like to, uh, talk to you for a few minutes. Do you have time?" A rather daring idea had struck her, and she'd decided in that moment to act on it. What was the saying? Fortune favors the brave. She was determined to follow through on this particular need for courage. She wanted more after their romp in the woods, and she was determined to know if her body's response was a fluke or if Bennett really could push her buttons like a virtuoso.

"Sure," he said when he saw her. "What's up?"

"Stuff," she replied. "Do you have time to chat with me for a while?"

"I guess." His preoccupied expression didn't stop her from taking Bennett's hand. She kissed him once, twice, and a third time tenderly on the mouth and then led him in a new direction. She felt like the iconic Mae West as his gaze focused on her.

By that point, his distant expression had changed to one of exquisite interest. His hands brushed hers now and then as they walked, and she adored the sparks it sent zinging through her body.

They headed down a series of hallways together, and it was dumb luck that no one else encountered them on their journey. All systems seemed "go" as they entered the antigravity locker room, walked through it, and ended up on the platform before a large pill-shaped metal chamber attached to spinning pistons at either end. It was the size of four recreational vehicles.

Kimberly was grateful that Melo hadn't been in here yet. She peeked in the window. Stretching out before them was a one-story weightless room, and it was blessedly empty and clean. The room was encompassed by a tank that could create a faux-weightless environment inside, different from the AG chamber in that no harnesses were required — and thankfully, no monitor or technicians.

She was pretty confident in her ability to sway him, because in truth, what she really wanted was to get him naked and fool around. "Let's go inside."

"Okay."

They entered. She closed the door behind them and locked it.

"Where did you do your training?" she asked for the third time as she set the controls that turned off gravity and had them both floating off their feet. Doesn't every girl dream of being swept away? She did, and this place was a fantasy destination she planned to check off on her bucket list—the one she had for her and the right person.

His eyebrows lifted. "Should I be offended that you aren't listening to my answer or flattered that you keep asking it?"

As she unbuttoned her blouse, she responded. "Flattered. NASA. I get it. I know the history of Frogmen—Underwater Demolition Teams, UDTs— meeting capsules and getting the astronauts out safely, and I know that a handful of SEALs go through astronaut readiness training as part of an elite group that's prepped for off-world duty. I'm familiar with space. I know you probably want to say more on the issue, but I don't know how much time we'll get. A stolen moment should be appreciated and used, rather than overanalyzed. What do you think?"

His smile lit his face slowly. "How many times have you done this…Dr. Warren?"

"Never!" She was appalled by the question, but given how brazen she was being, perhaps it was justified.

"Scratching an itch then?"

"Something like that." She was down to her bra and panties now. When she snagged her pants before they floated away and withdrew a string of condoms wrapped in foil, even she laughed. "Okay, maybe I was being slightly ambitious."

"If you think I can go five times without a break, have at it, my dear. I'm game to give it a try." His tone was low and sultry as he stripped his own clothes off and moved toward her.

As he passed by her, he laughed like a like an awkward teenager on his first date. The burst of enthusiasm made her giddy in return, and they chased each other around the chamber, floating here and there.

Her adrenaline pumped and her libido was hungry. She wanted him, needed him to make love to her. Grabbing the handholds above her, she locked her feet into a foothold and beckoned him. "Bennett. Come here."

His smile was wry, but he came to her all the same. When he grabbed the same hand positions, their fingers brushed. His mouth a hair's breadth away and his eyes searing hers, he said, "Yes, Kimberly. How may I pleasure you?"

"Be creative," she whispered against his mouth, loving his politeness. She licked her lips, and his eyes were suddenly tracking her movements. She took a deep breath, and her chest heaved with the intake.

A wicked gleam sprang into his eyes as his mouth slanted over hers. His tongue pillaged her own as he freed a hand to wrap around the back of her head. Her control slipped away as his hands and body demanded response. Arching her back and thrusting her body against his, she opened herself to him, willing him to take and to allow himself to be open too.

His mouth broke suddenly from hers. "So sexy," he said. "Where does all this passion come from?" That intense gaze was back, ordering her to answer, needing to know why.

"You," she murmured back.

"Truth," he said softly, stroking his fingers down her face and tucking a strand of hair behind her ear. It immediately floated back out, but he kissed it back into place, toying with the tender flesh of her earlobe.

Her hands slipped between them and her fingers slid

a condom into place, and then her legs wrapped around his waist. Moving her hips against the top of his cock, she teased him, loving the position of power.

He pushed off gently from the wall and they tumbled into the center of the chamber.

Holding on to each other, they kissed and explored, never letting go.

"Was this what you wanted?" he asked as he slowly thrust his hips, sinking himself deep inside of her.

Her breath caught in her throat. Words were forgotten as she nodded her head. Her body was too full for any other response.

He was very still inside of her, and her body stretched to accommodate him. When she could at last speak, she asked, "What's your fantasy, sailor?"

"This…" he said against her lips before he kissed her again. "You. A passionate woman who knows what she wants."

"I do." Her belly did a somersault as his words hit home. Had anyone told her that exactly what and who she was, was exactly what and who she needed to be? It was an aphrodisiac of the most explosive kind.

Her hips thrust against his, and their movements sent them into motion again. They went head over heels while caught in each other's embrace.

As they headed toward a wall, he caught a handrail and steadied them. He turned her around and entered from behind. All the while, he continued nibbling along the back of her neck and her spine.

Her sheath vibrated with excitement as the new angle hit not only her G-spot, but also her A-spot, and she climaxed several times. Her body was alive with electricity, and it shook with satisfaction as he turned her in his arms—toward him, reentering her slowly until she was moving wantonly against him again.

This time, he could not be contained, and he threw back his head and cried out, "Kimberly!" His body spasmed. The climax rocked his whole body, and she could feel his muscles reacting against her.

Burying his face into her hair, she relished the closeness of him inside her and wrapped around her. Nothing in her wildest imagination could hold a candle to this experience. It was lovemaking above and beyond what she thought possible, until now. The bar had been set very high.

Her fingers sank into his hair as her tongue traced the top of his ear.

He shuddered against her, spent, and laughed low and deep. "You might need to give me a few minutes."

"I have all the time in the world," she answered, pulling his head back so she could look at him. Her lips brushed over his. Her nipples, hard nubs, teased his skin as one of his arms wrapped around her and their mouths locked in languorous battle.

"Kimberly, you are needed in the center room. There's a heated discussion underway that you must handle." The computer's voice was an invasion into the sanctity of their private hideaway. Whatever was going on had better be worth it.

Kimberly hugged Bennett close, not wanting to let go.

"It's okay," he murmured. "We knew it was a stolen moment."

Her fingers trailed along his jaw. His eyes held hers,

and she wanted to spend an eternity exploring what happened in there. Strange, how this man had become as interesting to her as space itself. Never in her most inventive dreams had she imagined that happening. Men were beings that scratched an itch or satisfied an urge, but they were never—heaven forbid—a distraction from work. How had Bennett Sheraton made it under her skin so fast? And would she ever have her fill of him?

None of these questions would be answered today, and it didn't look like they were going to have a second act in their lovemaking session, so perhaps she should get to work. Heaven knew how much time she spent fantasizing about Bennett!

"Dr. Warren, your compliance is mandatory, by order of the manager of the Lester Facility, Dr. Hubbard," urged Sally. "He's an impatient person, as you know."

Kimberly nodded her head against Bennett's shoulder as her fingers slowly released her grip on his muscle mass. At the same time, other parts of her anatomy released their firm grip on his, breaking the physical connection they'd made.

Giving him a quick kiss, she pushed off with her feet, angling her body toward the doorway. Seeing the condom float off behind her, along with her panties, bra, and the rest of her clothing, she said, "I'll leave the cleanup in your hands, Boss." She winked as she used his Team nickname, and it was the worth it. The look he gave her would have sliced her in half if he'd had lasers for eyes. *Thank goodness for mortal strengths and weaknesses*. She laughed softly to herself.

Grabbing the handrail, she eased her body into the transition chamber, closed the door, and pushed the button to restore normal gravity. Her body was yanked back to the ground, and it took her a few seconds to reorient.

She checked the monitor on the other side of the door and saw it was clear. Not that she was a prude, but she didn't particularly want to answer any questions. The one she feared was "Is Sheraton the one?"

Walking out the other side completely naked didn't faze her as she headed to the locker room to shower. Barring nuclear disaster or a meltdown of something important, she was safe in thinking there was time to tidy up before she diplomatically handled the disaster that had Hubbard screaming for her. Given that she was not the most politically correct person in the world, it would to be a real stretch for her—a last-ditch effort for the Lester Facility, most likely—but, hey, it was never her choice to be thrown into the mix.

Walking into the middle of two grown men on the verge of a fistfight was downright stupid. Unfortunately, that was exactly what Kimberly did when she rushed between them and got caught in the verbal crossfire.

"The universe is thirteen-point-eight billion years old," Dr. Wang Lee shouted. His vehemence was punctuated with a raised fist that shook in the air.

"It's younger, around twelve. Haven't you taken a turn at the Hubble? No, I expect not, as you are of little importance in the space discussions we're having here." Dr. Yuri Pelsin towered over both her and Dr. Lee. He'd use anything to gain an advantage, she'd learned. Yuri was such an ass.

"Next thing you're going to tell me is that the solar system is only two billion years old, when I've proved it's four-point-five billion." Dr. Lee lifted both of his fists in front of him.

The man across from him responded in the same manner, and the two men squared off.

"Cool it!" she shouted at the top of her lungs. Taking a deep breath, she regretted it instantly. The room smelled like feet, or old blue cheese stuffed in a hot room for a month, and the bodies inside it didn't appear to have showered in quite some time. She'd had periods in her life where she enjoyed being a naturalist, but if there was ever a time to wear deodorant, it would be here, in a room full of thinkers, or at Comic-Con International. Hey, she was a geek at heart! "Sally, strobe the lights," she murmured into her phone.

Above them, the lights flickered on and off until the shouting stopped. Silence fell in the room. The silence was a welcome response and the one she'd hoped for. Now that she had their attention, she was going to use it.

Kimberly threw twin looks of disgust at Hubbard and Kess, neither of whom had done anything to solve the situation, but rather had waited and tossed the issue into her lap. Both of them looked away. Why did she have to be the one with the biggest balls in the room?

They deserved her ire, and she hoped they felt some kind of pain from her pointed look, but she highly doubted it.

"Thank you, Sally," said Kimberly, acknowledging the computer loudly. "Now, scientists, you all represent some of the greatest minds of our century, and we have serious hurdles to overcome before we can launch. The optimal window is Friday, and that gives us a very short timeline to make everything happen. So, put aside your differences and your debates, and get to work. Is that understood?"

A murmur rose from the crowd. Several faces turned red as their owners slunk toward the door, but most of the group remained.

"Combining our theories and these great minds will be a temporary situation, this is true, but we can create something long lasting with our work. This is what we need to help humanity. The resources we have access to right now are limitless."

Yuri scoffed at her words. "If you need a computer to help you manage all of us, I don't know how you achieved such a successful shuttle design, Dr. Warren. A girl, no less, designed this. I still don't believe it."

"The fact that I'm a woman has nothing to do with either brains or success. I'm not a closed-minded individual, and this allowed me to imagine and construct this amazing shuttle in a manner that only an open mind can conceive. Sally has been very instrumental, and insightful." She cocked her head to the side. "Only a fool throws away tools that are useful."

"Perhaps. There's integrity in doing it alone. Is it better to be a wise man among fools or a fool among wise men?" After delivering this biblical bon mot, Yuri stepped out of reach before she could strike out at him. She would have too, but the man was so obviously baiting her that she smiled at him. Kess would never allow Yuri to be removed. She couldn't put her finger on what was going on with those two. Spinning her finger in the air, she said, "To work, everyone. Move."

From the corner of her eye, she watched Yuri and Wang pass too close together. They exchanged a note, and her eyes widened as she realized how she'd been used. Stepping to a quiet spot in the room, she said softly, "Covert mode, Sally. Please monitor Yuri and Wang and tell me what the note says, the one they just passed."

Affirmative, Sally texted back to her.

Kimberly put her phone to sleep and tucked it back into her pocket. She gritted her teeth. One way or another, she would be outing those two and whatever they were doing. Given all the delays and problems, no one was above suspicion.

———ᴡᴡ———

Spending time with Kimberly had turned out to be a plus. Bennett had no idea what she'd planned when she pulled him away from his calculations, and yet he couldn't have been more delighted. Another hour or two together in the weightless room would have been ideal, but he understood that she had demands on her time. What was frustrating him the most about this place and the situation was that he hadn't made any progress in discovering the source of the sabotage or who had killed his brethren. He needed those answers.

His fingers rolled into fists. Allowing his feet to move him quickly to his destination was burning off some much-needed steam, but it wasn't getting him closer to the truth.

The hallways ran together as if a maze in a white-walled prison. The Lester Facility was a sterile environment, and without the handy-dandy map on his phone,

Bennett would have been walking back and forth, attempting to locate his Teammate. "Sally, show me where Melo, Kimberly, and Kess are located."

Mini versions of them showed on his phone. They were all in one place. *Well, that can't be good.* Just as quickly as they showed up, the images faded away, but it was long enough to figure out where they were.

He scanned his badge at the appropriate door and walked into a room that was filled with people. All of them sported some type of computer or tablet. Every nationality was represented. Spying Kimberly arguing with someone in Russian was interesting, and when she pulled another person into the conversation, flawlessly switching to Mandarin Chinese, he was duly impressed. Granted, he spoke Arabic, Spanish, and French, but he was always ready to learn more languages, skills, or pretty much anything useful in life.

His eyes moved to Melo, who was working his way through the crowd toward a door at the back of the room. Bennett followed, weaving in and out of the folks who could have been part of a United Nations delegation as far as he was concerned, and left them behind. His gut told him that the SEAL deaths were personal. They had to be. That meant someone in the Lester Facility knew something.

As Bennett entered the next room, he could see Melo with his phone to his ear. The frown and furrowed brow were not a welcome expression.

Bennet closed the door behind him and asked, "What did you find?"

"Listen for yourself." The phone played back a conversation between two very well-spoken individuals.

Very convenient that the record function was just a click away.

"Good call on covertly recording conversations."

Melo laughed. "Sally helped me. She can play back everything and anything. You just need a time and location."

"Good to know." Bennett leaned forward. "Wait, I didn't catch the last part of the conversation. What was it?" He had a sinking feeling about the voices. "Wait. I've heard one of those voices before."

"It's the IT guy who brought us laptops, and he's speaking with a scientist—Rigley—who's in charge of the manual-override system for the shuttle. He was confirming a piece of debris they'd retrieved from a test flight. It was part of an antisatellite weapon, but the country of origin is sketchy."

"Fuck. That's…unnerving. Uh, why do they think it's from another country?"

"You know that China launched several weapons into geosynchronous orbit in 2013." Melo looked peeved. "Something about that fight between Yuri and Wang was…off."

"I agree. But who doesn't know the facts of those weapons tests? It's old news. Public knowledge. Hell, *20/20* and *60 Minutes* covered it in lengthy segments," stated Bennett. "Maybe it's just a feeling, but I think there are more than one or two individuals. I think there's a group here that's trying to undermine this mission for their own purposes. Let's keep an eye on those two—Yuri and Wang—and add Kess to the mix. I don't trust that guy." Bennett chuckled to himself. "Sally, can you covertly monitor the activity of the IT guy who gave

us our laptops, and Rigley, too? Only share this information with Melo and me."

"Confirmed, Captain Sheraton." The computer's
voice was eerily sweet and amenable.

"Hey, I have to talk to you about the calculations I
worked out. There's something off with the weight allot-
ment and required fuel. I think someone's trying to haul
something else into space. We need to get in that shuttle."

"I'm working on it," said Melo. "Your best bet is to
go through Dr. Warren. Hate to put you in that position, but your friendliness with her could play in our
favor here."

"Maybe," said Bennett. He hated having to use her,
but they needed to get inside. There had to be answers in
the shuttle itself. "Let's see where we go from here." His
fingers flew over the keyboard as he typed in a series of
commands, attempting to uncover any data that might
have been left behind by his SEAL brethren. Leaving
Sally to work on the program he'd just entered, he
turned his attention back to the piloting specifications.

"Can you find Hubbard and get his permission to
enter the quarters of our deceased brothers? I need to
head back to the conference room and see if I can catch
Kimberly for a few minutes."

Melo smirked. "I bet." He nodded his head. "I'm on
it. Get out of here."

Bennett got to his feet and left. The conference room
was completely cleared out, as if someone had rung the
dinner bell. Toppled chairs and tables, ripped papers,
and abandoned coffee cups made the place look like a
geeks' abandoned war zone. He made his way through
the debris and into the hall.

Heading back to his set of rooms, he passed several interesting characters along the way: Yuri, who was smoking a cigarette openly as Sally berated him via his phone, and Kess, who was chatting with Rigley. Add Wang and few others who looked sideways at them, and that was a likely bunch to start with.

He pondered the probabilities of their involvement as he entered his room. Sitting down at the computer, he wrote several brief notes to himself and Melo.

—⁓—

Ring. Ring. The sound of the door chime shook him. He'd dozed off as he worked. Had he heard Melo come in? It felt vaguely familiar. He could see the man, lying prone. If there had been trouble, he would have come fully awake. Danger felt different, shocked the senses. Familiarity—or at least, calm situations—bred comfort. It was as if you could discern the energy charge in the air.

Rubbing the back of his neck, he chased away some of the stiffness. Both his mind and body were spent. Too little sleep and too much brain strain had him tied in knots. As his body stirred he noted that the side trips had been a workout too. Kimberly was a nice surprise after his long absence from the fairer sex, but how on earth was he going to plow through this mess in a short time frame? "Who's at the door, Sally?" he asked.

"The scientists for your next test are outside your door," said the computer-simulated voice. "Would you like me to send them away?"

He grunted. He wanted to answer in the affirmative, and yet he didn't want to jeopardize his standing in the competition for the pilot's seat.

A note fell off his chest. He recognized Melo's handwriting: *0700 Access Granted*. So Melo had sweet-talked the facility manager into letting them examine the quarters. Well, that was good news. He wadded up the note and tossed it at Melo's head. It bounced off and hit the ground.

Bennett smiled. Damn, that man was a good faker. Bennett knew he was awake. Grabbing his clothes off the chair, Bennett dressed quickly. Walking to the portal, he stared at the closed door for a few seconds, prepping mentally, and then said, "Open."

Chapter 5

BENNETT RUBBED HIS ARMS. COLD AIR BLEW continually through the hallways as wireless sweepers and mops moved soundlessly over the floors. At 0100 the three white-coated scientists led him into the bowels of the center of the building and, after a rather circular course, into a very small, strange room. Building materials poked out of the wall in an odd, symmetrical pattern of angles. In the center of the room was a tank full of water with two pieces of white cloth slung over the side.

Great! Was he going to have to bathe in front of these guys? How far up were they going to be into his business? Even he had a few boundaries left in life. Well, maybe…

One of the scientists cleared his throat. "Sir, would you please disrobe?" They pointed in unison at the tank, and Bennett wondered if he was in some kind of warped dream about lunatics and crazed scientists. Had Melo spiked his Tang? He wouldn't put it past his Teammate. This was a "race" to see which one of them was going to make the trip into space, and one of them wasn't.

Looking out of the corner of his eye at the men, he wondered if they were going to watch him. Was there some way to cheat when one was getting naked?

Bennett stalled for time. He made a show of scratching his nose, noticing that there wasn't any odor in this room. There was an industrial-cleaner smell throughout the Lester Facility, as though the place was continually being scrubbed and sterilized.

"What's up?" asked Bennett casually, trying to lighten the mood. "Or rather, what's down…there?" He pointed to the tank. "Can you give me an idea of what's going on here? What am I supposed to do?"

The three men frowned as if they were all Grumpy from *Snow White and the Seven Dwarfs*. This was a space-exploration group; there was a lot to be happy about here.

"Captain Sheraton, you've been asleep for fifty-seven minutes. Sally informed us of your rest period, and according to our tests, this is an optimal time to challenge your sleep deprivation, or Sleep Dep, skills," said the shorter man, whose ID badge read *Dorner, Caleb*. "This is a required test for our shuttle-pilot program. Did you or did you not agree to all of the testing for this assignment? Being a pilot is an honor any one of us would give our eyes, teeth…hell, our whole jaw for."

Bennett sighed. From the looks these men were giving him, the test was not optional. He needed time to discover who murdered his Teammates and find the saboteur. He made a last-ditch attempt. "While I can appreciate this test, you do know that I'm a SEAL. Sleep Dep is part of our training, boys. Dang, it's like the root of Hell Week." Of course his brain was still rolling around the fact that these men were monitoring him and his sleep patterns. Who else was?

The taller man tapped his electronic pen against the tablet. "We have four more of these to do, Captain. In or out."

Leaning forward, Bennett caught the tall guy's name. "I'm in. Allen, Parker."

"Everything off, and put on the white clothing," said the tall man as he gestured for the others to follow him. "All you are required to do is lie down in the water. We cannot explain anything further, as it would compromise the final result."

Bennett raised an eyebrow. "How long do I stay in the tank?"

Their faces were blank. None of them answered him.

Bennett shrugged and kicked off his shoes, then stripped off his button-down shirt and pants—not that he'd had much time to dress before these guys had rung the buzzer on his door. Melo! Sheesh! That SEAL who couldn't be bothered to crack an eyelid as Bennett was being dragged out. Bennett had seen the cruel little smile on Melo's lips and the way his body shook with mirth as if he knew something was going to happen.

Crap! Bennett hated being the last person to know.

He held up the white T-shirt. Hardware was laced into the cotton weave covering his chest and back, moving up his neck, and going over his head. If this stuff was on the white underwear too, he was not putting that thing on. Who knew what it would do? He was a commando guy anyway, sans underwear, and had been since Hell Week.

Finally, fitted with the hardware, he stepped into the tank. It sloped downward like a luge prepared to plummet down a mountain, or some other kind of tin casket. The water sloshed around him as he lowered himself until only his face was in the air and the rest of him was covered in water.

The men left the room, quietly satisfied that nothing had been secreted into the test. Of course, they hadn't looked that closely. He could be hiding things in places very few individuals would look, though he wasn't.

The hardware spun to life, creating a low, rhythmic vibration and hum, and then the noise and movement abruptly ceased. Bennett tapped his fingers on the instruments to no avail. He gave up and took in the room.

He studied the angles of the insulation around the room. It looked like a combination of fiberglass, concrete, and metal, and he sussed out the purpose as it dawned on him. He was in a small anechoic chamber, which changes the acoustics in a room, minimizing sound until there is practically none. He'd read about this type of chamber. His mind darted in a hundred directions as his eyes examined the layout. The angles and design were fascinating now, and he attempted to memorize the pattern and the manner in which the sound would hit the angles, be deflected and/or absorbed, and so on until there was no sound left.

The lights lowered, fading the images, and Bennett found himself eager to maintain a focus on those designs: the angles, the textures, and the shapes…something.

C-a-l-m. He mentally spelled out the word and his brain responded. Forcing himself to redirect his thoughts, he closed his eyes and slowed his breathing. Remembering a meditation he had done on the first night of a Sleep Dep test in training, he played with his breathing, listening to the sound, making it go faster and slower until he was so relaxed that his mind was eager to drift.

He didn't allow it. Instead, he tracked the blood flow and musculature of his body—wiggling his toes, feet, knees, hips, waist, etc., until he created waves.

The lapping was almost instantly absorbed, but he was ground zero, and the sensation begot the sound even if it was pulled away.

Moving to an old sniper trick, he recited the Declaration of Independence and the Constitution. Some guys liked to count or do arithmetic in their heads, but Bennett found it too distracting. Being a patriot and a history buff, he preferred the Founding Fathers' words, as they often gave him clarity during times in which there was none.

As his mind spun through each article of the Constitution, the lights sprang on suddenly, jolting him into a sitting position. Bennett sat up, shading his eyes so he could see who was standing in the doorway.

The man whose name he hadn't originally caught was walking toward him. "I'm Dr. Gary Leon. Absolutely amazing test! I've never seen anyone stay so calm. It's a record, you know. Over sixty minutes in the chamber and not one change in your behavior, heart rate, or anything. I'm astounded, simply at a loss for words. Congratulations, Captain Sheraton. Well done, sir!"

Bennett hauled himself out of the tank, stripping the cotton-covered hardware off his body. Despite his nudity, the other man did not stop speaking. Bennett toweled off his body and wrapped the cotton bath sheet around his hips, tucking the corner into a tight knot at his waist. One hand snagged his shirt and pants as he slipped his feet into the shoes. Who cared if he walked around the Lester Facility in a towel? At Zero Dark Whatever, who gave a crap about etiquette?

The scientist grabbed his free hand and pumped it heartily. "Amazing! I'm going to write a paper on this. I won't use any names or the fact that you're a sailor, but I know it will get a lot of tongues wagging. Perhaps after the mission we can talk about the methods you employed during your time in the tank. I'd be very interested."

"Sure." His enthusiasm was a little contagious, and Bennett found himself cracking a grin. What could he say? He'd been like this in BUD/S training too. Not once did he see little green men or hallucinate. Rather, he just maintained this methodical pace, and that had helped him climb the ranks of the Navy from enlisted to officer fairly quickly. Yep, it wasn't easy to rattle him, and he was grateful for that fact. But maybe he just didn't have anything important holding him hostage here on Earth either. He was unencumbered, without debt or asset, other than one vehicle and a stash of weapons, and it didn't matter if he lived or died, except to himself. He liked being alive, so that's what he was going to be.

At the back of his head, a voice kicked up a fuss. Those statements weren't exactly true. He did sort of "like" somebody, but that didn't really count. Did it?

Scratching his head, he pondered the idea of another person playing into the equation of his life. He wasn't sure he liked the idea. On the other hand, did he hate it? Not really, no, it was…okay, he admitted to himself. If he was being honest about it, that is.

All the way back to his room, Bennett pondered whether getting involved with Dr. Warren was a bad or a good idea. Granted, it had given him carte blanche to everything security-wise at the Lester Facility, and she really did have an inside track on the staff, but she was passionate, cute, smart, and funny too. Sort of a killer combination, if anyone asked his opinion.

Next to Bennett as he walked, Dr. Leon chatted away, his hands making large gestures. "When I first arrived here, I had no idea I'd be working with an actual anechoic chamber. The largest one is in Orfield Laboratories in Minneapolis. That's north of us, but you know that. You probably have a GPS or calming program built into your skull like a cyborg soldier. I've always wanted to see someone best that test. I tried it once, and it was an utter disaster. I cried and screamed and wet my pants like a two-year-old. Not that all two-year-olds wet their pants, mind you, but I did then. Who knew that silence could be a serious mind twist? When it comes to being trapped in all of that silence, I can't stop talking. But I think you've figured that out about me."

Sighing internally, Bennett wished that this particular scientist wasn't going to keep him talking all night. All he wanted to do right now was get some shut-eye, the kind that had noises in the background. With Melo's snoring, that was not going to be a problem.

—〰—

At 0400 Melo shook him awake. "C'mon, Boss. Prince Charming, it's time to wakey wakey. We need to get a few miles under our belt and do some CrossFit training before we tour the quarters."

Bennett groaned. He pulled the pillow from beneath his head, aimed it in Melo's direction, and threw it with precision. He'd slept less than he wanted to, and though he could handle it, he knew he'd perform better if he could get at least four hours without Melo's snaffling snores.

"Oof! Low blow, Sheraton." Melo leaned over,

attempting to catch his breath. Thanks to Bennett's good aim, he was going to run with a limp this morning.

Bennett stretched. Swinging his legs over the side of the couch, he rubbed his hands over his face and stood. He grabbed his shorts, T-shirt, and running shoes and was dressed and ready to go by the time Melo recovered.

"I didn't hit you that hard." The frown on his buddy's face was genuine. Bennett felt a pang of concern. "You okay?"

"Sure. I blew the antigravity test. Guess there's a problem with my middle ear as well as a burst eardrum." Melo scrubbed his hands over his face and then stared at Bennett. "Congratulations, man. You're the one that's going to be orbiting the Earth." He thrust his hand out.

"Sorry, my man. I feel for you. I know it was your dream as much as mine. I'll do us both proud." Bennett shook his swim buddy's hand. "Okay?"

"Yeah. Thanks." Melo gestured to his cell phone. "Probably for the best, I'm not launching into space. I'd hate to make that call to Alisha and get an earful on how I need to keep my feet on the ground. Wives, right?"

"I don't know, Melo. I never could make it work. My marriage was doomed and over in less than six months. She emptied my bank account and ripped my heart out. You've loved your wife for like, what, a half of a decade before you even married her. That's pretty special. Any man would envy a love and connection like that," Bennett admitted. Would he ever be that blessed? He doubted it.

"I suppose so. I wouldn't trade it for a ride to space. So that's a good thing." Melo gave a half smile.

Bennett considered lightening the mood by ribbing

the man about hurling in the Vomit Comet, because it had received its slang name for a reason. But he couldn't bring himself to kick a Teammate when he was down. Truth was…he'd be seriously bummed too, if the circumstances were reversed. "Anything else going on?"

"Nah. On the personal front, just missing Alisha. I got a text from her yesterday." They headed down the hallway, through the white room, and out the main door. Nodding at the guards, they took off on a fast-paced run.

Melo continued his train of thought. "She said it was *u-r-g-e-n-t*. Any chance I could meet her in town or bring her here?"

"I don't know, Jonah. We haven't determined the problems. I don't want either one of you to get blindsided. Putting her in danger, well, you'd never forgive yourself if something went sideways. And honestly, I wouldn't forgive you either," Bennett ribbed with an edge of seriousness. No SEAL wanted to put his loved one at risk. This was the very reason they left home to handle missions instead of staying put.

"Agreed. I'll call her when we return and figure out what she needs."

"Besides a booty call?" teased Bennett.

"Hell, we all need that," said Melo, laughing.

A sudden sound from behind them had Bennett signaling to Melo with a hand gesture and then peeling off and circling around. When he spied Kimberly Warren coming up behind Melo, he snuck up from behind and tapped her shoulder.

She squealed. "Don't do that! You scared me."

"Situational awareness, lady. I'm just saying." Bennett fell back in sync with Melo as Kimberly joined them.

"I, uh, couldn't help but overhear your predicament. Maybe I could help," she offered. Her breathing was paced, and it was obvious this lady was a runner.

"How?" asked Melo, looking at her from the corner of his eye.

"I have to visit a vendor in El Centro. She could meet us at a restaurant. I could stay in the car, or we could get separate tables. There's been something off in the quality of a product, and I don't trust anyone else to handle it." Her hands bunched into fists.

Bennett noticed the tension filling Kimberly. A wave of protectiveness slid through him. "I'll join you both. We can make it a foursome."

Melo laughed. "Whatever makes you happy, brother."

The look he gave Bennett twisted his gut. Melo knew that he and Kimberly were hooking up and was not particularly thrilled about it. Hooking up on a mission was a standard negative. Yet staying away from Kimberly was like giving up an appreciation for breathing and for the joys of life. Like leaving your Ka-Bar, superior technology, or cold beer at home. For a SEAL that was crazy talk and definitely not possible to do.

———

In fresh clothing and with the whiskers scraped off their cheeks and chins, Melo and Sheraton made their way to the former quarters of their fallen brothers. Scanning their IDs at precisely 0700, they entered the room together.

Bennett's mouth dropped open. The place had been hit. Cushions, pillows, and even the mattresses had been slashed. Stuffing spilled out on the floor, and there were broken computer parts littered all around the room. "Not what I would call 'preserving the scene,'" Bennett said.

"Nope," said Melo. His usual upbeat demeanor was sullen as he moved methodically around the room, checking places he might stash information. "I'm not finding anything. Are you?"

Having moved into the middle of the room, Bennett's eyes scanned the whole place. "Something's missing. What's missing, Jonah?"

"Besides their cell phones and weapons?"

Bennett nodded. "They both preferred the tiny stickers, not the big Ka-Bars our Frogmen fathers used. If those items aren't here and weren't on the bodies, then..."

"The killer has them," finished Melo.

"Let's write a program to scan for weapons and to turn those phones on. Those are good trophies too."

"I'm on it, but it will take me some time. I do a lot of it in my head." Melo tapped his temple with his finger. "By tonight, I'll have something for you."

"Good. We have a date to keep. Don't want to keep Dr. Warren waiting." Bennett stepped out of the room and closed the door behind his Teammate. He hated thinking about the position they were in. Being in the dark about who the enemy was could be very dangerous.

—∾∾—

They were finally out of the facility at 0950. A rash of calls from Hubbard and Kess had kept all three of them running around.

"What did Hubbard have you doing?" asked Bennett.

Kimberly sighed heavily. "Paperwork. As if it really matters. We are either getting the shuttle off the ground or not. Filling out forms isn't going to make a hill-of-beans difference."

"Kess asked Bennett and me to plot and then replot several alternative orbits around the Earth. He said it was a normal part of the protocol," Melo said, leading Kimberly to answer his question without directly asking her.

"It is, but it shouldn't have taken more than twenty minutes, tops. I wonder what he was really getting at. You never know with him." Her face settled into a frown for a few seconds and then bounced back as they reached her car.

"Meet my baby. I call her Bella. 'Cause she's beautiful."

Nothing was better than a road trip. The car seats had thick plush cushions. The seats were each a little different: the two fronts were blue and the one backseat that faced backward from the passenger side was green. If Bennett had to define Kimberly's vehicle, it would be as a cross between a hatchback and a VW, yet oval-shaped on the exterior like an egg.

"Thanks for letting me drive," she said, her voice filled with delight again. "I don't take Bella on the road very often. This is a nice treat." The vehicle was housed in a small covered garage to the left of the Lester Facility's parking lot. Kimberly started the engine, and as they drove down the long road, Bennett had time to appreciate the landscape of the property and the mountains just to the right of them.

"Is she a 'kit' car?" asked Melo, whose face was slightly pale. He was strapped into the backseat.

Man, he hoped Melo didn't lose his breakfast in the car. From what Bennett had heard, the Chamber Debacle was going to be fodder enough for ribbings over the next several decades. Bennett pulled a pack of gum from his pocket and slipped Melo a piece of spearmint from the front seat.

Melo tapped Bennett's hand, thanking him for the offering. The foil wrapper crinkled as he took it out. Shortly after he started chewing, the car filled with the sweet scent.

"No, there weren't any instructions per se," laughed Kimberly. "My mother designed Bella when I was five years old. Well, we sort of did it together. As I built the first incarnation of the space shuttle, I had a ton of spare parts, so I altered the engine design and the interior and made her fully functional all by myself."

Bennett pushed on his passenger-side front seat cushion with his fingers. "The material is recycled plastic. Right?" The color was bright blue with silver sparkles. Melo's wife, Alisha, would have loved the car. It looked as if Barbie had based her Dreamhouse on its color spectrum.

"Yeah," she said as she snuck a glance in his direction.

He smiled at her.

"I had this soft stuff that didn't work on the interior of the shuttle because it got hard in highly extreme temps. Not wanting to discard it, I molded it into these cushions. Quite frankly, having this car to work on—and the CarP, too—saved my sanity. There were a lot of problems with the first few versions of the shuttle."

"Mainly what?" Bennett was curious about the history of the vehicle that was going to take him to space and sort of in awe of this lady who simply made whatever she wanted and had such faith in her creations that she incorporated them into daily use. What better endorsement was there?

"First, there was the integrity of the hull—finding the correct mix of metals and fiberglass to withstand the pressures of launch, orbit, and return. I'm not fond of the clay tiles; they break too easily. So I made a new concoction for the exterior that could withstand a multitude of abuses. The second problem was securing the interior frame to the exterior shell. When we did the crash tests in Virginia—Bennett, you saw the footage—we kept killing the dummies. So I had to create a layer of material to insert between the interior and exterior shell. This was a sticky type of foam that has old-school fiberglass in the compound that could adhere to both pieces. It was the perfect answer, until we realized the door wouldn't open properly or even stay on until we figured out how to reinforce it, foam it, and then insert the interior and exterior locking systems."

She took a breath. Her car sailed over a bump, landing on the other side without even touching the ground.

His face turned toward her. "Magnets."

"How did you know?"

"It's the only thing that makes sense. Where did you source the materials?" He knew China was the leading exporter of rare earth metals. Did she know of a hidden stash? SECNAV would have loved to lay hands on those materials in large quantities.

"A ranch between Wyoming and Montana has a cache. The owners are space nuts, and they read a paper I did in college. Since they were my professors at the time, they were sort of obligated when they learned what I was doing with the shuttle. They helped me find a solution and provided the rare earth metals. You're the first person whom I've told. I don't want anyone else knocking on the door. They have over five hundred acres of mineral-rich land, and their first test spot yielded about three tons of materials."

Melo whistled. "That's hefty. They could make a pretty penny on that."

She shrugged. "They don't need the money. Their pursuits are more…intellectual in nature. When my mother passed, they helped me, raised me as their own child. I'm protective of them as much as they are of me."

"Did they invest in the shuttle?" Bennett wasn't sure if Kimberly was going to answer the question. Personally, it was none of his business. In terms of his investigation, it was imperative that he understand.

"At first." She pushed her hair out of her face. "They encouraged me to find investors. It was the worst advice… I mean, I understand it from their end; wealth is not infinite, but it wasn't the best path for me, though overall, one could argue that it's made the project move faster. The Warren Shuttle project progressed further, more efficiently and effectively, than any other on the planet, and that's why we have this opportunity to launch the laser array into space."

Melo whispered. "A possible heiress. Good call, Boss."

Bennett poked him with his finger. The man was oblivious to what was really happening here. He needed to brief him and get him on the same page. "This vendor we're seeing, the one in El Centro, what items are they responsible for producing?"

"BIST, that's their name." Her lips thinned. "The locking mechanism and a few smaller parts. At first, they were using high-grade materials; now, the handle practically falls off in my hand. I don't know what's going on with them. The specs I gave them for the locking mold are extremely specific, as are the items they are supposed to be smelting. We have enough of the smaller items, but the locking mechanism… I don't like the look of the one currently installed."

"Understood," said Bennett. His mind ran through a multitude of possibilities, from espionage to an incompetent quality inspector.

A voice piped up from the backseat. "I'm surprised you don't have a smelter at the Lester Facility," Melo quipped. "You have everything else there."

"I wanted to—to put one in, but Hubbard blew his top when he learned what kind of cooling and heating systems we'd need to put in place, so BIST handles custom molding for us. I've been calling them for weeks without a response. I don't know what's going on over there." Her hands gripped the wheel tightly.

He could see her knuckles were turning white. Her muscles tightened as she clenched and unclenched her teeth. "Hey, we're here with you," Bennett said. "We'll figure it out."

"Time is ticking away. It's an indulgence to go to the vendor's manufacturing plant, but I don't know if we can afford to launch without this part. If we do, we're sticking a pilot inside and welding the door shut. That can't be safe." Her skin was mottled with red. As her hand slammed on the steering wheel, the car lifted for a count of five beats.

"Does this thing hover?" Bennett needed to calm her down, change the subject back to something she could converse about easier. Going into an unknown situation with heated emotions was asking for trouble.

"I'm working on it. Why should Willie Wonka have all the fun?"

Laughter came from the backseat as Melo cracked up. "I'd love to see this thing expelling bubbles. Frankly, that would make my day."

"I'll work on it," she said. The tension slowly eased out of her body as she considered the prospect.

Bennett's hand reached out and covered her free one. He squeezed it before allowing her attention to go back to the road. Maybe part of his job was making sure Kimberly Warren got what she needed to make this launch happen. Seemed to him that she was the only one concerned with every aspect of the hardware for the space shuttle. The rest of the groups at the Lester Facility were just going through the motions. He hoped he was wrong about that, but his gut feelings were usually right. There was something going on, and several folks who wanted Kimberly to fail—who didn't want this craft to get off the ground at all. Yes, one of his priorities was protecting her, and in turn, protecting the mission.

———

BIST Manufacturing was housed on a concrete slab on the outskirts of El Centro. The air was dry and arid, redolent of cacti and dried sagebrush. The setting was more conducive to a shoot-out at the OK Corral than it was to a manufacturer of molded and drop-forged hardware.

Only a few cars were in the giant parking lot, and there was no sign of activity, even though it was a weekday. That in itself set off a number of alarm bells for

Bennett. He slid a glance at his Teammate, and they both scanned for hostiles. Other than a few chicken hawks circling the area, there wasn't much evidence of life.

Bennett walked slightly in front of Kimberly, ready to push her out of way if there was danger. He and Melo packed two SIG Sauer 9 mms each, knives, and extra ammo. They left nothing to chance.

Each step set his nerves on edge. He was prepped for a fight, and that might have not presented the best appearance as they stood at the front door, waiting for the overweight guard. Bennett knew his eyes were daring someone to push his buttons.

"What do you want?" the guard shouted through the glass door.

"I need to see Arnold Bist. Tell him Kimberly Warren is here." Kimberly was the epitome of calm. Either she hadn't noticed the tension building around her or she was ignoring it. Either way, she played her role perfectly: that of a businesswoman here to discuss business.

The guard hesitated for several heartbeats and then backed up slowly toward his desk. The large floor-to-ceiling windows along the front of the building gave them a perfect vantage point if he should draw a weapon. Instead, the guard picked up the phone. His hand shook as he hung up, and he sat down, heavily mopping his brow with a handkerchief. Looking nervously at them, the guard reached over slowly and released the lock on the front door. This man needed a stress-reduction class, or maybe he just didn't like the look of two large, muscular men flanking a powerhouse of a woman.

The three of them entered.

Without a word, they headed toward the elevator

and pushed the Up button. The front door slammed loudly and the front-door lock clicked in place. Bennett raised an eyebrow at Melo, who gestured at the largest front window; it was a single pane that had obviously been replaced recently, and they could shoot their way through it if necessary.

The doors of the elevator slid soundlessly open, and they stepped inside. As it closed behind him, Bennett was scanning for any out-of-place devices, such as gas nozzles, an elevator trapdoor, or anything else that could endanger them. The doors opened onto the fourth floor without incident, and he stepped out in front of Kimberly and scanned the room.

A tall woman dressed in a suit and three-inch heels said, "Nice to see you again, Dr. Warren. If you and your associates will follow me into the conference room…" She moved down the hall with alacrity. "Would any of you care for a beverage? If you need anything, I'm Greta. Push the pound sign and the number one on the phone and I'll bring you what you need. Mr. Bist will be with you directly." She closed the doors, leaving them inside.

Melo laughed. "Well, that was anticlimactic."

Kimberly frowned at them. "What did you think would happen? This is commerce, not espionage."

Bennett looked at each of them in turn. "I'll reserve my judgment until after the meeting."

Arnold Bist was a short, dark-haired man with glasses. He rushed into the room, shook hands with Kimberly, and didn't even utter a greeting. Sitting in the chair closest to the door, he said, "I know why you're here. I can't apologize enough. Shortly after we agreed to your contract, my resources manager switched vendors and began accepting inferior materials. I had to shut down our entire manufacturing plant, clear the faulty outputs and products as well as the supplies, and find a new source for materials. That's why we're shut down, so I can cast and manufacture all the parts in a stronger and more reliable form. I know you have extras and that you're probably using your backups, but I promise you I will have the contracted parts by tomorrow afternoon. Again, you have my fullest apology, Dr. Warren."

"Thank you, Arnold. I was wondering what happened. You don't seem the type to break your word. Not in this business, when most custom work comes from the recommendations of clients." Kimberly leaned forward. "I appreciate you making sure that you're using the finest of materials."

"Yes, of course." He opened the file in his hand and withdrew a piece of paper. "Here's the metallurgy of the part. I will double the amount we're sending you. The cost is nullified; this is on us." His hands shook and his face was a mottled red. "Now, if you'll excuse me." He stood, staring at Kimberly as he waited for her nod of agreement. The minute she gave it to him, he was out the door and practically running down the hall.

"Was it something I said?" asked Melo.

Kimberly smiled at him. "You two look like thugs. He probably thought I was coming to whack him."

With that comment, even Bennett had to crack a grin. "Are we all set?"

"What do you guys say—wheels up?" Kimberly tucked the metallurgy report into her purse and followed Bennett out the door. They walked down the hall in silence, waited for the elevator, and stepped inside. The minute the doors closed, she said, "So, tell me about Alisha? What's it like being married?"

Bennett took a long, slow breath and rolled his eyes heavenward. It was going to be a long trip to the restaurant. Or rather, a trip in which his Teammate was not going to shut the hell up. His wife was one of Melo's favorite topics.

—∿∿—

Half an hour later, Bennett was ready to jump out of the moving vehicle. Kimberly laughed, listening to Melo talk her ear off. Melo had gained the front seat as "navigator," and Bennett—Kimberly's lover extraordinaire, which obviously counted for nothing—was stuck in the backseat. His long legs felt like pretzels, and if Bennett had had to listen to one more word about lost loves, misunderstandings causing a separation, and being reunited during a Wounded Warrior Housing Project in Julian, California, he would have broken the back window and leaped out.

Luckily, they arrived at the restaurant within seconds of his last nerve's getting trampled to death. Shoving his way out of the car and sitting Melo on his ass again was slightly satisfying, but breathing in the fresh air and setting his eyes on Kimberly truly eased his cranked-up tension. She had a way of calming him.

Damn, he felt like an idiot. He walked around the vehicle and took her hand.

She smiled at him, a glint of joy in her eyes. "Lead on," she said.

His smile slipped away as he leaned down and kissed

her. His body was firing on all cylinders, and he wanted to crawl back into the car, without Melo, and make out. "Want to ditch them?"

"No way! I have to meet Alisha now."

His lips made a thin line as he tugged her toward the door Melo had just disappeared through. "Fine. But I'm taking this as a rain check."

"Absolutely."

The restaurant seemed dark inside after the daytime sunshine. California had a way of appearing perpetually bright. He blinked his eyes slowly, helping them adjust, and located his Teammate. Melo was "macking" on a woman who was way too beautiful to be his wife.

"Jonah, stop. We have company." The sparkling woman turned to Kimberly and hugged her. "I'm Alisha. I'm a hugger."

The look of shock on Kimberly's face was priceless. She managed to stammer out, "Kimberly. N-nice to meet you."

"Bennett," he said as Melo's wife squished her body against his. He knew he shouldn't think it, but he did: Melo's lady was stacked. Her personality was just as bubbly as Melo's. The two of them monopolized the conversation, and he and Kimberly sat back to enjoy the ride.

Buzz. Buzz. Checking his phone, he saw a text from Ouster. The man wanted a sitrep, a situation report, and that meant now. Bennett showed the phone to Melo. "Order me an iced tea, a spinach salad, and a turkey burger," he said to Kimberly before the men excused themselves from the table to find a secure manner to update the Admiral.

—˄˄—

Using a small scrambler he had in his pocket for emergencies, Bennett found a way to call Admiral Ouster. He wasn't looking forward to briefing him, but duty was duty, and he was known as a SEAL with follow-through.

"Sheraton, sitrep." Ouster's tone was tense and to the point.

"The situation report is as follows," said Bennett. "We followed a lead to BIST, thinking it might be espionage, and found out it was poor quality in manufacturing a part. That completes the leads in terms of physical parts for the shuttle. Melo is on the software angle, going over the specs, and hasn't unearthed anything anomalous. Both of us are reviewing personnel files, and we're watching a number of people including Hubbard, the facility manager; Kess, the project manager; and several of the pilots. We cannot rule out that there are additional accomplices, but thus far we've set up safeguards with the help of Sally to monitor unusual activity."

"Your job is to get that damn shuttle off the ground, Sheraton, so hop to it." Ouster coughed. "And…Dr. Warren, what's her medical readiness? How is she?"

Bennett paused. What did he say? That she was spectacular? That he looked forward to spending time with her, even when she frustrated him, and he craved holding her, protecting her, and making love to her? Hell, the Admiral didn't want to know that. Damn, he didn't even want to acknowledge it himself. "Sir?"

"Is she well?"

"I suppose so."

"Sheraton, I will be blunt. I want Dr. Warren to leave this project and get out of the Lester Facility."

"May I ask the reason, Admiral?" Bennett wasn't going to rip the rest of Kimberly's dream away from her without a serious reason. He respected Kimberly, and what she had done up to this point to make this project viable and it had been fairly miraculous.

Ouster cleared his throat. "She probably mentioned that she was a friend of the family's. I…I don't want her getting hurt. It's as simple as that."

Bennett considered his next words carefully. "With all due respect, without Kimberly, the shuttle will *not* get off the ground. She is a mission critical asset, Admiral."

A few grumblings came from the other end of the phone line. "Understood. It's up to you, Sheraton, to keep her safe and complete this mission. We're counting on you and Melo to succeed."

The line went dead before Sheraton could reply in the affirmative. He pocketed the phone and small scrambler. He wasn't looking forward to sharing with Kimberly that Ouster wanted her out, but at this point in the game, keeping secrets was a stupid way to create miscommunication and mistrust. Keeping things on track with her was much more important, both in terms of the mission and for personal reasons.

The restaurant was dark and smelled of fried food and beer. Kimberly wrinkled her nose, wishing for something more pleasant to smell.

Alone with a woman she hardly knew, Kimberly had no idea what to talk about or even what to do. She was horrible at playing the social scene. Small talk was not her thing.

They placed their orders for lunch and sat quietly for a few minutes. Kimberly stared blankly at the diners around them, not really knowing where to begin with Alisha. Several ideas ran through her head, but nothing seemed to fit.

There weren't a lot of women in the sciences, and she had very few female friends. She wasn't exactly sure what to talk about. Stars. Molecules. The weather.

"I'll begin," Alisha said with a friendly smile. "I don't mind. I'm a chatterbox. If I pry too much, just tell me to mind my own business. It's just that I really like seeing Teammates with cool women, and you seem pretty awesome. So, how long have you known Sheraton?"

"Not long," replied Kimberly, feeling the heat climb up her neck and cheeks. Though the length of their acquaintance had been short, it was as if she'd known him forever. "What about you and Melo?"

"Ages," replied Alisha, waving a hand in front of her face. "It wasn't until years later that Jonah and I actually admitted how much we loved each other. It was during a building project for a dear friend of ours. So much time wasted! If you want my advice, don't ever let it get to that point."

Of course, in the car, Melo had told Kimberly all about his and Alisha's union. Wasn't it polite to listen again? Besides, hearing it from another point of view provided a whole new kind of insight into their relationship.

"I mean…if I hadn't married Jonah, I probably wouldn't have found such incredible happiness—and don't get me started on the orgasms. I mean, seriously,

SEALs know how to bring it. Full attention, focused actions, and Jonah can make me actually squeal. It's crazy. I bet you and Bennett do well together. Right?"

"Uh, yeah. Thanks." Kimberly didn't know how to answer, so she just looked down at her phone, trying to cut the conversation short. It didn't work. She watched the woman blather on before she suddenly stopped and shifted nervously in her seat. She used the pause to ask, "Are you okay?"

"Yes, I just… Jonah is retiring after this mission. Honestly, I'm worried about being married to a 'docked' SEAL. They call them sea, air, land guys for a reason. With or without flippers, they need that adrenaline rush. Will I be enough for him?"

Insecurity. Did every woman embrace it, when it came to her man? Did she have it with Bennett? Not really. Going toe to toe with him was foreplay; it turned her on faster than his hands caressing her skin. Heavens, did that mean she, Dr. Kimberly Warren, liked Captain Bennett "Boss" Sheraton mucking around in her brain as well as her body?

She smiled to herself. The answer was obviously… yes. She loved it.

"What?" asked Alisha. "You have a funny look on your face."

Kimberly shook her head, chasing the images of a very naked, argumentative Bennett tempting her with his brain, brawn, and body. "Alisha, he chose you. Melo strikes me as a definitive person."

Alisha grinned. "He is." She touched a spot between her breasts as if hugging her hand there. "Jonah's my heart, my fantasy, my partner, and my only love. He earns the title of husband each and every day with his kindness, support, fidelity, and sense of joy. Having him in my world, and him wanting me to be part of his, is the very best part of my life." Her sigh was sweet, and the tenderness reflected in her eyes tugged at Kimberly's heartstrings.

"A very lucky man."

"Yes, I am," replied Melo from behind them. "Beware what you say, ears are always listening."

Kimberly felt the blood drawn from her face. She stood quickly, her chair toppling over and landing on the floor with a loud thud. As she backed up from the table, hands caught her, steadied her, and spun her around.

"What?" Bennett's hands held fast to her arms. "What dots did you connect?"

She couldn't speak for a minute. Her mind worked through the details, forming words. "I've got it. It has to do with…listening and Sally. I know at least one person who has more Intel than he's supposed to." Her voice was full of excitement. "And I know how to prove that he's part of the problem."

Turning to Melo and Alisha, Kimberly rushed on. "Do you mind if we continue this another time? I need to get back to work."

"That's how I learn the best stuff. Covert, remember." Melo nodded. "Of course, go to it. Just give me at least an hour to…"

Alisha pinched him.

"Ouch," he replied.

"Manners, Jonah," Alisha scolded. She turned to Kimberly. "He'll be right with you. Good luck. Break a leg. Or whatever they say to deliver success in your situation. I understand. I've enjoyed meeting you." She waved over the waiter. "Could you please put their food in a doggie bag?"

Kimberly gave her a half smile and then whispered to Bennett, "What does Melo's wife know about the issues at the Lester Facility? In truth, she isn't cleared to know anything, though she appears to be a pleasant soul."

"I doubt it's anything important," he whispered back.

She nodded. As Kimberly picked up her purse, Alisha whispered to her, "Those two have chemistry like nobody's business." The comment made Kimberly smile. She liked Melo's wife, and she admired the relationship between Bennett and Melo. They were Teammates, sure, but they were more than that—brothers rather than just friends.

The waiter presented the bags of food and a tray of drinks. Kimberly scooted past the happy couple as Bennett grabbed the sustenance.

Alisha looked over her shoulder at her. She smiled. "Nice to meet you. Let's do this again."

"Sure," said Kimberly. It surprised her that she actually wanted to meet with Alisha again, and her husband too, perhaps dine together as a foursome. Well, well, well, that was a future-based notion. Where was her head now? Not on the present—she had to tune into the now. Focusing on fantasy was only going to create false expectations. It was highly unlikely she'd ever see Alisha again. Kimberly allowed herself to be okay with that fact, and she stepped alongside Bennett. Was he a fleeting experience, too? Maybe, but she hoped that wouldn't be the case.

Melo waved his hands at Alisha, giving her the

"hush" signal. It was obviously not working. His wife was, as she herself had said, a chatterbox.

"If they aren't already a couple, they should be. I think they will be my very next project. Where's her home? I can give her a free interior-design mock-up..." Alisha chatted on.

Her husband gave up trying to wrangle his wife. Putting his arm around her, he signaled the waiter so he could pay the check. Melo kissed the top of Alisha's head and laughed softly along with her.

She whispered to him, and he grabbed her and kissed her. The blush rising up her cheeks had to mean good news. Only one thing could make someone glow like that. Kimberly would have to remember to congratulate him when they were back in the car.

She tilted her head, imagining their life together. She could only imagine these two individuals were quite a riot, happy and content in each other's company. Did she feel that way about Bennett? In many ways, the answer was in the affirmative. "Do we have to leave?" she asked. There was something wonderful about being around another couple that was so deeply in love.

Bennett's hand snaked out and latched onto hers. "Yes. We need to go." He tugged her along behind him, and they moved at a swift pace. When they were outside, he put the food down on the hood of Kimberly's car and pulled her into a shaded spot against the restaurant. Tipping her head up, he kissed her gently and lovingly.

Her breath caught in her throat. She struggled to breathe for a second and then relaxed. "I...I need to get back, or you do."

"We both do. I need more Intel. Can Sally help us out?"

"Yes, of course," she replied and kissed him gently, rubbing her lips against his. "What about Melo?"

"He can hoof it. Only, what, sixteen miles?"

She laughed. Her eyes locked to his.

His face sobered slowly. "I just needed something beautiful to remember this moment. With the shade enveloping you, your eyes open wide, you are sparking brightly. Your energy is electric, and I couldn't resist making this memory even more perfect by kissing you."

She touched his face with her fingertips. "You're right." She kissed him again. Who was hungry for food when Bennett was near?

Time was fleeting. She was determined to make Bennett the pilot who would be going into space, and who knew what was going to happen up there? She needed to cherish the present; all of their time together was precious. Another five minutes wasn't going to change their world. At least, this current stretch of time wouldn't affect them negatively. Bennett filled her life with positives, and she wanted as much as she could get of him before she sent him into the unknown on a shuttle of her creation.

Of course, in the end, they waited for Melo. The trip back to the Lester Facility was quiet, except for brief congratulations to Melo. Alisha was pregnant, and he was thrilled about becoming a dad.

All three of them ate their food in the car, and no one spoke.

Melo was less animated without his wife's presence, and Kimberly could see how the two of them fit together and complemented each other's personalities. Did she and Bennett do that?

Sliding a glance in his direction, she could see his pensive expression. "Anything I can do to help?"

"What? No. Just wondering how Melo was doing on his assignment, a small project I asked him to work on for me." Bennett elbowed the seat and heard Melo grunt behind him.

"Almost done. Hold your panties." Melo was frantically typing on his phone.

"Anything I can do to help? I'm good at other things besides design."

"Pfft!" The noise Melo made was rude. "Hardware and software are on opposite sides of the discussion, as estranged as designers and programmers. Stick to what you know."

"I programmed Sally. She's pretty amazing." Kimberly's hands gripped the wheel tightly.

"Speaking of which, I'd like to chat with Sully. Any chance I can access the shuttle before we finish the pilot-assessment process?" Bennett stared at her with that gorgeously penetrating gaze.

She wanted to say yes, and that she would take him inside her greatest design creation. But if she did, he might lose his place in line as he would have an advantage. "I'll work on it." If she could figure out a way to get the security off-line and sneak him in, she could make it work. Why was she jeopardizing everything for him? She bit her lip. Because she was sweet on him, wasn't she? No, that wasn't it. She really, really liked him…more than she should.

Going through the main gate and down the long

roadway to the facility, Kimberly wondered how she could keep her perspective when it came to Bennett. The best pilot needed to be behind the shuttle controls. He was trained for this type of thing, with years of flying and space training under his belt. Learning her system and getting behind the stick had to be something he fought for. She needed time to think this all through. She wasn't going to just hand it to him—or was she?

Chapter 6

KESS PACED THE PARKING LOT. THEY COULD SEE HIM from the windows of Kimberly's car.

"Do you need my help?" asked Bennett. He was calm, the kind of peaceful that let a fighter land significant blows and do serious damage to his opponent.

"Our help," corrected Melo from the backseat.

"I can take care of myself. He'll blow his top and then retreat." Kimberly waved a hand at the SEALs and pulled into her parking place. She set the brake and got out of the car. When the men were out, she pushed a button on her key fob and locked the doors.

As they walked around the car, Kess charged Kimberly, his hands outstretched and his tone high and squeaky. "How could you take off like that, without even leaving a message for me? I need to know where you are at all times. We're only days away, and you're gone…simply vanished… for two hours. I was losing my mind. How could you?"

Melo and Bennett eased in between Kimberly and Kess, forming a human wall. The man could still see her, but it forced him to back down and to lower his voice.

Kimberly sighed. "Now Kess, I did leave a message with your secretary—the one you hardly ever check with—that I was going to visit BIST."

Kess checked his phone and confirmed the message from her. He choked on his next words. "I didn't realize, I… BIST? What happened?"

"They had a few quality issues, and we'll have replacement parts by tomorrow. It's handled. Wrapped up in a bow." She couldn't help herself from adding that last bit. The SEALs forming a wall added to the humor of the situation.

"I, uh, you missed a meeting about the pilot results. The medical staff has notes for you on the candidates, and two systems are ready to be put online in the shuttle." Kess straightened the collar of his shirt. "If I had known where you were, then I could have kept you better updated."

She touched Bennett's back. He was staring daggers at the man. If Melo hadn't given him a warning look, which she had caught, this conversation would have ended at Kess's first charge. "I will send you a summary of my meeting. I'm sure Sally will update me on what I need to know when I'm back in my room. Thank you for your concern. Good day, Kess."

Sweeping past the SEALs and Kess, she walked regally into the building. There wasn't a chance in hell that she would let anyone see her sweat. Rather, she'd have more fun leaving them in the dust. "Choke on that," she murmured under her breath.

Stepping into the white room to get decontaminated, she smiled to herself. *Strength*, she told herself, *is the power behind courage and success*. Her mother had said that to her often when Kimberly was a child, and sure enough, it was proving true. She wasn't going to let anyone step on her ever again.

───※───

Watching Kimberly get bawled out by Kess had been tough. Holding his tongue had been significantly harder

for Bennett than he realized. Hell, it was right up there
with not punching out his BUD/S instructor during the
first week of training, at least until he had figured out
that it was all a mind game meant to separate the weak
from the strong. But here, Kess was a control freak without any real purpose.

Still, his fingers ached to be rolled into a fist and
shoved down that jackass's throat. But he couldn't show
his hand without getting kicked off this project. No, he
had to figure out another way around Kess, one that
allowed him to protect Kimberly, identify the killer of
his brethren, and get the shuttle into space to complete
the Op.

Bennett followed Kimberly back to her room, trailing
a short distance behind her like a protective Rottweiler.
He wanted to keep that jerk away from her, but he also
knew he needed to encourage a positive response about
his access to the shuttle. Life would be so much easier if
he could wrap her in cotton wool and put her someplace
safe. He was pretty sure she wouldn't go for that.

Melo went ahead to their rooms, nodding at Bennett.
They exchanged glances. So much was unsaid, but they
both knew that things had to change. Time was ticking
down to the launch and they needed to find answers.

Kimberly opened her door and gestured for him to
come inside.

He entered the room, heading toward the center of
it. He needed to find his bearings with her, and that
meant communicating.

She closed the door behind them and turned toward
him. "Did you need something, Bennett?"

"I wanted to brief you." Why hadn't he noticed it

before? Now was when his mind really digested the details of her personality, scattered around the room like hidden clues. The personal quarters of Dr. Kimberly Warren were more businesslike than traditionally feminine. She sported framed degrees on her walls and enlarged airplane and shuttle designs rather than flowers and lace. He liked her no-nonsense style, but could he handle the no-regrets lifestyle that had her constantly putting her mind and body on the front line? Was he going to have to prove himself to her, show that he was of like mind in order to get the pilot's seat? Was that being deceptive, or was that who he really was?

"Go ahead." Kimberly was more of a bold soul than he realized. Getting between the dueling scientists, flying the CarP, taking chances in confronting vendors…what else was on the horizon? Did it make her a loose cannon, or a good ally? Strength and bravery were definitely two of her greatest virtues. He wasn't sure yet, but he had to draw some kind of boundary with her. In a firefight, his aim was always deliberate.

"I updated Ouster on the situation, outside the restaurant. I couldn't tell you then, but he wasn't pleased. We're no closer to a solution—to getting the shuttle safely off the ground—than we were before." Bennett scratched his chin, stalling and searching for words to soften the blow he was about to deliver. "He, uh, asked me about your medical readiness."

"And?" She didn't even bother to look up at him. Rather, she shuffled papers into piles, shoving a select few into file folders.

The least he could do was give the news to her straight. Ripping off the Band-Aid, he blurted out, "He wants you off the mission and out of the Lester Facility. Feels it's too dangerous here."

Her eyes locked on to his. Sparks of heat fired in his direction. "I bet he does." Her foot tapped rapidly. "It's not negotiable. I'm not going anywhere! This mission isn't going to happen without me. That's my baby in the hangar, and I decide who goes up and who doesn't. So watch it on the orders, from Ouster or from you, Captain."

"Killing the messenger—nice. That's it, you're always right. If I let you out of here, you're going to blackball me from the flight. Is that right?" He closed the distance between them. "This isn't how the situation works, Dr. Warren. I'm in charge here. My presence is the result of an order. If you have a problem with that, contact SECNAV."

She stepped closer, her hands on her hips. Her mouth was mere inches from his. "Don't press me. I have that number on speed dial—not the official one, but the personal cell number."

The humor in the situation struck him suddenly, and a chuckle bubbled up inside of him. "I can't believe we're having a pissing contest. You're not the enemy, nor am I."

Her hands fell to her side and she laughed. "You're right. I've fought so hard for such a long time that I forget to dial it back sometimes. I apologize for being sensitive on the subject. This…is my life. My creations are Sally, the scanning device, the CarP, and the Warren shuttle. I will not leave my babies behind."

"I understand. I told Ouster as much. I stood up for you, Kimberly." He pulled her into his arms. "You want to live every moment to the fullest, regardless of the cost. What I need is…I need to know that you will listen to me. If I say no, then trust me and don't fight it. On the opposite side of that coin, I will listen to you. Okay?"

"Agreed." She nodded against his chest. "I…I need you to know that living on the edge…it's how I live. I'm alone, and I've had to pick and choose the important moments and fight for them. I'm managing my health issues. I really am. Yet, at times, I have to ignore it so I can go for my goals, too. I know it's a fine line, but I'm aware. I'm a very deliberate person."

"Just don't outsmart yourself, Dr. Warren." He tipped her head up so he could look her in the eyes.

"Fine! I'm bluffing! I wouldn't do it, pull you from the running. You're the only person I can imagine completing this mission. Not that you can tell anyone else I said that." She sighed.

"Roger that." Brushing his lips over hers, he kissed her tenderly until the tension eased from her body.

She pushed out of his arms and walked to her desk. She made a show of shuffling a stack of papers, creating distance between them. "I, uh, I have some messages to return."

Bennett didn't want to leave. He wanted her attention. "Is this you?" he asked. He examined the picture of a small child dwarfed by a giant stone statue, searching for a way to connect. Sharing his childhood—the story of how he'd gotten his name—had brought them closer. Would this situation do the same?

"Uh-huh." Kimberly crossed the room back to him. She took the driftwood-framed picture off the wall. "My mother took this shot at Easter Island. I was three years old. She used to talk about the substance of the statues, which was volcanic tuff—basically, compressed ash." She laughed abruptly. "The stories she would tell me about these statues were amazing. They were carved to honor and celebrate the spirits of ancestors, to draw them and keep them close, and welcome them as they returned. The religious rituals were extraordinary and private."

"You traveled extensively."

"She loved it. We each had one bag and one book that went everywhere. I was so enthralled by space. Even then, my favorite book was *Goodnight Moon*. I would take the book and read it to the statues. I used to call them the star gods. My mother never knew where I got that term, but it seemed to fit. When she passed so abruptly, I couldn't call them anything else."

She looked up at Bennett, her eyes lost in the past. "Maybe I knew even then that there was more out there in the universe. The day the Hubble Telescope discovered new solar systems and Earthlike planets, I wept with joy. I have a search engine on my computer that gathers all the information it can on space, planes, and new technology." Shaking her head, she finally looked up again and focused on him. "Sorry, I get lost in this... all of it. If I could travel to distant planets, or even just orbit the Earth once, my life would be complete. Pretty silly, huh?"

He pulled her into his arms. "Never. I understand completely." He kissed her and then pulled his phone from his pocket. He brought up an article from phys .org about a star that had three super-Earths. "We think alike."

"I saw this piece! It blew me away, considering three

new civilizations. Who could be on those planets? I'm in awe of the possibilities." She wrapped her arms around his neck and leaned up into his lips. She kissed him, and his world rocked on its axis.

"So we're on the same page," he murmured.

"Yes." She sighed. "I can't believe I'm saying this, but what are you asking of me?"

"Help me."

"How?" She leaned her body against his. "I'll do anything, except leave."

"Roger that. I get it." He held her close, relishing the woman in his arms. His feelings for her were immense. He hated dragging her further into the chaos and unknowns of this mission, but he couldn't figure out how to do it without her. "Just trust me."

Her eyes met his. "I do."

He held her gaze, amazed by the trust and the wealth of emotion. "Thank you." He kissed her. It wasn't an ordinary brush of the lips or a simple caress. Instead, he put the weight of his own feelings into that moment.

His arms wrapped tightly around her as hers cradled the back of his head. Her fingernails dug into his hair, turning his head slightly so she could pillage his mouth with hers.

Passion rocketed through his body as he held her tightly against him. Her strength and fragility, this duality, made him cherish her even more, as if she were the treasure he would protect with his own life and at the same time worship with his soul.

He caressed her hips with his hands before he cupped her bottom. The two beautiful rounds filled his hands as she drew her nails along his back until she reached his backside.

Clothes lay thickly between them, an unacceptable boundary. Together, they pulled at each other's clothing frantically, until they were standing naked in the middle of the room.

"Beautiful! I'm a blessed man."

She laughed. "Enough small talk, SEALman. I need you…inside me."

He saluted her. "Aye, aye." Grabbing a condom from his wallet, he slid it on and then took her into his arms. He lifted her high and she squealed excitedly. Then he slowly lowered her until she was poised over his cock.

She wiggled against him, squeezing his shoulders. "Bennett."

He kissed her, lavishing her lips as he lowered her inch by inch, enticing her body to welcome him, until he was fully sheathed inside of her.

Kimberly sighed with delight. She wrapped tightly around his waist and used his shoulders for balance as he used the power in his shoulders, biceps, and core to lift her up and down on his engorged shaft. The sheer sensuality nearly buckled his knees as they stared into each other's eyes.

"Kimberly…I…"

She pulsed upward.

It took his breath away. He opened his feet wider, for stability, and braced his legs, his hips moving in rhythm with her body until their mouths were frantic to touch, to kiss, to explore, and to share the moans of pleasure that escaped their lips. As their actions grew more eager and their passions rose, they climaxed together in twin cries of delight and collapsed onto her bed.

Entwined in each other's arms and legs, they closed their eyes. Sated. Complete.

They rested, trusting in the power and beauty of each other and their shared lovemaking.

Bennett's mind drifted as his body relaxed. It was the first time all day that he'd felt somewhat at peace. It didn't hurt that sex released the tension, but being with Kimberly was more than that. She wasn't just a part of the mission anymore. The woman connected with him on a deeply personal level. He found himself biting his tongue, wanting to share things that he had never shared with anyone.

Would he take that step with her? Could he trust another female after his ex hurt him? She'd been a nightmare, a gold digger on a mission, and he couldn't fault himself for being young and blinded by chemistry. They'd had nothing in common and even less to talk about.

With Kimberly, there were too many topics to discuss. Images played through his mind of the ways they had already connected. He wanted to know everything about her, and he yearned to bare his soul to her. *Heaven help me*, he prayed. His eyelids felt heavy, and he wanted to keep them closed and blot out the world temporarily. Even the best of SEALs could use some sleep to stay sharp.

The only sound in the room was Kimberly's rhythmic breathing, and it lulled him, called him to join her in sleep. As he drifted off, he could hear someone in the bathroom.

Light flooded the room seconds later.

Melo burst into Kimberly's bedroom through the

door to the connecting bathroom. "I did it. Get up. The phones—they're active."

Sitting up in bed, Kimberly pulled the covers over her breasts. "Melo? What are you doing in here? Why are you standing there?"

Bennett was already swinging his feet over the side of the bed, wrapping something in tissue, and getting to his feet. Wide-awake and ready for action, he was raring to go. "I'll explain when I get back. Get some rest." The moment would have been perfect if they hadn't been interrupted, but he would never turn down an opportunity to nail the bastard who took out his brethren.

He pulled on his pants and shoes and grabbed his shirt. Securing the weapons he had hidden under Kimberly's bed, he and Melo headed out of the room, made sure the door slid shut and locked securely behind them, and hurried down the hallway.

Glancing over at his Teammate, he looked at his phone and saw the dot moving on the map. "Where is that?" They wound their way through the building.

Melo shook his head. "I don't know. I asked Sally, and she said it was near the pump room."

Several robotic sweepers squeaked by them, diligently cleaning the floor.

"I wonder if they have cameras. Maybe they recorded something." It was a long shot, but Bennett asked Sally.

"Yes, they are equipped." She stammered. "Un-un-unable to access playback."

Melo led the way down endless staircases as they moved deeper into the bowels of the Lester Facility. Neither of them had even known this area existed. And it was doubtful any bad guy would be down there by the time they reached the place they sought. Significant time had ticked by, according to their watches, hours they couldn't use to their advantage now.

Just as they were about to backtrack, a streak of dried blood on the wall had Bennett drawing his gun. The sweepers couldn't reach up the walls—good to know.

He scratched the streak. It flaked off and its hue was distinct. Every SEAL knew the difference between blood and paint and this was the real deal.

Both men moved silently now, sticking to the shadows as much as they could. When they reached the spot where the map told them the phones were generally located, Bennett's eyes had already sighted a knife, tucked behind a drain. He crouched down, examining the floor beside it. "One of our SEAL brethren bled out down here. There were streaks of blood on the side of the pump. This is where the murder happened. Perfect place. No one would hear the incident. All the murderer had to do was wait until he lured him into the empty hall, kill him, and then move him to someplace else. Bastard!"

Melo took pictures of the scene for the NCIS folks who were going to be pissed that they were the last ones in on this Op. What could they do? The mission was imperative, sure, but so was identifying the killer. He wore gloves as he collected the knife and wrapped it in a plastic bag. He'd brought them for just this purpose: evidence collection. "Do you think one man did this to a SEAL? It doesn't seem possible that a guy from here could bring down a highly trained operative."

Bennett spoke through gritted teeth. "We don't know what kind of training any of these folks really have, and there might have been some kind of trap involved." He pursed his lips and blew out a slow breath. "One SEAL was killed in the CarP crash, and the other was killed by his own knife. Fucking assholes!"

"Well, that lets Kess out. Have you seen his limp?" Melo stood.

"It's an act. He feigns being weak and fragile, but the man is all lean muscle. Take another look at him. We can't rule anyone out." Bennett searched behind the next pump for the phones and found them. The screens were smashed and had blood on them, but the SIM cards were intact. "Let's hope there's some good Intel on these things. We need answers, starting with why two phones are down here. What was the last SEAL up to—what was his lead—that brought him down here?"

"Let's search the entire area and see what we can find."

"Agreed," said Bennett. "I don't like the looks of any of this. There are too many questions."

<hr />

As the clock rounded midnight, Bennett stood up and stretched. Caffeine had lost its hold on his senses, and he could feel the weight of too many nights without enough rest. He and Melo had spent hours searching the hallways under the Lester Facility. It reminded him of the subway system below Paris, the Metro was a warren of paths and rooms.

Afterward, they'd grabbed sandwiches, salads, and juices and headed back to their rooms to decipher the phones. That had taken up time, yet those devices had turned up very little data, other than lists of everyone in the Lester Facility with stars next to some names and a few photos. He and Melo had already identified the same souls. At least they were somewhat on the right track—unless there was someone they hadn't considered yet. "What do you think?" Bennett asked.

Pulling the second SIM card from the computer, Melo placed both cards into a small Ziploc bag and hid them in his wallet. He dropped the phones in another Ziploc for NCIS.

They had tried dusting the phones with talc, but there were no fingerprints. They'd worn gloves when they did. Maybe the NCIS lab would have better luck—not that they could wait that long.

"I'm at a loss. I was sure we'd find something useful. Those men died for a reason. What are we missing?"

Kimberly stood in the doorway, watching them. "My input. When were you going to tell me you found the phones?"

"Wow, you are a quiet one. You have a unique way of sneaking up on people," said Melo in a rather harsh voice. He refilled his mug with coffee and drank it down, despite how cold the pot had become. Shuddering as he set the mug down, he said, "Sorry, I'm tired."

"I'll bet. Listen, I've thought it over. The only way we're going to solve this mystery is by putting our heads together. Okay?" She stepped into the room and sat down on the end of Bennett's bed.

He stared at her. He hated the idea of endangering her, but they didn't have a lot of time. The launch was only a few days away, and he didn't want to blast off without tagging the hostiles. Identifying them had to be a priority before the launch.

Melo walked around the room. "I don't like it. We're used to getting shot at. You're not."

"I have better hearing, and I'm quiet. You didn't even know I was here. Of course, Sally helped me a little by forcing the air vent close to the bathroom door to shift to higher output. It hid the sound." Kimberly crossed her legs, tucking her hands together. "I've used the technique before to avoid Kess or sneak around him."

"Low blow on the hearing thing, Warren, but I'll give you credit on the sneaking around." Melo looked at Bennett, waiting for his acknowledgment.

How could he avoid it? They needed her to get to the bottom of this quickly. "Fine. But you're getting us on that shuttle tonight. However you need to do it." Bennett walked over to her and held out his hand. When she placed hers in his, he helped her gently to her feet. "And you're not to endanger yourself on purpose. Understood?"

The fact that she crossed her fingers before she nodded was not lost on him. Boy, she was a stubborn one. Hopefully, that streak didn't get her—or them—into hot water.

Chapter 7

GETTING TO THE SHUTTLE WITHOUT SOMEONE watching their every move was easier said than done, but by sneaking in, they would have the place to themselves to investigate whatever they wanted.

Kimberly mapped out a plan with Bennett and Melo and then set out to implement it. Since she was smaller than both men, she was presently crawling through the air ducts. Being blasted by the chilly stuff didn't ease her nerves. Instead it ramped them higher, sending shivers racing down her spine every few seconds.

Her teeth chattered by the time she reached the center of the Lester Facility's ductwork. Working her way through to the next set of ducts, she pulled herself through as fast as she could.

She heard voices now and then and paused to allow them to pass before she resumed her path. Unfortunately the hangar was on the far side of the building, and the plan didn't take into account how long it would take her to crawl there on her hands, elbows, and knees.

As she reached her destination, she again heard voices. Pulling herself slowly closer, she realized they were familiar: Yuri and Wang. She couldn't make out their words, but neither of them had been approved for shuttle tours, due to the safety precautions, nor was anyone allowed to be alone with the vehicle.

Withdrawing her phone from her pocket, she keyed

in her request. Sally, page Yuri and Wang to meet Kess in
the conference room. Acknowledge my request with a text.

The computer responded instantly, and an announce-
ment went out over the loudspeaker. The two men left
the room quickly.

She pushed the grate open and lowered herself to the
floor. Closing the grate, she texted Bennett and Melo
and then keyed in an access code to open the door.

Ten minutes passed before the men arrived. She was
getting worried when they rounded the corner.

"Did you see Yuri and Wang?" she asked.

"No," said Bennett. "Were they in here?"

"Yes. It pisses me off too. They don't have approval.
There seem to be a lot of people coming and going
without my knowledge, and that's not part of my agreement with Kess and Hubbard." She closed the door and
crossed her hands over her chest. "Have at it."

Melo leaned down and said, "Good job. Even though
you look like a dust collector."

She frowned. "Right! You'd think it would be cleaner
in there, given how paranoid they are about particles."

"How often do they clean vents?" asked Bennett.
"Not very, from the look of it."

"And since I've gotten covered in grime, then I'm the
only one who has accessed the shuttle in this manner.
That's a helpful fact to know," she added.

"I agree."

Uncrossing her arms, she brushed off as much of the
"filth" as she could reach. Then she shadowed the men
as they walked around the shuttle, examining the outside. "What are you looking for?" she asked.

"Anything out of the ordinary. Of course, you're the

perfect person to ask. Does anything stick out?" Bennett swept his arm wide, inviting her to take the lead.

She bit her lip as she examined the outside. "Everything seems fine here…" She turned her head to the side. "Wait, you remember how the door lock was an issue? That's why we visited BIST. Well, I placed my initials under the handle of a solid one, and this isn't the right side." Pulling out the door, she examined it. "It's been put on backward. Someone took it apart to get inside and messed up the reinstallation." Looking up at Bennett, she said. "I wonder why."

"A better question might be, what did they do inside?" Melo added.

They walked around the inside of the shuttle.

"It matches my design," Kimberly said. She sat down in the pilot's seat. "Of course, the laser array isn't loaded yet. That goes in tomorrow. Things might change."

"Did you notice a box in your crash test, one that took out a pilot?"

"No, but I only watched the video once. Was there a box? I didn't put one in." Kimberly stood. "I'm going to go back to the room and access the video."

He grabbed her arm and gently tugged her to a halt. "Wait. Before you do, I think we should watch this room and find out what's going on. If we can access it after the array goes in, we might find the answer we need."

Melo's mouth changed from a thin line into a wide grin. "So you think whoever is responsible for the box might be sabotaging the project as well as causing the deaths? Let's set a trap and see what we catch."

"Agreed," said Bennett as he escorted Kimberly off the shuttle. "Time for a new game—one of our creation."

—∿∿—

Melo sat in an R & D cubicle and pulled apart the laptop. As he opened it up, he found several interesting items, including a tracking chip and a second chip that mirrored all information and sent it wirelessly to another device. Without dislodging those, he laid out all the tools he needed for his ruse.

"Sally, call Rigley. Tell him Melo needs him in the R & D Center," Bennett commanded. He added one last order. "Can you covertly share any communication—outgoing or incoming—from his phone and direct that info to my phone and Melo's via text message?"

"Affirmative." Sally created new icons on Bennett and Melo's phones. To keep the good doctor safe, they'd all agreed that Kimberly should stay in her room and return the many messages that had piled up while they were gone. None of them wanted to see her pulled from the decision-making role for the pilot position due to negligence.

Messages scrolled across the screen...

Rigley: Being called to R & D by Melo.

Yuri: Why?

Rigley: Don't know. Will update you.

Yuri: Watch yourself. More at stake than you. Remember that.

Bennett whispered into his phone. "Print this conversation and send copies to Kimberly's room and mine. No one else is to view this."

"Affirmative," replied Sally.

The room was filling up with scientists. Men and women chatted, raising the decibel level in the room.

Rigley entered and wound his way toward Melo.

Staying out of sight and keeping an eye on Rigley was optimally effective in his position to the front and right of Melo. If Rigley tried to bolt, Bennett could nail him easily.

"What do you have for me? Is it a solution to our problem?" Rigley stood with his hands crossed over his chest. He stared at Melo for several seconds.

Every scientist in the room was working on the same project: a new chip and hardware design to assure that the array could stay in a locked position. Putting all different types of tech heads together to find the answer was why there were so many cubicles shoved into one room.

Unfortunately, the technology of some countries lagged behind that of others, and no one wanted to share designs at this point. Hopefully, that would change if and when a solution was found. If it wasn't, Bennett knew he could come up with an option on the fly. He trusted his skills.

Melo gestured at the table in front of him. "I didn't get a chance to thank you for the computer you lent us."

Rigley's face paled. The guy looked like he was going to wet himself. Whoever chose him as a partner in crime had picked poorly. His mouth opened and closed as he gulped air. "I, uh… That is… I mean…"

"Who told you to give us this particular computer?" Melo leaned forward. "Or was this your brainchild?"

"What? Me? I gave it…to you." Redness climbed the man's features as he shifted from foot to foot. "I mean…I don't know what you mean."

Melo cleared his throat. "Correct me if I'm wrong, but this chip allows all information to be mirrored to another system, and this allows it to be sent wirelessly. Where is it going?"

A text from Kimberly popped up on Bennett's phone. Sending reinforcements.

No! Bennett gritted his teeth. He needed more from Rigley than just a copy of a text. It wasn't conclusive enough. Hold off, he texted quickly.

Too late, she replied.

His eyes caught movement. Bennett saw the action unfolding before anyone else did. The door on the far side of the room opened. Hubbard and several security guards entered, looking angry. They rushed through, making their way to the back of the room where Rigley and Melo were talking.

Rigley's eyes darted to the men coming his way. His agitation escalated, and he stumbled backward as he moved away from Melo's cubicle. When his back hit the wall, he took several short breaths. Pulling his phone from his pocket, he pushed a button and said, "Erase."

"Sally, stop Rigley. Whatever he's erasing, halt it." Bennett moved, grabbing the phone from Rigley's hand and pushing him to the ground. He had spotted the bulge next to the phone: a gun. Was this guy going to pull a gun on a SEAL? Damn, bad idea. If the shot didn't take out the target, a SEAL would pound him into snot.

The guards took Rigley in hand. They weren't gentle either.

Bennett emptied the gun and handed it to the tallest guard. "I'm going to want that back. I recognize it." This was a 9 mm SIG Sauer, standard issue in the Teams. Leaning down, he held Rigley's gaze, giving him the icy eyes he'd perfected after years of interrogating the enemy. "Where did you get the gun?"

"I found it." Rigley was shaking. "I did. Really. The gun was in the staircase leading to the basement. Thought it was a good idea to keep it, given that there are so many…international types running around." He swallowed hard, his eyes darting from Bennett to Hubbard. "Believe me, please. I've provided years of service to the Lester Facility. I'm a good employee."

"One that was passed over for a raise two years in a row," Hubbard said, shaking his head. "I'm disappointed, Rigley." He added to the security guards, "Take him to my office and keep him secure. Call the police, and let the front gate know that we're going to have company."

"Wait," said Kimberly, who had run into the room. She was panting, holding a hand to her chest as she said, "Wait, please. You can't call the cops."

"Dr. Warren, I don't see how waiting will aid anything." Hubbard pushed his shirtsleeves farther up his arms and put his hands on his hips. His frustration was evident.

Bennett scratched his chin and gave a quick nod. "As much as I'd like to disagree, calling the police will delay the launch until an investigation is complete. There's a time crunch, right?"

"Let us move forward on this lead and see where it takes us," Melo offered.

A murmur rose around them. Several of the scientists, designers, and engineers were standing in their cubicles and watching the action. One of them was filming it on his phone and adding commentary. What had the world come to?

"Quiet!" Hubbard shouted. "Sally, by order of the facility manager—match my voice print on this—move all recordings of this event in the R & D Center to my computer only. Do not leave any material on any other devices such as phones, tablets, computers, et cetera." Pulling his handkerchief from his pocket, he mopped his brow. He murmured under his breath. "Why people need to record every moment of the day is beyond me—as if we'd allow them to get one iota of info out of this place. Thank God we have several levels of blockade to keep it from the outside world. Hell, there's no live streaming from inside the Lester Facility anyway."

Melo pushed past the guards, getting to within a hair's breadth of Rigley. "Wait! That was the whole point. You found a way past the information blockade. You were sending data to the outside. What was it... espionage or the highest bidder?"

"No, I can't. You don't understand. You wouldn't be able to protect me if I told you some...of the truth. That's all...I can share..." Rigley was sweating up a storm. How could someone sweat that much in such a short time? He had to be up to his eyeballs in this whole mess. His clothes looked like a hiker's after several hours of walking through a lake or stagnant pond with pit marks, slime, and other stains. Wasn't there water about two miles from here, but still on the facility's property?

"You want to bet?" added Melo. "Visit any nice bodies of water?"

"How did you know?" Rigley asked. "Were you watching me? I...can't talk to you."

"Hold off there." The guards made a move to pull Melo off Rigley. Bennett stopped them, grabbing their arms and pulling them to a halt. He gestured for them to give Melo a minute. When Hubbard nodded his consent, the guards complied.

"I can't handle the stress. I don't sleep. I just…" Rigley said. "Fine, fine. I'll tell you everything. The first part is, yes, I'm selling information to the highest bidder and I was meeting someone by the far pond. But I'm not alone, and if you want all the information, you need to speak to…" Rigley sucked in air as if he was deprived. His hand pushed hard against the wall of Melo's body without budging it.

Bennett reached back and eased his Teammate until they were standing next to each other. Melo cut him a glance that said he was none too happy about being pulled off Rigley and that he would get further with some bodily harm.

Suddenly, an odor that smelled like burning hair permeated the room.

Rigley's eyes bulged. His body jerked and spasmed. "My p-pacemaker." His mouth opened, and foam came out the side as he shook and then went limp. He crumpled onto the ground.

Melo stepped toward him. Pulling a pen from his pocket, he touched the man. A shock came from the body.

Kimberly leaned down and touched Rigley's neck. "Move over. He doesn't have a pulse." She did chest compressions until the medical staff arrived. They took over for her, but it was clear the man was deceased.

Rigley was removed on a stretcher.

No one spoke for several minutes.

Static broke the silence, followed by a buzzing.

Her attention went to her phone.

"Kess, come to R & D. We need to talk," Hubbard said into his phone. "Kimberly, I'm ready to close up shop and call it a day. We cannot continue this way. I understand this launch is of national and international value, but how many lives can we risk on it?"

"Please, give me some time," said Kimberly. She wiped tears from her eyes, obviously moved. Whether it was the death or the threat of canceling the launch, Bennett didn't know. "We're close to finding answers."

Bennett listened to their conversation for a few seconds and then noticed a black spiral pattern around a wall socket. He nodded to Melo. The two of them inspected the area where Rigley had stood. A small silver device was set in the wall, plugged into the socket. The device on the wall—this silver box—had given Rigley a fatal dose of electricity that made his body dance and his hair fry.

My p-pacemaker. These were the only words Rigley had managed to add before he died.

"Sally, what does this silver box do?" Bennett was careful to ask very quietly via his phone.

"It is a projection/speaker amplifier for the room, controllable by any device." Sally went on to explain how it could be used as a speaker for music or to project information or as an extra electrical conduit.

Melo furrowed his brow. "Great. So anyone in this room could use this device."

"Correction," said Sally. "Anyone in the Lester Facility can control it."

Bennett sighed. *So much for our pool of suspects, It went from smaller to larger again. But what about Yuri? Was he involved in this, or was his text conversation with Rigley more misdirection?* They couldn't afford any more red herrings if they were going to stay on track.

He watched Melo pull the pieces of the computer together and place it in a bag. Whatever they planned next, it had sure as hell better work out more effectively.

───※───

Kimberly stood with her hands on her hips in Hubbard's office. Her anger was practically producing steam out of her ears. To keep herself calm, she was tapping her foot and trying to ignore the strange rotten-egg odor in the room. "If you invited me in here to take away my control over who becomes pilot, you have another thing coming."

Hubbard sat unmoving behind his desk, taking the silent route. His half-eaten lunch of Caesar salad looked like it had been sitting there for hours.

She wrinkled her nose, but it wasn't just the meal that made her queasy, it was the two backstabbers confronting her. "This is my shuttle design. Without my solving the return-trip safety issues with the shuttle's unique combination of hardware and software, none of us would even be here. We have one more change for a safe and effective round-trip. So do you want to tell me why I'm getting berated by Kess? I'm doing my job, and I'm doing it well."

Kess smiled at her. That idiot was sitting nonchalantly in a chair by the window, sipping coffee as if this discussion were a commonplace chitchat between friends. He was the enemy, and nothing was going to make her give up her ground.

"I'm simply saying that if Kimberly cannot respect our rules, why should she be making the big decisions?"

She spun in his direction. "So, I go to a vendor's to check on a part, and I'm the bad guy here. What a load of crap!" Her laughter started slowly and grew louder. "I'm not giving up my role of choosing a pilot, so you can suck it, Kess!"

"Miss Warren..." began Hubbard.

"*Dr*. Warren," said Kimberly through gritted teeth. "I've earned the right to be here, and if you have a problem, call the Secretary of the Navy. Now, get off my back and out of my way." The last line was shouted, and she knew her temper had taken control of her, but she was done with them. Whatever was going on, she had had enough.

The two SEALs decided it would be a good idea to conduct interviews with the trainees. Each trainee would be brought to them one at a time, without prior briefing, and they would be separated until the questioning was over.

They were given a small room—basically a shoe box with one door—containing a small table and two chairs. Hubbard had told them to "be gentle" with the pilot candidates. Bennett didn't give a rat's ass about their comfort. He just wanted to get to the bottom of the deaths and the issues with the shuttle.

After a brief discussion with his Teammate, they decided that Melo would do the questioning and Bennett would observe. Melo was a talker, and he chatted away as he positioned a chair on one side of the table and took a seat on the other side. Bennett took up residence in a far corner. It was in shadow, but it gave him a great view of the door and the interviewee. He was a visual learner and preferred this role, as it gave him greater insight into the involuntary emotional cues tied to body language.

The first man in the hot seat was a man with the singular name Nyambi, an African astronaut who nodded at them both before he took his seat across from them. "What topic will we be discussing?" he asked.

"Several. What brought you to the Lester Facility?" Melo kept the tone casual. There was no time limit for the interview, so they were going to make the most out of it.

"I arrived a few days before you. Our first representative took ill. An emergency appendix operation, I'm told. I was asked to come out here and represent our country and am pleased to do so." Nyambi spoke with animated hand gestures. "We've been performing similar simulations. Several private corporations are having their own space race, but as a soldier, my first duty is to my country. Monetary concerns come very far down the line. I'm sure you understand."

"Married?" Melo asked.

"Engaged." Withdrawing his phone, he showed Melo several snapshots of a woman with short hair. "Ella. Isn't she beautiful?"

"Yes," agreed Melo. "What do you think of your fellow candidates?"

Nyambi's face fell as he pocketed the phone. "I expected like-minded individuals who were fascinated by space. Instead I have faced tremendous competition and ungentlemanly behavior."

"How so?"

"The first set of shuttle specifications was outdated.

I check such things. If I had gone into the flight simulation with the old specs, I would have failed. When I brought the issue up to Kess, it angered him. He said there were several issues happening and I should take care to double-check everything. I did." Pursing his lips, Nyambi considered his words. "I did not want to be suspicious, but I have had items stolen from my room too, including my computer."

"And you brought this computer from home or received it from…"

"What was his name…like the gum, perhaps?"

Melo leaned his elbows on the desk. "Rigley."

A smile lit Nyambi's features. "Ah, yes, that is the IT person who gave me my equipment. He appears nice enough. Do you need me to do an assignment with him?"

"Not exactly. Where have you been for the last hour?" Melo didn't let anything show. Rather like a conductor leading his orchestra, he led the conversation where he wanted it to go.

"I was spending time with Donner and Leon, having my test in the anechoic chamber. A strange place—felt like I was in a tomb, though I suppose that is the point. My time was twenty-two minutes. I'm told it is acceptable. Dr. Leon was escorting me back to my room when I was redirected here." Nyambi looked at Melo and then Bennett. "What has happened?"

"Where were you before the test?" asked Melo, sitting back in his chair.

"Playing Beethoven's Fifth and attempting to gain a few hours of rest. My roommate snores." He placed his hands on the table. "How does any of this concern Mr. Rigley?"

Melo glanced at Bennett. This guy knew nothing.

It was clear. "It does not. Thank you for your time, Nyambi. You are welcome to leave."

Puzzled, the man stood, nodded at each of them again, and walked out of the room. The door closed behind him.

The room seemed bigger with only the two of them in it.

"Do you think they will all be like that?"

"Mostly transparent?" Bennett shrugged. "Perhaps. All we can do is interrogate them and find out. The good part is, we can ask them anything we want."

The next six interviews yielded nothing useful. Five men and one woman from different countries, and they all had verifiable alibis. There was only one interview left—Yuri Pelsin, the astronaut from Russia.

Of course, when they'd asked the security guards to bring him in, the man had already gone back to his quarters and wasn't answering any pages. So Melo and Bennett trekked the length of the Lester Facility to reach Yuri's quarters. It was a tediously long walk.

They passed several of the astronauts and a few trans-lators. Assistants trailed along with a couple of them, and one of them took dictation as he moved.

Finally at Yuri's door, Melo knocked. Nothing. He rang the buzzer on the side of the door. Nothing. Looking at each other, they silently agreed they weren't going back empty-handed. They were going to find some information on Yuri Pelsin.

Fed up with wasting his time, Bennett said, "Sally, let us in to Yuri's chamber." They had been given carte blanche, and this seemed like a good opportunity to take advantage of it.

"Affirmative." Sally accessed the door and it slid soundlessly open. Bennett decided she was an excellent computer and a decent force for good in this crazy place.

He stepped inside. The room was dark. "Lights."

Instantly the lights lifted to full, showing Yuri stretched out on his bed, wearing earphones and with a surprised look on his face. "Did we have an appointment?" he asked, and then mumbled, "It appears to be a strange time, when people are allowed access to what should be a private chamber."

The room was large, almost as big as Kimberly's. Someone had assigned Yuri a generous living space. The furnishings were plush, with two overstuffed chairs, a table with bottles of vodka, and a humidor most likely filled with premium cigars, probably Cubans. The color scheme was different from other personal quarters, as though it had been professionally decorated in tones of gray and black. The bed was a California king, unlike the queens in all the other rooms. Even Kimberly had a queen, and she'd said that was standard.

The black carpet was thick and well padded under his feet, and the ceiling had a modular set of planets set into it, positioned directly over his bed. The mobile reminded him of something a baby or child might have in their room. There were no paintings on the walls.

Instead, photos dotted one of the bookcases, mostly of a pretty blond woman who looked Swedish and two matching blond children with big smiles. On the desk were manuals and books similar to the ones Bennett was reading about piloting the shuttle and the types of problems one could encounter. Well, that was interesting. It looked like Yuri intended to sit in that pilot's seat.

The notes on his desk were similar to Bennett's, except the calculations were definitely wrong. It was easy to read at a glance. Yuri hadn't accounted for the gravitational pull of the Earth or for any drift, especially if the shuttle was struck by an object big enough to move it or give it momentum. Of course, the onboard computer could correct drift, firing the engines, etc., but one needed to take all of that into account in case the onboard systems failed. Hell, Yuri needed more experience. Make a decision tree, use some statistics—it would have yielded better results than the ones he'd arrived at.

Bennett finished his circuit of the room and went back to the center, preferring his vantage point on both the doorway and the jerk on the bed. He nodded at Melo, who was waiting for his cue.

Melo walked to the desk and pulled a chair over to the bed. He sat down and smiled. "I spoke with your friend, Wang." Nice opening—the bait was set.

"He's *not* my friend," rushed Yuri. "He's my—" Abruptly his words ceased, as though he was about to blurt out something he didn't want to. The look of frustration on his face indicated some kind of guilt.

"Your what?" prodded Melo. "Are we soliciting sex?" Of course, Wang had said nothing interesting or out of the ordinary, except that Yuri had helped him with a project to plot the telemetry of the communications array—step one in the pilot's mission after he breached the atmosphere and reached the appropriate orbit. But there could be more to the situation. Bad guys rarely announced their diabolical plans without the appropriate prodding.

"No!" said Yuri, pushing off his bed and getting to his feet. He looked offended. "I have a wife and children."

"That does not preclude a relationship, not in this day and age. Whether that is a friendship or something more…"

"Nothing more." Yuri scowled as he walked to the small table, where a small coffeepot and cups sat, and with his left hand, he poured a cup of dark, syrupy dregs that had to be cold, given their consistency. He took a sip, frowned, and put it down. Opening his full-size refrigerator—another thing Bennett hadn't seen in a personal room—he withdrew a carton of orange juice, drank it down in several gulps, and dropped it in the trash.

"What are you doing with Wang?" asked Melo. "Sharing notes? Trading secrets? Espionage?"

Yuri's eyebrows shot upward, shocked by the implication, even more so than the question about sex. Nope, that wasn't the right direction either. Or, he thought, studying Yuri's face, maybe it was the right question.

As if Melo had plucked the thought from Bennett's head, he asked, "How did you meet Kess?"

"At Space Command many, many years ago, before it was replaced by Stratcom." Yuri waved a hand in front of his face. "We were working on projects similar in nature, but were not permitted to share information at the time. Our technology was half a decade behind yours, and the information was proprietary, until Russia caught up."

"Interesting. So Kess slipped you the data and the technology blueprints…" Melo stood and took up a position at the wall across from his interviewee. He cocked his head to the side and waited, leaving the idea to dangle in the air, another hook and another worm.

Yuri crossed his arms and looked up and to the right, undoubtedly tapping into his imagination. He spoke with his eyes still averted upward as he shifted his weight from foot to foot. "I don't know what you mean."

Lie! Body language was such a giveaway. Pelsin's personnel records indicated he was a lefty. If he had been looking to the left, Bennett would have given the man the benefit of the doubt, as most individuals looked in the direction of their dominant hand or side. But those looking to their nondominant side, especially upward, were clearly thinking up a story. Combined with Yuri's changing his weight from foot to foot...well, it was clear that this man was a liar.

"I can't believe you would accuse me of such a thing. I need you to leave my personal chamber. Now." Yuri shifted his eyes toward them, and his anger was evident. He was daring them to start something.

"How well did you know Rigley?" asked Melo.

Yuri's lips thinned. He walked to the door and pointed. "Out, now." When neither man moved, he added, "He gave me my computer and updated my phone." He gritted his teeth. "Leave. I need my rest for the next set of tests."

"We're allowed to hold you, to detain you, and to keep you from being considered for the pilot position of the Warren Shuttle." Melo swept his arm dramatically, indicating that all of this could go bye-bye, and then he smiled.

Yuri's fingers rolled into a fist and his arms stiffened. The man looked about to blow his top, but then something stopped him. He laughed, a burst of a strange, maniacal sound. "You gentlemen can *try* to do whatever you want." Then he strode past them and lay down on his bed. He put the headphones back on. Closing his eyes, he blocked them out, the odd smile still on his lips.

Bennett gestured with his eyes to the door. What an odd person Yuri was!

Melo left the room first, skirting the edge of the bed with his foot and sending a shimmer of movement along the mattress. Ah, he was a mischief maker.

Yuri didn't move. He winced and then resumed his "cool," supine posture.

As Bennett crossed to the door, about to walk out, he looked over his shoulder. Ah, there it was...

Sure enough, Yuri had one eye open, watching him. The expression on his face was one of deep satisfaction and relief. The Russian had won this battle, but the war wasn't over. Yuri wasn't going to win the next one. Bennett would make sure of that, if he had to die trying.

Kimberly was bored to death. Waiting outside Hubbard's office was a tedious taste of retribution. She could imagine that was exactly what Kess was thinking. It was her turn to pace back and forth while she waited for some kind of communication. Nothing good could come from having the facility manager and the project director chatting one-on-one.

The hallway was bleak, devoid of people and any other human touches. Hubbard preferred the place sterile, so it didn't have so much as a kitty poster on the wall. Well, there might be one in someone's personal quarters, but not out in the open. Actually, given the collection of individuals housed in this place, "warm and fuzzy" probably wasn't on anyone's priority list.

"C'mon," she said softly. "Let me in."

Well, maybe being left in the cold was her fault. Originally, they'd kicked her out of the office when she started a shouting match about this being *her* shuttle. Neither Hubbard nor Kess had taken very kindly to that notion. She had to admit that many people had contributed bits and pieces of the inner shuttle workings to get the project moving faster, but the overall hull design was hers, and it did bear her name.

"Am I that much of a tough cookie?" she asked herself. Of course, she would rather be made of tough stuff than be soft and squishy. If there had ever been a learning curve for her, this was it: standing up for herself.

She straightened her spine and took several long, slow breaths. When she grew tired, she leaned her head against the wall and wondered where everything had gone wrong. Somehow, she had been losing control an inch at a time, and Kess had been gaining ground. Would it solve anything if Kess left? As disheartening as it was to admit, it wouldn't accomplish anything... not at this point. They needed to finish this work and launch this baby.

She checked her watch. It had been hours. Perhaps she should just head back to her room and let them page her when it was time to return.

Abruptly, the door slid open. A voice beckoned from inside. "Dr. Warren, please join us." It was Kess.

She cringed. She'd never get used to that man. Pasting a pleasant smile on her face, she pushed off the wall and went inside.

Sunlight poured into the room from the large windows along the eastern wall. The sunrise was a welcome sight after such a long and complicated night, and it reminded her that she hadn't gotten much sleep. And when that was added to the emotional upheaval of the last few hours, it was no surprise her feelings were a tad raw.

Seeing the two men hunched over a computer screen next to each other made her feel excluded—as if they had a secret. Yellow pads of paper filled with notes sat on either side of them. Pencils sat abandoned, as if all the hard work was already done.

"Take a seat," Hubbard said, pushing back from the table. It wasn't a question, but she wasn't used to accepting commands, so she paused for several seconds before she chose a spot.

Kimberly ignored Kess as she focused on Hubbard. She only wanted the answer to one question, so she took the initiative and asked, "What did you decide about the launch?"

Her nemesis grinned wickedly at her. "I'll let Hubbard explain. I have work to do." Kess shook hands with Hubbard, got up from the table, and paused in front of her. "You know that we have cameras everywhere." He smiled again and lifted his hand to touch her shoulder before thinking better of it. He went out the door. It slid soundlessly shut behind him.

"What does that mean?" she asked. "As far as I know, we don't have any footage of the murders or any other illegal activity." She didn't understand what was going on. What did these men know that she didn't?

"We don't," replied Hubbard. He made a noise

somewhere between a choking sound and speech. "Excuse me." He crossed the room and helped himself to another cup of coffee. "Do you want some?"

"No. Thank you. What I'd like are some answers. I've been outside waiting for over an hour. Are we launching?" Her impatience was getting the best of her. She tried to rein it in, but it didn't work.

Hubbard sat down again. He took several sips from his coffee cup and then placed it on the table. "The short answer is yes, we will launch. The long answer to a very complicated issue that Kess brought to me is that *you* will no longer be in charge of pilot selection."

"Why? Give me one reason."

"I can provide several, but this is perhaps the most poignant." He turned the computer screen toward her. Photos sped across the screen, ones of her with Bennett in some seriously compromising positions. The word *naked* didn't even begin to cover it.

Her jaw dropped open. When she found her voice, she asked, "Where did those come from...?"

"At Kess's request, we added cameras to several additional places in the Lester Facility, and he's been monitoring them. He captured these photos and didn't think it would be an issue until he saw how emotional you were in the R & D Center. That's why we talked first. He's in charge of the launch; I owe him that." Hubbard spread his fingers. "You understand, of course, that Kess will be going forward with his choice of pilots."

She laughed, softly at first and then louder, until Hubbard moved uncomfortably in his chair. "You bought that?"

"Dr. Warren, are you okay?"

She presented him with a wide, toothy smile. She leaned forward, putting her elbows inelegantly on the table. "I had an itch and I scratched it. Men do it every day. So why discriminate?" She rubbed her hands together and stood. "It's not your decision, or Kess's choice. SECNAV appointed me the decision maker, and if you want to change that, then either one of you can go through the proper channels. Until then…" She walked to the door and opened it. Looking over her shoulder, she said, "Don't threaten me."

Hubbard sputtered as the door slid shut, closing him inside.

As Kimberly walked down the hall, she said, "Sally, delete all images of Bennett and me together. Make sure you check for backups."

Cold air blasted down on her from above.

"Hey, Sally, make sure you check the temperature. For some reason, it's like an iceberg in here."

"Done. Confirmed on images, and temperature is adjusted to a comfortable seventy degrees Fahrenheit," said Sally.

Kimberly sneezed. It didn't feel different. Maybe Sally needed a diagnostic, or some kind of checkup.

She headed straight for her room. Upon reviewing the discussion with Hubbard, her anger bubbled up inside her, so hot it could melt steel. This was the fuel she needed to get over the hump. They were going to solve the issues that faced them—or else.

Chapter 8

KIMBERLY SAT IN HER QUARTERS AND STARED AT HER phone. She'd already fielded two calls from SECNAV and three from Ouster.

Somehow she'd let slip about her involvement with Bennett, and they'd all freaked out. First of all, she didn't expect that anyone would find out or that she'd be so angry that she leaked it. Second, weren't her bedroom activities private? According to Ouster, the answer was no, and she had jeopardized Captain Sheraton's position.

SECNAV was leaning toward allowing Kess to choose the candidate. She knew Ouster would support her, even if he didn't like doing it. The Admiral was so overprotective, and had sought someone for her more stable and ordinary than a SEAL. But she had never been a regular soul, so how could the person she dated be?

Dated. Huh? Were they actually dating? She'd have to think about that.

She stood up and paced, checking the clock on the wall. Time was speeding by, and she hoped Bennett would arrive on time for his pool simulation. His score on this test would factor into the final decision, and she needed everyone to see how well qualified he was. In her mind, Bennett was the only man for the piloting job, but she knew she'd have to justify her decision.

Her phone signaled a text, and she smiled as she

looked at the screen. Several individuals were on her side. She guessed her situation was making the rounds on the gossip train. Also, the monitor from the pool sent several of the candidates' results to her. Yuri was in the tank, and Bennett was next up.

"C'mon, Bennett, kick ass," Kimberly said. She sat back down in the chair and waited.

—∿∿—

The heavy door slammed shut behind him. The smell of chlorine stung his nostrils. His eyes scanned the pool area. It was packed with people. Bennett was less fond of man-made swimming holes than he was of rivers, lakes, and oceans. Give him salt water any day, even with the threat of toothy predators, and he was a happy guy. This place was hardwired, with a shuttle structure sunk into the pool. Frankly, for an astronaut, it was an ideal training area.

He shook his head, trying to dislodge the order stuck in his head. Ouster had called right before he entered the pool area and insisted he stay away from Kimberly on an "intimate" basis. How had she spilled that fact! He'd almost told the Admiral to screw himself but had held his tongue. SEALs were known rule breakers, and he could just ignore it. But it was impossible to argue with the notion that hooking up with Kimberly endangered the mission. He was better off sticking to the parameters of his assignment, and so was she.

It was hard to ignore how angry it made him. He liked Kimberly, but he had to break it off. Was there any other way to get through this with their psyches and the mission intact?

He stepped in a puddle of water, and it splashed him. The cold spray was just what he needed to focus.

Concentrate, Bennett! Do your job.

Focus was a favorite word of Gich's, as in "be present in a situation"—in other words, do what you're doing when you're doing it. Stay grounded in your tasks, and focus your mind on the matter at hand.

Bennett pursed his lips. He needed to do that right now.

He pulled his sweatshirt over his head and slipped his legs out of his sweatpants. He was going to ignore Kimberly until the mission was sorted. It was for the best. He dropped his sweats on an empty bench, and his flip-flops smacked loudly on the tiled floor as he approached the monitor and checked in. "Captain Bennett Sheraton for the two o'clock slot."

The monitor looked him up and down. "You're early for the simulation. Take a seat over there, or you can observe from the far wall."

Bennett preferred standing and watching; it was a better view. He wondered who was down in the pool right now. Whoever it was had lost two of his tools and was doing the steps out of order. The dexterity rating was going to be nil. Didn't anyone read instructions anymore? Being a sailor had taught him that there were actually right and wrong ways to perform tasks. Knowing the difference saved a lot of pain. Research was the first step to every success.

The safety diver signaled from below, and three more divers jumped in the pool. They released the man in the space suit and brought him up to the surface. Popping off the mask, they shoved an extra mouthpiece into the wearer's mouth. As they turned to the elevator launch and a large set of stairs, they hauled the man and his giant space suit out of the water.

Bennett was there to lend a hand. Locking his arms under the man's armpits, he aided the divers' movements, and they thanked him.

The man inside the space suit didn't say a word. He was too busy sputtering and coughing up water. He looked up into Bennett's eyes with a sneer. It was Yuri.

It took much longer for Yuri to be extracted from the suit and for a new space suit to be located and the mock-up reset. By then, all of the candidates were arguing with the monitor.

Staying out of the melee seemed like a wise idea, so Bennett mentally practiced what he was going to do in the pool. It was probably why he was ignoring Yuri when the man came up to him and started pelting him with questions.

"How many hours have you logged in the water?" Yuri spat out the question, sending a spray of spittle with it. "How can you be considered when this is your first time in this pool? You don't deserve to be here. Why don't you quit already?"

"Oh, but I have been in this pool. Not for this particular task, but I've been through many like it." Bennett brushed the droplets off his skin. "Most of my career has deployed in and around the water, so let's say I've spent roughly twelve thousand hours in the drink."

None of the men around him commented further. Yuri was still finding his tongue as Bennett secured the space suit and entered the elevator, which lowered him into the pool. It took him a few minutes to get used to the gloves, but he was able to secure the safety line to his suit and get to work.

The simulation to set up the array in space was contained in a rather deep pool. The mock-up was simple. With all the parts color-coded and labeled, Bennett was able to assemble it quickly. The difficult part came when he was turning the array and trying to lock it into place. No matter how he shifted the hardware, it wouldn't stay aligned. When a diver pointed at his watch to tell him that he'd reached the time limit, frustration set in.

Bennett was tempted to pull off the suit and perform the task without the gear, but this action would have disqualified him altogether. At this point, he had one more chance to pass the test.

Making his way along the bottom of the pool, he followed the protocol, securing his tether to the elevator and activating the Up function. Slowly, he was hoisted out of the water.

When he placed his feet topside, he unclipped the tether and stepped clear of the elevator. The test was officially over now.

Pulling off his gloves, helmet, and suit, he waited for the monitor to approach him. Several people were gathered around, and their voices were raised in disagreement. The monitor stepped clear of them and headed straight for Bennett. Ripping a piece of paper off his clipboard, he said, "You passed, Captain Sheraton."

"Wait," said Bennett. "The array didn't lock into place. I failed the second part of the task requirements. I'd like to do it again."

"Do it as much as you want. But hear me on this…" The monitor shook his head and said, "The gear is not functioning correctly. No one could have locked it into place unless they cheated and took off their gear, which would essentially kill them in space or allow water into their space suit, creating a dangerous situation." He threw a glance in Yuri's direction.

"Interesting." Bennett was curious as to why the array wouldn't lock into place.

"In terms of training, you're the best-qualified person in this facility. Good luck, Captain. I hope you get the mission." The monitor hurried away, leaving the pool mock-up and testing area.

Bennett looked at the diver sitting on the edge of the pool. He spun his finger in a circle. "Rack 'em up. Let's do it again. Nothing better than having muscle memory."

The diver nodded. He gave Bennett a thumbs up before he pulled on his mask, secured his mouthpiece, checked the air on his tank, and hopped back into the pool.

The room was emptying out. It appeared that everyone had come here to watch him fail, or maybe they were here for Yuri.

Funny how nothing ever went well for those tragic types, like they invited pain into their lives so they had something to complain about. That was the opposite of how Bennett dealt with life—magic came from hard work and the belief in one's own power and capability.

Time to muster his magic skills. Bennett made sure nothing would get in the way of his pool time as he secured the space suit, helmet, and gloves and made his way to the elevator. Blissfully, the only people in here now were the on-site medical team, the divers, and himself. Using the precise protocol again, he secured the tether to the elevator and sent it down into the pool. "Time to make the doughnuts." He chuckled at his own joke and mentally prepared for his tasks. Having them fresh in his mind kept him directed and gave him the edge he needed to improve on the timing of his first test.

If he practiced a few more times, he knew he could make it even better. SEALs rehearsed over and over until they could perform an action in their sleep. Bennett was going to make sure he had every action nailed down. Though the odds of his return were not favorable, given the danger involved in the mission, he was going to give himself the best chance he could...to come home alive.

—⁓—

Pacing in her personal quarters, Kimberly was more than prepared to talk to Bennett, who had been out of the test hours and hours ago. She had called him and sent texts without receiving any response, and she needed him. If it hadn't been for Sally's regular updates, she would have worried that Bennett had been killed or hurt. According to the computer, Bennett's life signs were fine, and the tests were performed within acceptable limits and currently complete.

Well, for now he was okay, but when she got a hold of him... What? She'd kiss him! Apologize for spilling the beans. Shout at him, because she wanted to yell at herself. Oh hell, what a mess!

Footsteps from the bathroom alerted her to Bennett's approach as the door slid open and he poked his head in the door. "I'm picking up my notebook," he said.

"That's all you're going to say? Why didn't you come straight here after the test? " She blocked his path out of the room. "Where have you been?"

"Busy." He stepped around her without a second

glance. "I have to go. This isn't the time to canoodle, as much as I enjoy it. There are problems to solve to stay on track for the launch."

"Hold on there, SEAL. No word from you in hours and hours, and you give me a lame line and leave?" She had to stop him in his tracks and force him to talk to her, so she grabbed his arm. "I get it…that we need to keep our minds focused. But what about us?"

The look he gave her was laughable: as if she could stop him. She didn't care! Her whole life she had dated men who couldn't handle strength and courage wrapped in brains and common sense. Her instincts told her that Bennett would be the exception to the rule, that he could handle whatever she dished out. "Want to play? Fine! I'm not sorry I told SECNAV and Ouster. Just so you know, I could have skewed those tests in your favor, Bennett. Just made you look like the king of all the tests and sent everyone else home."

"So why didn't you? Because you don't have the guts to skew anything."

"I don't need to. You *are* the real deal, Bennett." The weight of everything she had said and done hit her. She might not only have jeopardized the launch, but Bennett's career too. What a diva she'd been.

In his jaw, a muscle spasmed. "I don't believe you. You love this—all these individuals competing for your attention. Who will win Dr. Warren's favor?"

"How can you say that? It's uncomfortable, almost painful watching everyone compete."

"I disagree. I think you like it. The all-powerful Dr. Warren." Bennett's words were cold. "Ouster has ordered me to stay away from you for the good of the mission. Your superiors want us apart, so here I am, I'm following orders."

"The mission. Seriously! That's the excuse. If you don't want to be with me, just say so. Or are all SEALs famous for their sly talk and their 'fuck 'em and flee' flight plan?" She stomped her foot. "So, just get on with it, if I'm the reason you need to ditch. Go!"

"SEALs have honor." He spun back toward her, a look of pure male anger on his face. "Don't go there. Slurring my brethren or me is uncalled for. I've been honest with you. Besides, it's you. You don't really want me. I'm convenient."

"Don't I?" She grabbed his hand and yanked him closer toward her. Her fingernails dug into his flesh until he responded. "Don't walk away from me. Don't you *ever* dare to do that, *Boss*!" No one likes getting yelled at, but it was even worse when your lover gave up "for the good of the mission." She wasn't going to let that crap stand. "For the record, there's nothing easy or well-timed about you. Convenient, my ass! Do you think love comes every day? No! It doesn't. It's rare, you idjit!"

He stilled. Something in his gaze softened. "Kimberly, I can't protect you if I'm falling for you. Love… I… Let this—us—go." The pain in his words was clear. It was impossible for him to hide his emotions.

Love. Did she love him? Christ, he loved her. Bennett wanted her. He desperately needed to hold her and touch her. It felt like his heart was being split apart. This thin slip of a woman, a female like Kimberly Warren, was no match for his physical strength—though her emotion and her mind, with that unbridled passion and darned logical thinking, teased his soul. He knew as he tilted her chin up toward his lips that this "fight" was about to change direction.

He brushed his lips over the tip of her cheekbones, and then her nose, before he caressed her lips.

She moved closer, winding her arms around his neck, and her fingers slid from his skin like butter on a hot griddle.

As he grabbed her waist gently, almost reverently, he said, "Are you sure you want to go down this path?"

"Yes, I am. I'm not fragile. I'm strong." Her lips brushed over his. "Keep that in mind. I'm not someone you can just thrust aside. I fight."

"I'm getting that." His eyebrow rose. "What about the mission? No one wants us together."

"I do. Isn't that enough?"

"Yes." Relief flooded him. It was clear she was as committed as he was. With her by his side, he could defy any odds.

"I love the way you look at me like you're seeing into my soul." Her eyes flashed with heat before closing to half-mast. She licked her lips and then held eye contact with him. "You're stuck with me, Boss. I'm never going to let go. The mission will work out. I have faith—in you and me and this project."

"I apologize about before… I believe you, Kimberly. More importantly, I believe *in* you." He held her gaze, opening himself to her. This woman was under his skin in a way he could never have imagined, and if he walked away today, she would still be there for the rest of his life. How could he deny that truth…about her?

"Can we get naked now?" She cupped his bottom and squeezed.

"I think that's my line." He laughed. This sexy woman wanted him as much as he wanted her. He pulled his shirt over his head and dropped it to the floor, then brought his face close to hers.

Her lips brushed his, teasing him. She pulled out of his grasp easily, as if he hadn't been holding her at all.

What was she doing to him? His eyes scanned her. He could see the hunger in there, the warmth, the want, and the need.

"Kiss me. Really knock my socks off, and don't hold back." She stood there, waiting and wanting.

"Aye, aye." He grinned as hunger rose to the surface. He lifted her into his arms and then laid his mouth against hers, drinking from, pillaging, and dueling with hers.

Kimberly's arms twined around his neck at first and then her hands moved, gaining greater purchase. Her fingers dug into the muscle mass around his shoulders. The small bursts of pain as she changed her grip added more levels of heat to his already boiling desire.

Hands fumbled with clothes, tugging and tearing until they were both naked.

Their primal natures took over as Bennett carried her to a desk full of books. With one arm, he swept them aside. They crashed to the floor, and he laid her down on the bare surface, moving between her legs. His hands needed to stroke her, his mouth and tongue to touch her, taste her, delve into the sweet depths of her pleasure.

"Bennett," she moaned, thrusting her body down, toward his tongue. "More."

The movements increased as he drove his tongue faster over her clit. As she came, he buried his mouth between her legs to drink deeply of her passion.

Her breath shuddered out. "I'm never letting you go."

"Me neither." Coming from between her legs, his mouth slick and eyes blazing, he grabbed a condom from his pocket, covered his cock, and then primed himself at the sweet, silky slick of her opening. He gently slid himself inside. Pushed all the way to the hilt, it felt like coming home, a connection he'd never had with anyone else. He wanted to deny he had it with her, a stubborn and oftentimes obstinate woman like Kimberly, but he did. She challenged him in a way no other had before, and her sex drive, her heated passion, always simmered just below the surface of her skin.

He thrust his hips and watched her eyes widen and then go back to half-mast. A wicked smiled played on her lips as she beckoned him to her.

Leaning down, he touched his lips to hers.

"I can taste me on you. I like that."

"Have you done that…tasted yourself before?" Curiosity might have killed the cat, but this tidbit was sure to give him additional fuel for his fire.

"I'm a woman. We all know how we smell and what we taste like. We appreciate our own deliciousness." Her hands locked around his head, forcing his lips to hers as she kissed him with wild abandon.

Sure enough, his satisfaction with her answer only made him want her more. Nothing was sexier or more attractive than a woman who was comfortable in her own skin.

His hips picked up the pace, rocketing in and out with long, deep strokes until he could feel the moans coming from her throat and the convulsions tightening over his cock. He didn't want it to end, not this soon.

Pulling out, he felt her body shake and shiver. "Bennett?" she said. He knew she needed more; so did he. How had he gotten into this situation, where his mind and body were so drawn to her that he could defy orders from his Admiral and his own good sense about the mission to be with her? Dwelling on it right now wasn't useful. He'd examine that motivation another time. As his favorite instructor had always said, "Be in the moment. Whatever you are doing…give it one hundred percent of your attention." And that was exactly what he was going to do.

Picking her up, Bennett carried Kimberly to the couch and sat down with her still in his arms. This time, face-to-face and eye to eye, neither of them could deny how they affected each other. Body language didn't lie.

She was mounted on his lap. "Thank you for staying…for not running away when I shouted at you. You're the first man to appreciate my strength."

"I better be the last." The comment was out of his mouth before he realized it. The shock of it was reflected in her face. He cleared his throat. "Your turn."

That wicked gleam was back in her eyes. "My pleasure." Her voice was deep, arousing, and sultry. He wished he could bottle that sound; he only heard it when she was in the throes of intense pleasure. God, it was an aphrodisiac!

Her hips lifted up slowly and came down even slower. It was almost painful how pleasurable it was.

His eyes started to close.

"Uh-uh-uh…" she said, touching her fingers to his cheeks. "Watch me."

He nodded and forced his eyes to feast on her.

Those creamy, silky breasts with their gorgeously pert areolas—he needed to taste them. He pulled her closer to lock his lips over each of them in turn and pulled tenderly at their darkness as his tongue laved the tips.

Her motions changed, became more frantic, as he tended to her. Kimberly tried to bat him away, but he was unrelenting. She finally cried out, and her body pulsed up and down his cock.

He flipped her then, putting her back onto the couch and priming himself over her. "Have you had enough?"

Her eyes were sleepy as they looked up at him, but fire still blazed in them. She dared him: "Never."

His own mischievous grin met hers, and he slid his cock in and out of her until they were both on the pinnacle. As an orgasm broke over him, he could feel her completion too. Together, they collapsed on the couch.

Carefully putting the bulk of his weight on one side of her, he cuddled her close. "Dr. Warren," he murmured, "you can fight with me anytime."

Her small fist punched the side of his chest. "Thanks, Boss."

He lifted one eyebrow. "Will you ever say my nickname without sarcasm?"

"Never."

His fingers found a tickle spot at her waist. "Maybe," he said as his fingers made her squirm, "I can change your mind."

She smiled. "Perhaps." Her head nestled under his chin. "Catch a few winks with me. Please, Bennett, hold me."

"As you wish, Doc." His whole body was spent and highly relaxed, but sleep was nowhere near coming.

There was a lot on his mind: the flight, the race to space, the murderer—and her.

What had he gotten himself into? It was impossible to keep his distance from her, no matter how hard he tried, and obviously the same was true for her. Dr. Kimberly Warren was a handful, and he honestly did not want to let her go, not ever. Did that mean he needed to make peace with it? Yes. Otherwise, how was he going to be able to focus on the mission?

God help him. Hugging Kimberly tightly to him, he closed his eyes and allowed himself a few seconds of comfort.

Chapter 9

SITTING IN A CUBICLE IN THE R & D CENTER OF THE Lester Facility, Melo finished his fourth cup of coffee as he reviewed the hardware and software issues associated with the Warren Shuttle. The brain of the shuttle kept shorting out.

He could sympathize. His brain had been going down so many different roads, he felt as if he were spinning in circles, too.

He closed his eyes and rubbed his thumbs over his temples. He let go of all predetermined parameters and allowed his brain to move wherever it needed to go—*romping free* was the term his macroengineering professor had used. By releasing the tension and going beyond the current focus, an answer oftentimes presented itself. It was usually that simple.

Simple. Simplify, he thought. *Back to basics. One foot in front of the other. Walk. Don't run. Keep it simple, stupid—KISS—the term many people use in advertising and in life. Simple.*

Nothing in the tests or associated paperwork suggested that it was sabotage or any kind of hacking problem. Check.

In Melo's opinion, the underlining enigma was actually something easier to define. Much more simply, keep it singular. Right! The demands being made on the technology exceeded its scope. In other words, he needed to delimit the array of tasks demanded of the current hardware by writing code that asked it to do less, and then develop a separate technology for each remaining task.

He picked up his notebook, a small black school one, and took it down the hall to a room holding twenty of the greatest design and engineering minds in the world. He handed the notebook to James Henner, team leader for the first part of the problem. He didn't envy the individual attempting to keep the engineers and the designers speaking the same language. It was akin to speaking English to a room full of French and German speakers: only a few words made it through. Melo presented the data to Henner and watched as the man shifted from exhaustion to excitement and exuberance.

"Hold up. We have a new attack. There are three systems that need to be changed. The electrical is going to be single-tracked with these chip sets." Henner held up a circuit board. "The fueling system will be set up on this one"—he pointed to another—"and the manual extras, such as the enlarged wings, et cetera, will be on this set." He raised up a third board. "Then and only then will we link them into a motherboard for 'monitoring' only. In that way, if one subsystem gets overloaded or shits the bed, there are easy options to reroute it." He smiled at Melo. "Now, does everyone know what they are supposed to be doing? Because each group has four hours to implement it before testing."

Henner patted Melo on the back and said, "So simple. I don't know why I didn't see it before. Somehow we were asking the system to do too much, and that was frying it. Now we should be right as rain."

"Glad I could help. Sometimes you just need fresh eyes and a different perspective." Melo shook hands with Henner and headed over to the next group, which was meeting in a room down the next hall.

Shouts of frustration came from the ten souls meeting in there. This group was tackling the problem of keeping the laser array locked in one position without the possibility of its being hacked or changed by someone else.

He opened the door and peered into the room. It looked like the Sunday morning after a Saturday keg party, at least the way Melo remembered it from college. The men wore stained shirts, nobody had showered for what smelled like days, and crumbs of food stuck to their mustaches and beards.

A brief image of hosing them down and adding some soap zipped through his mind, but given how heated the group already was, Melo did not want to test their tolerance.

His eyes sought the leader, Ula Parks. She was in charge of this cacophonous group, which was attempting to lock the array in place.

Advances in technology were happening too fast to assume that today's secure devices couldn't be overcome by tomorrow's brilliant minds. At least here they were tapping a lot of experts for a solution.

"Frankly, all that needs to happen is that an object with enough mass hits the array, and all of a sudden it's turned toward us. Boom! Lasers are blasting all over the place, and we're the ones hiding from our own creation. It's too easy for this whole plan to backfire," shouted George Quoag.

"Hold up, everyone," said Ula. "Let me talk to

Melo and see what he's found out." She turned to him. "Thanks for visiting our dungeon of gloom. I thought I was going to see you only in the R & D Center." She gestured Melo closer and examined his notes.

She smiled and then chuckled. "This is good, Melo. It's a great idea! I'm glad you're on our side." She turned back to the band of the great unwashed and said, "Okay, geeks. Listen up. What if we did a combination of the two? First, the array is set up—that function works well. Second, it is shifted into an outward position—yes, it is physically moved. Third, a chip is put into place that forces the telemetry to be set outward from Earth in order to function. And here's the kicker: this chip has a bio element that cannot be duplicated, so it becomes unhackable."

"Damn, that's good," said Quoag. "It's almost like making it analog, but without the wires. It needs a specific signal; otherwise, it just shuts down—that's the fail-safe. I like it. I can work with it. What do you guys think?"

Murmurs of interest rose in the room as the group divided up by task to write the program and develop the software. For a place that had seemed on the verge of a riot, it was amusing to see everyone quiet and calm.

Ula hugged Melo. "Damn, that was good. I was considering having Sally flood the room with happy gas so I could take a break. This could work, but, uh, what type of biological element should we use?"

Melo slapped his arm. "Take as much as you need, and the Navy has more of me too."

"Done! Your blood will be the DNA element in the brain chip of the array and in the screwdriver used to turn it on and off. Thanks, Melo." Then Ula laughed. "I'm not sure I'd let these geniuses take a needle to my arm, mainly because they're geniuses and not IV techs—they have no bedside manner. Well, only a few of them do." A blush rose in her cheeks as she waved him away. "Go to the med lab and get me a half a pint."

He nodded. "Will do."

His eyes scanned the men and women who filled the room. These minds were some of the greatest of the century. He'd read many of their theories and most of their books and papers on design and engineering. Wouldn't he love to spend a day with them just shooting the shit? *Another time*, he thought as he made his way to the med lab.

Nearly stepping on a floor sweeper as he rounded a corner in the hallway, he stumbled. "Damn things."

He found his feet again just in time to turn right into the medical area. The front desk was empty. Voices drifted to him from the back.

Huh, guess everyone's busy. No matter.

Melo did what he did best and helped himself. He went into an empty room, found IV tubing, a butterfly needle—a reminder that small is still powerful—and an unused blood bag.

SEALs had more options these days. Like many in his Team, he went through an advanced medical training so he could do more in the field, even operate, if necessary. Not that he'd be doing a triple bypass, but he could suture the crap out of almost any wound.

Thus, he didn't think it strange to perform a simple procedure like drawing his own blood. Step one: wrap a piece of latex around the bicep and then tie it off.

Step two: pump the fist a few times. Step three: push the needle into a prominent vein, preferably the one just inside the bend of the elbow. And step four: watch the red stuff go.

Blood flowed just the way it was supposed to. When he had enough to suit his purpose, he pulled the needle out. He stuck a cotton ball over the hole with adhesive tape, untied the latex, and sealed the bag of blood. Being a stickler for such things, he disposed of the needle and tubing in the appropriate containers and walked out of the cubical, feeling pleased with himself.

"Hey, where did you come from?" A nurse dressed in a midthigh blue dress with white tights and shoes—and a definite swing to her hips—stopped Melo. "And where are you going with that?"

Damn, now I'm running into people. Where's my stealth mode when I need it?

He decided to go with the lighter approach. Pasting his "homeboy" smile on his lips, he lifted the bag of blood. "Just making a withdrawal."

"Wait! You can't just leave!" She looked torn between wanting to physically stop him somehow and running to the back for reinforcements. Frozen with indecision, she stood there.

Waving at her with his free hand, he left. He double-timed it down the hallway and back the way he came.

Melo smiled. He couldn't imagine there were too many people who walked in and treated a medical area like a self-serve pump, but he wasn't an ordinary soul. He'd been taking care of himself for many years, even before he married his lovely Alisha, and he was proud of being effective and efficient.

He stopped off in the room where the group was working on the biochip for the laser array and dropped off the bag with Ula. "That was fast," she said.

He nodded his head and left. Afterward, he stopped at the cafeteria for an orange juice and an apple, and then he went back to work in the R & D Center. While he walked around, his brain created, thinking up a new design approach for a different kind of biochip. Most engineers would call it a unicorn—a design so ambitious, it was unobtainable. Chuckling to himself, he decided that if this worked, he was calling it the Melo, or if that didn't work, the FrOgMEn.

Opening a fresh black notebook, he picked up a pencil and sketched out a design. It was crude, but good enough. Then he started in on the math. Whoever had told kids that math wasn't going to get them far had never learned the art of a great equation! Math could be as delicate and beautiful as a paintbrush's stroke on canvas, and it could do the most amazing things: unlocking possibilities and probabilities that might never have been examined if someone had not been brave enough to tackle them.

Munching down on his apple, he finished it in no time and tossed the core into a wastebasket across from his cubicle. As he did, he had a "lightbulb" moment. Eureka! That was it. He knew how to fix the biochip and have an unhackable element. If he created a chip that had to be used with another chip to modify it, then they had an easy-to-use key too.

He'd got all of that from making the basket with his apple core: a key in a lock. Picking up his phone, he dialed Bennett. His Teammate needed to weigh in on this action. "It's Melo. Head to the R & D Center. I might have solved one part of our problem—or actually, both parts."

Grabbing another cup of coffee from the constantly filling pot, Melo went back to his cubicle and sketched out several sample scenarios in which to use the chip. He could hardly wait to go over them with Bennett and then hustle all of his notes down to Ula. Would she like the key-in-a-lock concept—a biochip that had to accept another biochip to complete a circuit and make it alterable? Hell, he did!

Less than five minutes passed before Bennett strode into the room. He stepped inside the glass-walled room, his bulk filling the small enclosure, and asked, "What have you got?"

"Something good, my brother. Just you wait." Melo filled him in on his plan and the manner and means to implement it.

Bennett scratched his chin, and he looked impressed. "Not my area, man, but it sounds good. How long until you have a prototype and we can beta test it?"

"Approximately two hours, max. I'll make two chips, and then we'll test them out on the simulator. If it works, we're changing history. Rather, I'm changing it." Melo tapped his temple. "Ingenuity."

"Yeah, it certainly is," said Bennett, raising an eyebrow. "And with such great humility too."

———

The two-biochip concept was a go. Ula not only liked the concept, but she invited Melo to join their group for additional construction, implementation, and testing. Melo, who had been itching to spend time with these brilliant folks, jumped at the chance. With all hands on deck, the chips were completed in less than an hour and the key-in-a-lock concept was banged out shortly thereafter.

The whole group headed to the R & D hangar where the simulator for the laser array and the shuttle systems were housed. It was a home-base laser array—the structure that was practically identical to the one going into space—and the best place to beta test the two-biochip concept.

Ula geared up the appropriate computer simulation. "We're ready, ladies and gentlemen. Melo, if you'll do the honors."

Melo took the two biochips, inserted them in the board, and stepped back. He was going to see his babies in action.

Ula pushed the Engage button, and lines of data scrolled across the screen. There wasn't room for all of them to see it, so she gave a blow-by-blow account. "The first biochip has been tapped. Engaging. Working. Yes, it's effective. Now it's running the second part of the protocol, assuming the array has been turned and it's…it's engaging. Working. Locked. The chip can be removed and the laser will not move. If it gets pushed out of orbit for some reason, it will resume the position or disarm—completely disabling all functionality for the entire array."

Smiling at the group, Ula said, "Adding that last element was a nice touch, everyone."

A small cheer went up from the group. Success was a contagious and elating emotion.

Melo couldn't stop smiling. He had done it. They had done it. This was one of the most important pieces of technology to date, and he was a part of it. Hooyah!

Building on their momentum, they loaded into a small tram and took it all the way to the hangar deck where the shuttle was being stored. Along the way, they all agreed that the part should be called the Melo, after its creator. He couldn't have been more thrilled. A part of him was going into space.

They entered the hangar and piled out of the vehicle. There were so many people and so much equipment, they had to squeeze through it all to locate the shuttle itself and then climb into the bay where the laser array was stored.

Melo was given the honor of installing the biochips. He patted the machinery, and then the group hustled out, closing the shuttle bay door behind them.

With Melo in tow, the group left the hangar on foot and headed for the cafeteria. This was essentially the break room for the entire Lester Facility. They were going to raise a toast for all the great work done today. After so much turmoil to complete this essential work, they were all ready to celebrate.

<hr />

Melo was elated about the success of the biochips. He sat down with a group of his peers, feeling he'd earned a seat among those geniuses who surrounded him. The cafeteria was packed with facility employees. His eyes scanned them briefly, and he paused on Kess, who was walking toward a large table. Thank God that jerk wasn't joining his group.

When Ula placed platters of burgers and fries in front
of them, it could have been mushed bananas and he'd
have been thrilled with it. As he lifted a burger heaped
with toppings to his mouth, the sound of a chair getting dragged backward on the floor—that high, squeaky
sound—had him abandoning his food and taking to his
feet to investigate.

Finding Kess at the center of the drama was a plus,
as it gave him more Intel on the man. This guy had been
on their radar for a while. They were just waiting for
him to overtly mess up so they would have a reason to
question him. Could this be the opportunity they'd been
waiting for?

Conversations were hushed around the two individuals who were standing and arguing. One of them was
being yelled at, and he was denying he was at fault.
Melo found an empty wall close by and leaned against
it to watch.

Kess's face was mottled with red. He looked as if he
were going to blow a gasket or a heart valve any minute
now. "You need to complete all tasks before you even
think of heading to the cafeteria, Browner. What do you
think, a pilot just says, 'I know we're taking off, but it
doesn't matter if I'm actually doing my job to get us
safely into the air'? No! The entire flight would be dead.
Burned to cinders, and that poor jerk who didn't do his
job would be responsible. So get your butt in gear!"

"I did! The tasks were completed. Look at the checklist." The tall man with receding red hair and tons of
freckles shrank back. His name tag said *Browner* and
his frame was thin and slightly hunched. His skin was
pasty too; it was easy to see he was not the sporting,

outdoors type. Reaching toward the table, he picked up his checklist and presented it to Kess. "See…I did as I was told. Saul even signed off on it."

"Saul isn't your boss. I'm your boss's boss, so I'm your boss. Get back down to the hangar and go over that list. On launch day, do the entire list exactly as it is written, not how you remember it, and don't ask other people for their input on *your* job." Kess hissed out the last line so softly it was hard to hear the words. "Proprietary things are a part of every job; those tasks are kept secret for national security."

Huh, thought Melo. *Now that's interesting. What national secret is Kess referring to? Wouldn't two SEALs working for the U.S. Government know about it?*

As Kess turned to leave, a woman who was in conversation with someone else bumped into Kess, spilling her drink on him. "Sorry, sir." She ran her hands — which were holding napkins — over the front of his shirt, attempting to blot the liquid away.

His jaw was open, and he looked too shocked to reply. He closed his mouth, took a step back, and walked around her and the spreading mess on the floor. He walked out of the cafeteria without uttering a sound.

Melo withdrew his phone and sent a text to Bennett with notes on the scene he'd just witnessed. It might have been nothing, but his gut was telling him there was something significant about the confrontation.

Chapter 10

AFTER A LONG DAY, HAVING TIME OFF WAS NOT ONLY necessary for sanity's sake, but also a welcome reward for work well accomplished. Kimberly filled a cooler with beer, wine, and water and packed a hamper full of food. With a blanket in hand, she reserved several hours on her, Bennett's, and Melo's schedules. As the three of them walked through the parking lot, it was hard not to appreciate the beautiful sky. The moon waned and the stars were bright.

"This is going to be the perfect night for stargazing," said Kimberly with a small hop in her step. Both she and Bennett were aware that Melo missed his significant other, and they had a surprise for him.

Melo grumbled.

"What was that?" asked Bennett, baiting him. "Sorry, I didn't quite hear you."

"Nothing," replied Melo sullenly. Not that Bennett blamed his friend. Nothing was less romantic than being a third wheel on a night like this one—clear sky and starlit.

"What vehicle are we taking, or are we walking to our destination?"

Kimberly looked at Bennett, and he smiled innocently and said, "Let's take yours, buddy. We can stretch out in the back and look at the stars." She rolled her eyes at Bennett and shook her head. He was being a wicked soul.

The crickets and frogs were already serenading them, and a cool wind blew in from the west. It was refreshing.

They deposited the hamper and cooler into the back of the truck, and the three of them piled into the cab. They buckled their seat belts and drove off the grounds of the Lester Facility. After about twenty-five minutes of driving, Kimberly pointed.

"Take the next road on the right. It's a dirt road going straight up." Kimberly gave directions as Bennett sat quietly, holding her hand. His thumb traced over hers, and she glanced at him now and then and smiled. "Go slow over this part. Sometimes there are cars in the road."

Sure enough, a small car was tucked off to the side and a woman waved at them. As the dirt cleared, it was easy to see Alisha waiting.

Without even stopping the truck, Melo hopped out, ran around the back, and took her into his arms. "Alisha…" The kiss was one of the most romantic and grandiose in the history of kisses and belonged in an old MGM black-and-white, silver-screen movie.

Bennett grabbed the steering wheel as Kimberly released her seat belt and scooted into the driver's seat. She found a safe place to park, pulled the car into the turnoff spot, set the brake, and turned off the engine. "I'm glad we could arrange this surprise for Melo. He needed the break, and she was thrilled to have an opportunity to see him. Boy, she's a talker. I could hardly get off the phone with her."

Bennett laughed. "Yeah, she's pretty perfect for Melo that way. He says very little and she chats on."

She turned her body toward Bennett. "I'm glad…we have some time together."

"Me too." He reached out and pulled her toward him, kissing her with a tender touch that resonated in his soul. He released her and said abruptly, "What's for dinner?"

She smacked his chest playfully. "Really? You have me in your arms and you're asking about food? Fine! I raided the cafeteria and picked out chicken, raw veggies, potato salad, Julian apple pie—the one with the crumb top—and…me."

"I'll start with you." He made a motion with his mouth as if he was going to bite her. "Seriously, I am starved for food too."

"Men!" she said as she leaped out of the truck.

It felt normal and fun to be bantering with each other, as if this is what their normal life would be like. Easy. Companionable.

They left Melo and Alisha to their own devices, knowing they would come find them when they were hungry or needed to leave, and set off on the trail to the top of the mountain.

"Kids come here a lot to neck," Kimberly said. "You know, make out."

"Good Lord, I'm not that old, Kimberly." Bennett swatted at her behind and only partly connected.

The smell of fresh air, the sense of space… It spoke to the spirit in a way that rejuvenated him. He was not one of those individuals who could spend endless hours inside. He needed the sounds, the openness that being outdoors gave him. He took a deep breath. "It's beautiful out here."

"Yes, it is." She laughed and pushed her fanny out again. "One more try…"

Coming up behind her, he leaned down and kissed

her neck. "Let's get up the mountain before I do something on this path that isn't appropriate for kids. Besides, we don't know who or what is up there."

Her breath quickened. "Race ya!" She took off like a shot.

With the hamper and cooler in his hands, he was at only a minor disadvantage. He passed her at a full run that had her shouting at him to wait up.

Reaching the top before her, he placed the items on the ground and looked around. No one was in sight. The view was incredible, and they had the place to themselves. There was no way to see the Lester Facility, as it was set in its own valley and surrounded by a sheer-cliff rock face on both sides of the mountains, but they had a great view of the lights from San Diego. Down to the south, he could even see Tijuana.

Footsteps sounded behind him, and he turned toward them with open arms. He caught Kimberly and hugged her tight. His lips grazed hers. "This is a welcome break," he said. "Thank you."

She hugged her body to his. "You're welcome. I wanted time together, doing something other than the work. Something besides the mission." Her eyes lifted to his. "Unless this is just…a mission to you."

He stroked her back. "It's not. I believe you know that."

A smile filled her features and she leaned up and kissed him. "Yes. I guess I just had to hear it from you."

"Eeew! Gross! Stop that! You're going to make me go blind," said a voice approaching them. Melo and Alisha strode into the clearing, holding hands. The looks on their faces were of pure joy. "What do we have to eat?" Melo asked. "I'm hungry."

Bennett shook his head, taking a step back from Kimberly and putting himself between the food hamper and Melo. "You're always hungry. Ladies first."

"By all means," said Melo, taking a bag from Alisha. He pulled a blanket out of it and spread it on the ground. "Ladies."

Kimberly and Alisha sat down and pulled the food out of the hamper, placing it in the center of the blanket while Bennett and Melo grappled on the ground, attempting to see who would reach the cooler full of beer, wine, and water first. Bennett was taller and won by an arm's reach.

"Get off me," said Bennett, rolling Melo to the side. He opened the cooler and tossed a beer to his Teammate. "Guess this old man still has it."

"Hell, you're in better shape than I am. Too much broken-down shit in my body." Melo caught the beer, popped the top off with a rock, and sucked down half before he added, "Glad your bones are going to be rattled. Better you take the knocks than me."

"Gee, thanks." Bennett lifted his beer. "To the stars." His eyes caught Kimberly's, and they locked to each other for several heartbeats.

She blew him a kiss and went back to setting out the picnic food. "I'll have wine," she said. "Alisha, I put two kinds of water in there—bubbling and flat."

"Oh, bubbles. Definitely." Alisha opened her hand and waited for her husband to fulfill her request. He did just that, but he kissed her dainty palm before depositing her requested beverage. "This was a great idea," Alisha continued. "Thanks, Kimberly. When I received your call, my first thought was bad news. But this...

this is wonderful. I know you can't discuss anything, and I'm not asking you to. I just want you to know...." Pulling out her phone, she showed Melo a picture. "To see this…"

His eyes brimmed with unshed tears. "It's the ultrasound photo. Damn, that's incredible. There's my slugger. Boy or girl, you're going to be a baseball player."

The tears spilled as Melo turned the phone toward them.

Bennett squinted his eyes, but all he could see was a picture of a blob and a few dots.

"Congratulations," said Kimberly with a bright smile. "That's such a gift."

Bennett really didn't know what to do, so he shrugged at Kimberly and said, "Yeah, congrats. You both will be wonderful parents. Melo told us on the car ride home, but I guess this makes it…more real." He knew they would be great too. It was just a different stage of life, one he hadn't made the leap to yet.

"My morning sickness makes it even more real," said Alisha with a laugh. "But telling friends, talking about it…adds to the anticipation and excitement." She grabbed Melo's hand and urged him to sit down beside her. "I've already started my 'honey-do' list, so when you get home we can paint the spare room and put the crib together…"

The two were very doe-eyed and seemed to focus in on their own world.

Bennett took his cue and reached out a hand. "Come with me. I'm not that hungry…for food anymore. Are you?"

"No." She grinned at him and dropped the chicken

leg she was munching on, wiped her hands on a wet wipe, and took his hand. He pulled her to her feet and wrapped an arm around her shoulders, escorting her to a secluded grouping of rocks.

He sat down and pulled her onto his lap. "Just needed a little time alone with you."

"You can capture me anytime," she said and then saw something out of the corner of her eye. "Look at that."

A meteorite flared on its path toward the Earth, crashing some distance away.

"I wonder what treasures are aboard that rock."

Bennett nibbled at her earlobe. "Sorry, Doc, I'm more concerned about the treasures here on Earth. I'm holding the most precious one in my arms."

Chapter 11

BENNETT WANTED MELO'S LIFE RIGHT NOW. HIS Teammate was dry and tucked into think tanks with some of his favorite heroes in the engineering and design fields, and Bennett was stuck here, sick to death of tests. At least the laser array was good to go and the shuttle issues were being fixed now, thanks to Melo. Yep, that man was sitting pretty.

Water. Water was everywhere, and though he loved the stuff on a normal day, his skin was beginning to look like a duck's butt underneath the feathers.

His mind wandered. He didn't know what to think about Kess and how that guy fit into the issues surrounding the shuttle, but he agreed with Melo that they had to be related. With Bennett stuck here, how could he follow Kess or uncover additional facts? Besides, with the shuttle timeline so short, why keep doing these tests? He'd been shoved through more analysis than he knew possible, and his brain had been stretched with three psych evaluations. His body had been wired up while he ran three ten-mile stretches and more. Hell, he couldn't remember the last time he'd peed in private.

Everyone knew where Bennett was and what he was doing 24-7, which didn't leave any time or leeway for solving crimes. After he'd finished the spatial-awareness tests, he'd almost considered punching out the monitor. The man had injected him with a mild sedative and left him wired up to a game that zapped him with a current when he veered off the path, and then the man had gone on a break. Bennett's anger had kept his exhaustion at bay, but he desperately wanted to wire a part of that man's anatomy to see how he liked being zapped. The test seemed more fictional than real. Who was going to fall asleep during one of the most exciting experiences of their life?

Bennett sighed. Opening his eyes, he looked up through the water at the faces and shapes above him. Right now he was doing an oxygen-deprivation test— holding his breath. As if a SEAL didn't know his limits with every element, especially water. He told them he could go almost five minutes, if no one bothered him. Learning to slow your pulse rate and breathing was one of the first things instructors taught the tadpoles in BUD/S. If you didn't master it, you pretty much didn't make it through the phases, let alone Hell Week.

He counted to himself, figuring out how much longer he needed to stay under. If someone could best his time…have at it. He doubted they would, as he gave everything he focused on his *full* attention.

The gear holding him down helped. It might add a few more seconds to his time. Truth was…in the quiet of the water…this was the most relaxed he'd been all day. But who knew what was next? Maybe he should just stay down here.

—⁓—

"They're tormenting and torturing our boy." Melo stood in the doorway of Kimberly's quarters. He crossed his arms over his chest as he said, "It's time to call it."

"Call what?" Looking up from her desk, she stared at the broad-shouldered SEAL. She'd been so engrossed in her reading that she hadn't heard the door open. "What do you mean?"

"Look." He took a seat in front of her. His face was grim. "I know my shit tolerance for tests. I'm pretty sure that Sheraton reached his…like ten tests ago. You need to put a stop to all of this testing. Wrap this puppy up. You know who you're sending into space. Put everyone out of their misery and choose." Melo scratched his nose. "Believe me, it's for the best. Besides, he needs to have something left for the flight. Let him conserve whatever energy and brain power he has left."

"I never thought of it that way." Kimberly smoothed her hair. "I just wanted everyone to know that Bennett is the right candidate—mainly, because he outperformed the others."

"He's already done that." Melo waited for her to speak or take some kind of action, and Kimberly knew it was time to be more decisive.

"You're right," she said. "No more testing. It's time to make the decision…official."

A hand smacked the top of the water. It was time to come up. Bennett released himself from the gear and swam upward. As he broke the surface, he headed for the stairs and walked out of the pool.

Several of the other piloting candidates pointed at the scoreboard and argued. Bennett glanced at it, though he didn't need a tally to tell him that he'd kicked ass on this test.

A short man wearing the name tag of Johnny Grisnor handed him a tube. "If you'll open it and suck on the oxygen for five minutes, I need to score your blood-oxygenation levels," Grisnor said. He held up an oximeter. "We've had two candidates exhibit hypoxemia—where the blood oxygen falls below normal levels—and one person has showed signs of oxygen toxicity, or…"

Bennett finished the sentence. "Hyperoxia. I dive."

"Right, right. Of course." Grisnor pointed to the spot where the oxygen would be triggered. He looked at his watch and said, "Whenever you're ready, we'll begin."

His fingers triggered the oxygen tube, but as Bennett brought it toward his face his nostrils flared. He pushed the tube back and quickly shut it. "It's ammonia."

"What?" asked Grisnor. "Let me see that." The technician looked shocked as he retrieved the tube and checked for himself, and then he put it aside and took out another tube. He assured himself that it was indeed oxygen and handed it to Bennett. "Captain Sheraton, I'm very sorry! I don't know how that gas got into our stock. If your olfactory had not been so well developed, you could have been poisoned."

Cautiously lifting the proffered tube of oxygen to his mouth, Bennett took a tentative half breath. Yep, that was O^2. When everything went well with that breath, he slowly increased his inhalations until he breathed normally and fully utilized the device. In the meantime, he watched Grisnor calling frantically on his phone about the ammonia tube. It was obvious this individual had nothing to do with the mix-up, but who did?

After the five minutes passed and the test ended,

Grisnor took Bennett's vitals. "You're good to go, Captain. Right on track, though I'd prefer you stay here for a few minutes and take advantage of the oxygen." His hand touched Bennett's forearm. "Sorry again, sir."

Nodding his head, Bennett accepted the apology. "Sure. Thanks for the oxygen. Oh, by the way, who, uh, who was in charge of filling and/or distributing these?"

"A variety of people were involved in the process, though I believe ultimately Mr. Kess was in charge of making sure we had enough stock for all the candidates, as well as adding the labels to the equipment." Grisnor pointed to the sticker. "See, your information is right there." A phone beeped emphatically. "That's my supervisor. I've got to go. I'm going to file a report about this. Take care, Captain Sheraton, and best of luck. Hope you make it into space."

"Thanks. Me too." Bennett watched the young man hurry away. His lips thinned. He picked up the oxygen tube and took a few more breaths. Even though it wasn't really necessary, it was calming. This was pretty much the reason why there was oxygen on air flights, so that the passengers were calmer when a plane plummeted. Horrific as that was…it was the truth.

Allowing his mind and body to relax, Bennett considered the situation. He could make a big stink about Kess and whoever else might be involved, but that could also chase away a lead. In terms of attempts on his life, this was a fairly lame one. He'd seen hostiles with more determination, so this "poisoning" only registered about a two on his one-to-ten drama/action scale.

Yes, it was a better plan to remain low-key. Bennett made several mental notes on the event. If it ever came

up in the future, at least he'd remember the chain of
events correctly and the reason he'd made his present
decision. He'd update Melo and record it for his After-
Action Report, the damn document he'd be writing after
his return from space. But if he didn't make it, the next
group would have an idea of where to pick up a lead.

Kimberly walked out of her office, a woman on a mission. Melo was wise to push her. She'd hate for Bennett
to get the mission and have nothing left in the tank to
act on the role.

She gave herself a pep talk as she went. It was time
to take charge. This was her shuttle, and she was the one
who decided the role of pilot.

Adrenaline surged through her body as she pushed
herself to a faster pace. She could feel her heart thudding against her chest as she rounded the corner. One of
two things was going to happen: either she'd talk herself
out of what she wanted to do by taking the long walk
to Bennett's test, or she'd become more adamant about
ripping his clothes off and taking advantage of him.

Smiling to herself, she wondered if the word *advantage* was the best choice. What man didn't like being
wooed, touched, and made love to? Seriously, though,
would a SEAL really turn down all of this?

She looked down at her white lab coat and utilitarian
gray skirt. Okay, so maybe she wasn't sporting super-
model attire, but she definitely had the secret-identity
look nailed. Underneath, she had quite a surprise.

After pulling open the last door, she walked into
the holding room of one of their sterile rooms and

punched the button on the intercom. "I need to speak with Boss ASAP."

Inside the room, four techs worked with one pair of trainees. The point of the exercise was to deprive the trainees of a certain amount of oxygen and have them perform a series of tasks. A scoreboard held their current rankings: Navy was way ahead in first—go Bennett—and the internationals, listed in order of their best times, lagged behind.

A bell rang, and the Army guys sprang into second. The rankings altered again as Boss was pulled out of his gear, given a small tube of oxygen, and led to the door.

One of the programmers waved at her, signaling that he didn't need Boss to come back. The tech mimed scratching his butt and she smiled. Dressed in head-to-toe white suit and helmet, he looked like a science-fiction character, and she pursed her lips to hold back a humorous retort.

The tall SEAL stared down at her as she walked to him, grabbed his elbow, and steered him out of the room. They went down one long corridor and then another one. Few people greeted them as they went farther into the bowels of the building.

She was surprised that Boss let himself be led. He continued to suck on the oxygen as his eyes studied their surroundings. When she stopped at a large door, he looked down at her with a raised eyebrow.

When she swiped her badge over the scanner, the door opened and she led him inside. The lights sprang on, and she pushed a red button to the right of the door, locking it. There would be no mistaking her intent as Boss took in the mock-up of a bedroom in space.

"It's a model for a new space station, one being developed for commercial use by private financers. They wanted my input, so I made them an actual physical room to check out. What do you think?" asked Kimberly.

Glunk.

Boss had placed the oxygen tube on the table to his left. He looked amused. "Is there a test that you need me to pass...here?"

"I don't know that I'd call it a test..." She was being evasive on purpose.

He took a step closer to her. "What do you want to call it?"

"A stress reliever."

He smiled and closed the gap between them. His mouth was only a hair's breadth away. "Thank God! Do you need someone to open your pressure valve, Doc?"

"Yes," she said, meeting his brashness with her own. "I want to see you put your words into action. Isn't that what you often taunt me with?"

He pulled her into his arms and kissed her. *Passion* was not the word for that kiss. Heat. Demanding, concentrated force that searched for a target, and she was it.

Every ounce of her want pulsed in her actions as she pushed his clothes off and sought his mouth. Their tongues dueled as their hands ripped, tore, and released the barriers until they were both skin to skin.

He lifted her into his arms and walked them to one of the space chairs. Designed for an astronaut wearing a bulky space suit, it was an easy fit for two. He seated himself, situating her on his lap.

She pointed to one of the slots on the armrest.

Boss was curious enough to delve into the slot. His fingers withdrew a condom.

Her body lifted with the reaction of Boss's belly laugh. She joined in, as he fit the sheath over his cock and then gave his full attention back to her. "You're full of surprises," he said.

"Aren't I?"

With Bennett tucked into the model bed of the mock-up space bedroom, and with her stress level in check, Kimberly walked with a small bounce in her step toward Hubbard's office. She was on her way to share the good news before she lowered the boom on Kess. It seemed fitting that way, or maybe she was just being petty toward Kess. Either way, it worked for her.

She passed several assistants who scurried past, laden with dry cleaning and packages, and she smiled at them. They nodded back politely.

Maybe it was outside of her character to be so overtly friendly. It didn't matter, because all was right with her world at this exact minute, and she wanted to enjoy that.

Outside Hubbard's office door, she scanned her ID and requested entrance. The door slid open. Deciding to leave him a quick note, she walked to his desk and was about to sit down when she saw Hubbard's body covered in blood. Tucked into the alcove below the desk, he lay there like a discarded piece of paper. His throat was slit, and his eyes were wide open, as if he had been caught unawares. The horror of it was too much to take in immediately.

Shock and panic struck Kimberly in stages, and when

she had finally digested the scene of the murder, she screamed at the top of her lungs.

Sally's voice came over her phone. "Do you need to call security, medical, or something else, Kimberly?"

"B-B-Bennett and Melo," stuttered Kimberly. "Tell them I f-f-found a body." She stepped away from the body, careful not to upset anything. She swallowed nearly twenty times, trying to keep the bile from rising into her throat.

Seeing a dead body was enough to make anyone swoon. She made it all the way to the far wall and collapsed into the chair nearest the table. "Oh, God, this is where I sat earlier."

"Kimberly?" Melo was the first to arrive. "Good. I'm glad it's not you. Sally needs to be more specific when she pages us." He squeezed her shoulder and slipped past her. Bending down, he looked over the body.

Bennett came next, out of breath. His shirt was on backward and his pants were only half-zipped, but Kimberly didn't care. He was already pulling her into his arms and hugging her.

The tears she'd kept at bay burst out. She knew part of it was nerves, and she reined it in as soon as she could, but the other part was a real sadness. Hubbard had been kind to her, for the most part, since she had been here. It was only recently that he started leaning more toward Kess, and perhaps that was his way of balancing the scale, since she had the government in her corner.

She looked up at Bennett. "I'm okay. Go do what you need to."

He kissed her forehead and moved to where Melo still knelt. "What have you got?"

"Looks clean. His throat was slit. I'm not in forensics, but given the angle, I'd guess it was left to right, so the killer is a righty or is posing the scene to look that way." Melo pointed to the raised edge that was slightly wider. "I'd posit that Hubbard knew the assailant and was comfortable around him, enough so that his back was to him, and the person surprised him. Slit his throat and eased him onto the floor to delay discovery."

Bennett stood. "Kimberly, does Hubbard have a secretary?"

"Nothing regular since Gretal, who is on maternity leave for another month. Hubbard has had different assistants substitute when he needs help. I hear he's pretty self-sufficient. He likes the protocol of having his own assistant, though." Kimberly mopped her face with a tissue she took out of the box that sat on the far end of the bookcase shelf. As she reached for another one, she dropped the used tissue into the trash and missed. Leaning over to pick it up, she saw a small thumb drive on the floor, hidden in the shadows under the edge of Hubbard's desk.

She picked it up and took it over to Bennett. "I found this on the floor. Seems like an odd place for it."

Bennett traced the path from the drive to Hubbard's body. "I bet this was in his hand when he fell or close enough by that he knocked it away."

"Perhaps the murderer was looking for it." Melo inserted it into Hubbard's desktop and accessed the files. Bennett and Kimberly huddled around him. There were at least a dozen files.

"Do you recognize any of the names?" asked Bennett.

Kimberly shook her head and then stopped. "Wait. That one. It's from the test flight, the one Kess and Yuri did together. Open it."

Melo clicked on the folder. Only one Microsoft Word document was inside. He opened it, and it showed two different sets of data for the same flight. "Is that significant to you?" he asked.

Two sets of male eyes turned toward Kimberly. "Maybe," she said. "But I'd like to get the answer from both of those horses' mouths."

Bennett touched his phone. "Sally, can you locate Kess and Yuri?"

"Searching…" The computer worked for several seconds, and then said, "Yuri Pelsin is in his quarters, and Kess is off premises. There is no message as to when he will return to the Lester Facility."

"Sally, seal the door for NCIS," Bennett ordered. "Also, please alert Melo, Dr. Warren, and me when Kess returns. In the meantime, guide us to Yuri's location. I have a few questions to ask him."

—⁄⁄⁄—

Throughout the long walk to Yuri's quarters, which were on the other side of the Lester Facility, Kimberly argued her need to confront Yuri. Neither Bennett nor Melo would agree to her terms, nor could they dissuade her from her desire. Regardless of her wishes, the good doctor was staying in the hallway, at least until the situation was handled, and that was final.

Bennett stood at the corner of the hallway that led to Yuri's quarters. "We're not moving one more step until you promise to stay here."

Her lips thinned. She was angry, and her cheeks were flame red. "Fine."

Luckily, the hallway was clear. He and Melo made their way down. It was easy to tell from the phone app that Yuri was in the bathroom. "Sally, open the door. Divert noise for us, so he doesn't hear us entering." He liked that trick, the one they'd learned from Kimberly when Sally blew the air loudly to cover any noise.

Soundlessly, the door slid open. The lights were on. They were dim, but there was enough light to see that Yuri was still in the bathroom.

The only way they could catch Yuri in the act was to barge in. If they saw something untoward, well, they were all men. There was too much at stake here to be polite.

Melo counted off on his fingers: three, two, one.

They opened the bathroom door and entered.

By the shower, Yuri lay dead on the floor. His eyeballs were plucked out, and his throat was ripped open.

A strange device sat in Yuri's hand, and its razor-sharp talons were covered in blood. It moved toward them, and Melo crushed it with the sheer force of his boot before it could strike. So this machine had killed Yuri—but who was controlling it?

"Deadly toy. I wouldn't want to feel that thing scratching my back," said Melo as he scraped off the bottom of his shoe with a towel from the rack by the door. Tiny fragments of metal rained on the floor, including a small camera lens. "Too bad we couldn't have followed that thing home. The owner would need to be fairly close to control it."

"Yeah. We can have Sally run the monitoring feed and see what we find." Bennett backed out of the bathroom. He dislodged a board on the wall by bumping it accidentally.

"What the hell…" Bennett's words trailed off as he took in a collection of items. There were photos and small trinkets taped all over the board: chunks of hair, glasses, pieces of fabric, jewelry, and…skin. "God, this guy was sick! He kept trophies."

"I bet if we traced all the deaths associated with the project, we'd find pieces of them here." Melo checked Yuri's pulse just to be sure. "He's still warm, but he's definitely dead. He could have done it. Killed Hubbard and then come here."

"It's too tidy. I don't like it. We're missing something." Bennett stepped back, pulling Melo with him. He snapped pictures of the entire bathroom, leaving nothing out, and then the two of them withdrew to the bedroom. "Lock the bathroom, Sally, and don't let anyone in until NCIS arrives."

"Affirmative," the computer replied as the bathroom door locked with a loud click.

Melo walked to the bookcase. "Damn, he appeared ordinary on the outside, and on the inside he was a psychopath."

"Probably a sociopath. They can get by in society fairly undetected for a time. If he was this crazy up front, Yuri would never have passed all the psych evals." Bennett took pictures of the Yuri's bedroom, and the two SEALs stepped into the hall.

"Sally, lock Yuri Pelsin's quarters until NCIS arrives. Double-locking the place should keep it extra secure, right?" Melo scratched his neck.

"One would think," Bennett said.

Again, Sally did as requested, except this time, the loud click echoed down the hall.

"I'm glad Kimberly didn't have to see this," said Bennett.

"Me too." Melo shook his head. "I think I just saw something out of the corner of my eye. Was it...did I just see...Kess?"

The two men took off at a run. When they rounded the corner, Kimberly wasn't there.

"Help!" Kimberly's voice echoed down the hallway.

They ran toward it and reached a place where four corridors met.

"Crap! Which way?" asked Melo.

"I don't know." Bennett pulled out his phone. "Show me Kess."

"He's not in the building," said Sally.

"Where's Kimberly?" Bennett redirected the computer.

A mini version of her showed up on his phone. "This way," he said. They headed down the second hallway on the left, turning and winding their way through the building.

Running through the Lester Facility at full speed felt more like a thriller movie than it did real life. Unfortunately, they'd performed more than their share of athletics in chasing down targets, and Kess was not going to get the better of them.

Bennett leaped over a sweeper mop, glad that he was keeping his eyes open.

"Damn it!" A thud sounded from behind him and Bennett, without turning, knew that Melo hadn't been so lucky. His swim buddy had just been taken out by a sweeper maid. He couldn't wait to rib him about that one.

"Move," yelled Bennett over his shoulder as he dodged past two medical personnel deep in conversation. *How can people walk and talk and not get into accidents?* Those two were so thickly in it that they barely even saw him burst through their tête-à-tête.

"You're getting slow, old man," said Melo mockingly as he sprinted up beside him.

"Gee, thanks," said Bennett.

They rounded the corner, and shots zipped past them. Finally they caught sight of Kess, who had his arm around Kimberly's throat. He aimed a gun at them.

Bennett pulled Melo back around the corner, but one round had already caught his buddy in the shoulder. "Hell's bells, Melo, did you have to collect more metal for your collection?" Bennett asked.

"What can I say? The scars make me prettier." Pulling a gun from the back of his waistband, Melo held it in front of him. At a glance, the bullet hadn't gone through, and the bleeding was minimal, which was good. It meant nothing vital had been hit.

"I'll shoot her," yelled Kess.

"No, he won't," said Kimberly. "He's in love with me."

"Now you admit it. Why didn't you say it before, you—you damnable woman!" shouted Kess. "For as long as I've known you, I've wanted to be your lover. We could make magic together."

Bennett had his gun in hand. He pointed to the far column. Holding up one hand, he counted down. Then he launched himself to the other side as Melo held himself at the ready to lay down suppression fire.

Kimberly kept Kess talking. "Why not tell me that, instead of trying to control me?"

"You need controlling. Why can't you see that?" Kess shook with rage and emotion as he confessed his feelings. "You're mine, and you're going to be mine… and everything you have is mine too, including the shuttle—the Kess Shuttle. Isn't that beautiful? We can launch together and circle the planet, ruling from the stars… That's the reason I did this, killed those men and hid the truth from you. I need you to accept what has to happen. I'm going to rule everything."

Aiming his weapon as he moved, Bennett fired in midair, hitting both of Kess's legs and his firing hand. Blessedly, he missed Kimberly. Kess landed against the far wall with the force of a linebacker. The impact forced the breath out of his lungs, but Bennett was still moving. He was up and hurtling himself toward Kess, who managed to push Kimberly away and grab his gun with his unwounded hand. Kess fired at Melo, who was also charging, and close.

Bennett's buddy went down. Damn it!

Bennett never took his eyes from Kess. He knew he should capture and question him, but this guy was too unpredictable, a loose cannon. Before he knew it, his instincts had commandeered his brain, and he fired one more time—a headshot. The finality was true.

This time the man was gone. Bennett had wanted to question him, to wring a few truths out of the son of a bitch who masterminded a ton of crap around here, but that possibility was gone now. What had he done? Damn it!

He grabbed Kess's gun and pocketed it. A small controller was sticking out of Kess's pocket, and he grabbed that, too.

Bennett knew he'd have to live with the consequences of his actions. But there was a large part of him that felt better launching into space knowing that Kimberly would be safe on the ground. Kess had been a bad man, and there was no doubt about his guilt or his actions.

As Bennett pulled Kimberly to her feet, his eyes momentarily scanned her for damage, which she was blessedly free of, and then he quickly went to Melo. Fuck, his swim buddy did not look good. He'd gladly have given his own life to save Melo or take away his brother's pain.

"Sally, we need a med team." Bennett was already on the ground assessing the damage to Melo as he said, "Melo's been shot in the thigh, and he's bleeding fast and furiously." Bennett pulled his shirt over his head and tied it around the wound, pulling it tight and putting the weight of his entire body onto the bullet hole.

Melo groaned. "Damn, you need to go on a diet. I had to get…the SEAL…who weighed a thousand pounds."

"You're going to be happy I'm fat and fast," Bennett said as he kept the pressure on, stanching the bleeding.

Kimberly tore off her shirt and held it against Melo's shoulder. Her voice shook as she said, "I waited. I did as you asked."

"I know, Kimberly. I know. You did fine, honey. Just what I asked you to, and the way you kept him talking was smart. Very wise," Bennett murmured to her as he watched Melo. His swim buddy was hanging in there.

Stretchers arrived with doctors and paramedics quickly. Bennett felt that Melo was going to get good treatment here. That boded well.

"I'm benched," Melo said. He attempted to lift his

head, and his body spasmed with pain. "What about the launch? You can't stay here alone."

"I've got Kimberly. No worries. Okay?" Bennett signaled the paramedics to take the stretcher. "Just don't rat me out to Alisha. You know how wives are about their husbands getting hurt."

"Fine, but you'll owe me one," said Melo, his voice hoarse.

"I'll owe you two," said Bennett, gently butting his fist against his friend's and then holding up two fingers. "Heal swiftly, my brother."

They hoisted Melo onto the stretcher. They'd do the surgery there, where they had some of the best doctors around, and then he'd be transported to Balboa. Alisha was going to have his hide, and there was nothing Bennett could do about it. Shit hit the fan, and it went where it did sometimes. There was no rewind function, and overthinking it didn't change the outcome. Hopefully, the woman wouldn't take too much skin. He was partial to everything below his waist.

Bennett watched his friend disappear down the hall, then turned to Kimberly. "Can you make it to your room?" he asked. He wanted to escort her, but he had to finish necessary tasks. The rooms were close; he knew they were.

"Yes, it's just down that hall and to the right." Some color returned to her cheeks as she replied, "I can do it."

"Good." He hugged her close. "I'll be there shortly, okay?"

His eyes followed her to the corner. His heart went with that beautiful woman. He could hear her scan the badge and go inside. There were no threats to Kimberly in this place anymore. The only one who could have hurt her was dead. Bennett had made sure of that. He felt a lot safer about her being in the Lester Facility, but there was still work to do.

Looking back at the scumbag who was responsible for the death of his brethren made Bennett's blood run cold. At least the bastard was dead. He'd have some good news to tell Ouster, and though it would bring little comfort to the families of the victims, the overburdened judicial system wouldn't waste its time handling this jerk.

The security guards walked up and stood beside him. "What do we do with him?" one asked.

"Put him on a stretcher and lock him in a room. I might need access to him later. And revoke any badges, passwords, or pass codes," ordered Bennett. He bent down to close the man's eyes and swiped Kess's ID. He pocketed it and headed for the man's quarters. There was no telling what he'd find there.

—◦◦◦—

Bennett scanned Kess's ID to get in and then stood there for a few seconds. Searching a dead man's room was never as thrilling as one might think. The place had a finality to it that made it sort of eerie.

There was a method to the search. Take in the entire room visually before touching anything. If possible, take pictures or record a video, and then choose the top three to five places you would consider hiding something, starting with the obvious. On the second attempt, Bennett found a SIM card. Turning on the computer, he said, "Sally, access the SIM."

Kess's face filled the screen. "If you're watching this, then I'm either dead or I've succeeded in my quest. I planned and executed a rather intricate operation that brought down many lives, and this video describes what will go down in history as the day I bested the United States and all the countries of the world. I'm now the new ruler, the dictator of the Earth, and here is my manifesto…"

Bennett listened to the video rattle on for several minutes. Kess took responsibility for all the lives lost in association with the project, and Bennett concluded that Kess was definitely insane. This guy's manifesto completely sucked.

Without realizing it at the time, Bennett had followed Ouster's orders and taken care of the person responsible for the deaths of his brethren. There was some satisfaction there, but it would have felt better if Melo were still by his side. He had no doubt that his swim buddy would survive and thrive, but it would have been good to have him still there, guarding Bennett's six.

His phone buzzed like crazy—messages from Ouster. The Admiral had a sixth sense about action. Ignoring the phone for now, Bennett played the video again while he searched the room one last time. Nothing special was in there.

Thank God Kess wasn't a trophy collector like Yuri— guess there was room for only one sociopath. If there were additional documentation or clues, Bennett had no idea where they were hidden.

"Kess and Yuri… If only we had cornered them sooner." Bennett shook his head.

As the mastermind of this whole charade, Kess had roped poor Yuri into this mess using Yuri's sociopathic behaviors against him. Kess had a lot to answer for. But how do you ask a dead man a question? Maybe things would have had a different outcome for Yuri if he'd come clean about Kess's involvement. Instead, that guy had gotten in over his head too, and had only seen one way out. For both of them, it was a bad way to go: violence for violence.

Bennett stood and stretched. He thought about the particulars some more.

The impending launch must have escalated Kess's timetable, forcing him to tie up loose ends before the big day. Did Kess really think he could bully his way onto the flight and rule the world from space? Yikes!

Ejecting the SIM, Bennett pocketed it and took the ID too. "Sally, seal this room like the others. Same instructions: don't allow anyone in until NCIS arrives."

"Affirmative," said Sally. As the final locks clicked into place, Bennett walked down the hall. Right now he needed one thing, and one thing only: to hold the woman he loved in his arms. Damn, he had come close to losing her. She'd never know how his hand had shaken as he lifted that gun to shoot at Kess. The bad guys were gone. No more targets. At least there was comfort in that fact. Now he just had a mission—to launch into space. That was going to take him away from Kimberly.

He double-timed it down the hallway until he reached her door. He paused and gathered himself. Calmed his breathing. What would he say, he loved her and he was leaving her because he had to complete this mission? His gut clenched. How could he say good-bye just when he had found the unthinkable—a woman to love with his entire heart?

Chapter 12

THE DAY WAS FILLED WITH PREPARATIONS. THE TONE around the Lester Facility was a combination of shock and relief. Everyone had been on edge with the sabotage, and knowing it was over brought an overwhelming sense of ease to their actions. But the betrayal of Kess and Yuri… That was something no one would be getting over anytime soon. Over sixty announcements had been made, and most folks were putting their phones on mute to avoid the calls and texts.

The psychology staff was already booking appointments for an evaluation of the remaining staff, but first, the entire focus was turned to one thing…the shuttle and it's newly appointed pilot. The rest of the candidates were in agreement on Bennett's qualifications, and they were lending a hand where they could to expedite the work.

Launch was to be at 0400 the next morning, and the list of what still needed to be done was long. Besides going over the laser array instructions and hardware again, Bennett wanted to walk through the shuttle alone. He needed to visualize everything he was going to do. That's what SEALs did: when they could, they practiced.

Last night, he and Kimberly had held each other. They had spoken very little. Words just couldn't convey what they needed to. Over and over they had made love until they were exhausted, but they never let each other go. Now he sipped coffee, alternating between staring at her and scanning the long list of items to review for the flight.

A new project manager was being brought in by the Joint Chiefs, a man name Fraz Gorsk, but it was unlikely he would make it in time for the launch. That was for the best, in Bennett's opinion; he'd rather his life was in her hands. He knew she'd protect him, the same way he'd always protect her. Why couldn't the Joint Chiefs just leave well enough alone and keep Kimberly in charge? It wasn't his call, but he wished it were.

Hell, he didn't have a lot to complain about. He was about to go live realizing one of his greatest dreams, being in space. That was a lot for any soul to take in.

He stretched his fingers. He needed to go over everything again.

Why could he hit anything he aimed at with a gun or knife? It was practice. He'd worked and worked at each skill until it was a muscle memory.

Scratching the back of his neck, he knew he could recite everything he needed to know. That wasn't the problem. It was the unknown. He had to keep his doubts away and trust his training. As his mentor, Gich, had told him many times, "The ability to act comes out of belief in self." The advice had helped him in tough pinches, like the time he'd stepped on an IED, or improvised explosive device, and had to figure out how to defuse it without setting the fucker off. As many an EOD— Explosive Ordinance Disposal—expert would say, the odds are about one in one hundred, and it's scary as hell.

"Kimberly, I'm going down to the shuttle. I'm going to sit in the pilot's seat and visualize running through the procedures and the entire mission," Bennett said. He was already on his feet. Coffee in hand, he walked to her for a kiss. They locked lips for several seconds, and then he left.

He was torn between spending every second he could with her and focusing on the mission. "Be present," his instructor had told him. That's what he would do. He would take each moment one step at a time.

The hallways were busy, filled with people rushing from one place to another. He scanned his ID.

"Captain, we're done with the interior for now," said a man whose name tag read *Orly, Wilson*. He gave Bennett a clipboard with all the recent readings of the instruments, fuel intake, etc., and left him.

Entering the shuttle for the first time by himself made the mission real. Bennett inspected the entire ship and then sat down in the pilot's seat. Closing his eyes, he ran the steps of the launch through his head.

His phone buzzed several hours later. He'd been so caught up in his visualization, he hadn't realized how much time had passed. He looked at his phone. It was a text from Kimberly.

Meet me on the roof at 6 p.m.

He replied, OK.

That gave him the rest of the day to review the equipment they would install in space. He was going to review that installation, but do as much as he could physically or using computer simulations. Practice makes it reflex.

On the roof of the facility, an empty blanket waited to be used. Sally had secured the doors for them. Only

Kimberly and Bennett would have access to it tonight. This was a going away that she hoped meant "until we meet again" rather than "forever." She wouldn't allow herself to dwell on it either way. Instead, she was going to enjoy their time together.

Bennett's fingers entwined with hers. Kimberly looked up into his heated gaze. Emotion welled in her heart as she saw the openness in his eyes, as if he were beckoning her to look into his soul. Was this what it meant…to be truly connected to someone? This was her way to say good-bye.

How could it be that she had never felt this way before? Perhaps there was something to this whole soul-mate thing. Being someone's other half had never been so appealing…as long as it was Bennett.

His hand squeezed hers. "I only have a short time, and then I need to get back to…prepare."

She nodded. There was so much she wanted to say to him, a breadth of sentiment that was probably too silly or emotional to say out loud. Swallowing the words she wanted to share, she leaned up and kissed him.

The tender brush of lips was electric. His free hand snaked out and grabbed her waist, pulling her close.

As soon as his body touched hers, her own need blossomed. It was as strong as his, as noted by her pelvis pushing against his.

"Kimberly, I feel like a teenager who might get caught at any moment," he murmured against her lips.

She giggled. "Me too."

"We're too old for this shit."

"Tonight we're not." She rubbed her hands along his muscled shoulders. "Enjoy it. I am." Placing her hand at the back of his head, sinking her fingers into those luscious locks of hair, she moved him toward her. Their mouths met, a war of tongues, heat, and hedonistic delight.

She tugged at his clothes, rushing to experience his skin against hers. He fumbled in the dark with her bra.

She laughed. "SEAL, you don't have game." With one finger, she popped the clasp open.

"Gee, thanks, lady. You should be flattered I'm out of practice, or maybe it's you. The fact…that you make me nervous sometimes…" His voice dropped off.

She stilled. "What do you mean?"

"I've never felt this way before. With anyone," he admitted. "Pretty macho, right?"

Her hands cradled his cheeks. "Actually, I think it's the sexiest thing I've ever heard." She kissed him with all of the emotion she'd been holding back.

"Wow," he murmured.

Leaning her forehead against his, she said, "If you haven't guessed, I long for you. Together or apart…I'm yours, Bennett."

His arms wrapped tightly around her, cuddling her close. "I love you, Kimberly."

Her heart thudded in her throat. Never had those words so deeply touched her that they seared into her soul. Her emotions spanned from extreme jubilation to tremendous sorrow when she imagined what she could lose now. This man was the one person on Earth she would give her life for, and he was blasting off into space. When she found her voice again, she shared from her heart. "I love you, Bennett. More than I realized possible."

There the two of them stood for a long time in a state of undress. They were still and quiet, enjoying each other's energy and presence. This moment was one she'd tuck away in her heart and remember.

—◇—

He lowered her onto the waiting blanket. He needed to be inside of her, and he had to tell her, to share in the sentiment she had expressed. "You have me too. I am yours," he said. Her words had so deeply touched him that he needed her to know he didn't take her or this relationship for granted.

His thumb stroked along the side of her cheek as he placed his lips against hers. The tender touch sent a wave of passion through his body, heating his blood and making his heart race. She was intoxicating.

Removing the rest of her clothing, and then his own, he placed a condom on his cock and wrapped his arms around her. Naked skin rubbed against naked skin. Flesh ignited flesh as nerve endings sang with excitement.

He held her breasts cherishingly, raining tiny kisses and caresses along the glorious orbs until her nipples were hard and extended, begging for his mouth. As he laved the tip of a nipple with his tongue, she arched her back, thrusting her pelvis against his.

Her hands rubbed along his arms and back, exploring, kneading, squeezing. As she tilted her hips up, he lifted her straight into the air and lowered her slowly onto his waiting cock.

All she had to do was touch him, and he was rock hard. *This lady is incredible.*

Her legs wrapped around his waist, squeezing tight,

as her hands found purchase on his shoulders. He cupped her buttocks, such perfect orbs, helping her to set a rhythm. His body ached to release.

As he kissed her, he became lost in her lips, her mouth, and her tongue. The sweetness of her breath became his as they made love with their entire bodies.

Too soon they were both climaxing. Together, their souls were united in bliss as they rocked to pure satisfaction.

Holding her against him, he could feel her legs weakening, unable to stay set around his waist. "I have you," he whispered. "You won't fall."

Instantly, she let go. Her trust was not lost on him. Instead, it fed something inside of him, a hollowness that he hadn't realized was there. That place where something had always seemed missing was suddenly very full…of her, Dr. Kimberly Warren.

He hugged her tightly, burying his nose in her hair. Drawing in the scent of her, the essence of lovemaking, the lavender soap, and the lingering scent of jasmine. His soul was quiet: no running forward with a need to go, or to find action. Rather, he was content to simply hold her. Even the memories were quiet, the ones that played over and over of friends dying, missions gone sideways, and things he wished he'd done differently in his life. For now, this peace was so consuming, he felt himself drifting off to sleep, holding the woman of his deepest desire. Truthfully, that fact scared the hell out of him. Launching into space seemed tame in comparison.

Shifting to his side, he held fast to him. "I love you, Bennett," she murmured. "Forever."

"Forever, my love." The sentiment warmed his heart at the same time it chilled his blood. The weight of what he had to lose now had increased tenfold. Before their declaration, their time together had been a memorable collection of moments, and now he was leaving her behind with an unknown future.

He forced himself to push the emotion away, because in his heart he knew the truth. He loved her too dearly to go and too dearly to stay.

——~~——

Launch day was upon them. After making love on the roof for several hours, cuddling, and talking, Bennett and Kimberly had entered the facility building and gone back to work. Their brief time together was the only thing that seemed real to her. Everything else was a blur of activity.

Going through the motions of the day, they ate breakfast together, showered, and dressed. They smiled at each other and held hands or touched when they could. Neither of them would say good-bye—that was the word they didn't want to utter. It stood unspoken between them.

Earlier in the day, the Warren Shuttle had been taken outside. It was amusing to watch a small truck tow the amazing space vehicle, parading it before them on the way to its launch position.

The fuel had been checked and the systems reviewed. Everything was a go, and that included the weather. With clear, bright blue skies above and no wind, they couldn't ask for better conditions.

"Keep your eyes peeled," Kimberly said. "That comet we've been watching is still moving away from your direction, but it could change its course." Her facial features were tight with stress and worry, and an under-lining excitement for him too. Of course they'd talked about all of this before, but it was nice of her to remind him that she'd be here, waiting, and that he needed to stay on his toes. "We'll be monitoring you from here."

"I will be vigilant in my awareness." He smiled softly and tilted his head in her direction as if to say, "You be careful too."

Last-minute technicians moved in and out of the vehicle for a final check, including Browner, who was sweating bullets over something on his launch list. No one had time to review everyone else's job. They just had to trust them.

Too soon Kimberly was standing before Bennett, and he was ready to leave.

Pulling her into his arms, he kissed her in front of everyone and said, "I love you, Kimberly." Her heart melted.

She knew interest would be written over all of their faces, but she didn't care. The warmth in her heart was all that mattered. "I love you too. Be safe, Bennett."

This was it, the moment he had been working for and had dreamed about all of his life. The hobby of studying the stars and keeping up with all the latest information and technology, along with his piloting and his physical SEAL training, would serve him in this. And he didn't just want to succeed, he needed to. Also, he had a reason to return to the ground…to Kimberly. Emotions welled up inside of him at the weight of this present.

He couldn't speak, and after he kissed Kimberly, he simply nodded at the others surrounding them and entered the Warren Shuttle. From now until he landed back on Earth, his entire focus would be on piloting the shuttle and performing the mission as planned.

The door closed, blocking the view of those outside, but not severing the connection.

He moved to the pilot's seat and strapped himself in. He reviewed the controls and double-checked all the monitors one last time.

Knowing Kimberly as well as he did, he understood the shuttle much better now. It was a sleek, sexy design that cut down on wind shear and had several unique innovations.

He smiled to himself and hoped she knew she was right there with him. Melo and his biochips were there too. Traveling into space with the hopes of his country, his Admiral, and his brethren made him feel like he had an army at his back. Now it was up to him to take charge and follow through with the mission.

As the shuttle door closed, everyone retreated inside except for the emergency medical crew, who took up a station right inside the bay doors. With this much fuel on board, a fireball could be devastating.

Kimberly waited for several seconds and then rushed to join the others in the Command Control Center. It was filling up.

She found an empty terminal and sat down. Flipping the switch, she watched the monitor spring to life in time to see the engines come online. She said a silent prayer for Bennett, the shuttle, and the mission.

Fears ran through her mind and she allowed them to keep going out of her brain. Nothing was going to stop her from relishing the experience of watching her own design launch into space.

"Captain Sheraton, you're cleared for takeoff when you're ready," said the mission leader from the Command Control Center.

"Roger," replied Bennett.

Kimberly bit her lip as she watched her screen. Heat filled her face as her heart raced out of control. She wanted to yell, "Stop! Wait! I don't want you to go." And yet, she did want him to fly the shuttle. In her head, she knew he was the only one who could make this mission happen. The man could think his way out of anything.

The live feed from inside the shuttle showed him pushing the yoke forward as the shuttle blasted off into the sky. It arced above the building and headed into the troposphere. The screen showed only a slight amount of turbulence, and the readings were steady. As the shuttle disappeared into the sky, the feed faltered and then cut out completely. Now they had to trust that its design was sound and that Captain Bennett Sheraton would make it safely into space.

Chapter 13

THE FORCE OF THE ROCKETS AS BENNETT WAS THRUST upward reminded him of his first parachuting high jump, except there was no wind batting his body around as if it were a rag doll. Instead, the shuttle was defying gravity and lifting him into the unknown.

Rocketing through the atmosphere and emerging into the vastness of space was one of the three coolest things he'd ever done in his life. It was right up there with receiving his Trident and meeting Kimberly. It would have been impossible to explain to a layman what it was like going up, up, up and then transitioning into this great immenseness, as if he'd burst through a bubble and entered an endless, infinite cavern of stars and wonder.

Bennett stared. His eyes went everywhere at once, trying to take it all in. Perhaps that was what saved him. As he looked around, he saw something moving. It was crawling out of the small wall-mounted box near his head. The box was very similar to the one he'd seen on the Langley crash-test video, which had then disappeared from all logs.

The night before launch he'd checked, and there was no box. So it had to have been placed in the shuttle and attached the day of launch. His eyes tracked the movement of the contraption as it crawled free of its housing. It was a silver device, some kind of small robot.

Damn, he'd bet that Kess had had Browner install the

box. Melo had told him about the incident in the cafete-ria, and this must have been the reason for the yelling. Browner was told to follow some kind of list, and he'd bet his eyeteeth this box was on it.

Shit! The mechanical robot moved like a spider, gaining momentum. A creature like this had killed Yuri. It was headed for the brain of the shuttle. There was no camera this time, only a small chip on its back, so it was preprogrammed.

Didn't Melo crush the last one with his foot?

Reaching a hand down toward the strap on his leg, Bennett withdrew a slim knife and tossed it at the spider. The momentum had the knife flying backward, and it missed its mark. That spider still moved. "Fuck," he said.

"Nearing destination," said Sully.

If the spider reached the brain first and switched to manual controls before Bennett reached the first orbit, he would drop out of acceleration and start falling toward Earth. There would be no recovery. It might take a while to die, but the shuttle would just plummet downward. What a slow and painful way to go!

"Not on my watch! Kess, you bastard," Bennett mut-tered. "Reaching up from the grave, you son of a bitch. Well, it isn't going to work. I'm not giving up without a fight." He connected the dots from the manifesto to the shuttle, visualizing the box clearly now. This thing might be a part of Kess's plan, but he could end that once and for all. "Sully, artificial gravity."

"It's unadvisable, Captain," the computer explained.

"Do it now."

Reaching his hand toward the sheath on the other side of his thigh, Bennett grabbed the other Ka-Bar knife and threw it at the spider. It slammed into the center of the creature and sparked. For a second, the robotic creature flailed its legs, and then it fell to the ground with the knife still stuck in its core.

The smell of burnt copper filled the cabin. At least it hadn't started a fire; he'd be hustling his ass to the fire extinguisher otherwise. Relief flooded him.

"Clean the air, Sully," Bennett ordered. He turned his attention back to piloting, tuning out the distraction. Touching the first button of the panel in the center of the console, he marked the time until he cut the rockets and switched to engine bursts.

In the Command Control Center, Kimberly sighed with relief as the shuttle cleared the atmosphere. They'd lost contact while Bennett traveled through it, and she was anxious to see his visage or hear his voice.

"Come in, Captain Sheraton," said Liaison Jennie Jarvis. "Please respond."

"This is the Warren Shuttle, Captain Sheraton speaking." Bennett's voice was sound and clear.

A shout went up in the room.

"We're picking up several gasses present in the cabin," said Jarvis. "Please report."

"Nothing," Bennett said. "Just, uh, venting some smoke. It's handled, and all systems are working correctly. Coming up on first orbit. Going radio silent to prepare for first task."

"Copy," said Jarvis. "Good luck, Captain. We'll look forward to hearing from you on the next check-in. Over and out." The woman looked up at Kimberly and smiled.

Kimberly gave her a thumb's-up in return. In her mind, she was already reviewing the words *smoke* and *vent*. What could possible cause such a thing? She sucked her lower lip into her mouth and chewed, running through the possibilities.

Bennett turned the Command Control Center radio to mute. Checking the proximity of the area, he could see a ton of space junk, but nothing that would interfere with the deployment of the new communications satellite. He pressed the button that would record the distribution and positioning.

Upon reaching the appropriate orbit of most normal or commercial satellite communications arrays, approximately twelve thousand feet above the Earth's atmosphere, Bennett oriented the shuttle. Opening a side bay door, he pushed a button that jettisoned the newly updated communications array, which launched flawlessly. Its side flaps opened automatically, revealing solar panels, and the device sprang to life as it maneuvered into position.

He closed the bay doors and waited until the array had moved out of range. Then he fired the engines, turning the shuttle away from the device. A series of commands scrolled across the monitor to his upper left, and he watched the feedback from the satellite. The system connected directly with the satellite, and the complex list ended with one word, *Complete*, proving this part of the mission was successful.

Sending a test signal from the Warren Shuttle, he received responses from facilities all over the planet, including the Lester Facility. He checked the readout one last time and could see that the array was functional and in good working order, so he closed the bay door.

He blew out a long, slow breath he hadn't realized he

was holding. One task down. Now it was time to take the shuttle upward into geostationary orbit and tackle the next hurdle.

Kimberly had tuned out everyone in the Command Control Center. Her entire focus was on reading the plethora of information from the shuttle. She was relieved when she saw that all systems were working well and that the burst of smoke had not been from anything in the shuttle's payload but rather from some device that had been added on board.

Looking over her shoulder, she wondered who had added something that shouldn't be there. She picked up her phone and said softly, "Sally, I need you to trace all devices loaded onto the shuttle and tell me if something was added that was not on the manifest."

"Working..." Sally was quick to respond. "Captain Sheraton concealed several weapons on his person and within the shuttle. Shall I show you where?"

"No," said Kimberly with a half smile. Nothing could take the "prep" out of the SEAL. "Did anyone else add something?"

"Only Browner. He placed a metal box containing an object onto the shuttle wall." Sally brought up a visual as she spoke. "It was approved by Project Leader Kess but was not added to the manifest."

"Where's Browner now?" asked Kimberly.

"Browner is located at the back of the Command Room. His vitals are elevated and he's on the verge of passing out." Sally showed a live feed of Browner's face.

Kimberly frowned. "Sally, send this footage to security and tell security to detain Browner immediately." Giving her attention back to the shuttle readouts, she added, "What does Sully say about the item that was in the box on the wall?"

"Working…" said Sally. Then she showed a picture, a paused frame of footage from Sully's onboard recorder. A knife was sticking out of the center of a small robot spider.

Kimberly laughed. That was her man. He handled whatever came along, didn't he?

"According to Sully's log, the item from inside the box is no longer operable. Is there anything else you require?" asked Sally.

"That will be all." Kimberly logged off and sighed with relief. She looked up at the big screen at the front of the room, which was tracking the shuttle's movements. "Keep going, Bennett. Keep on moving."

A small blip at the top of the screen caught her eye. It was so small that if she hadn't been paying direct attention to every inch of what should be where and when, she might have missed it. Kimberly was pretty particular about details, and to her, that blip stood out like a sore thumb.

She walked over to Jarvis and pointed at the top of the woman's terminal. "What is that?" When the woman didn't respond immediately, Kimberly said, "You need to get Captain Sheraton on the comm, now!"

Bennett fired the engines again, and the Warren Shuttle moved upward, farther into space. The Earth grew smaller as the shuttle progressed. He had to admit, flying the shuttle beat the hell out of flying a regular plane. He didn't know if he'd ever be able to appreciate going back to one.

"We will be reaching geosynchronous orbit in ten, nine, eight…" Sully said.

Bennett flipped the switch off, cutting the engines and turning the shuttle to the side. When it didn't move to precisely where he wanted it, he flipped the switch again and fired several small bursts.

"…seven, six, five, four, three, two, one. This shuttle is now in geosynchronous orbit at the designated spot for deployment," said Sully.

The area was clear. There was very little up here, only high-grade military hardware, and it was ideal for the laser array.

Putting the controls on automatic, he said, "Maintain the helm, Sully. Keep me apprised of incoming messages and any change in conditions inside and outside the shuttle."

Releasing his harness, Bennett reviewed the oxygen and power levels in the cabin, which were normal and working efficiently. He then he grabbed the broken spider, secured both knives in a storage container, and locked it down before dropping the spider into the transition bay for disposal.

Bennett ate a power bar and sucked down liquid, fortifying himself for the work ahead. After he'd relieved himself, he let himself into the transition bay, through which he would exit into space. Reviewing the list of instructions was a secondary concern, but he did it anyway. He'd rather have it fresh in his mind before he went out the door than need to come back inside and take off his suit again to do it. Though he could probably download it to Sully, he wanted Sully's full focus on the shuttle and the area around it.

He went into the back portion of the shuttle and checked the oxygen tanks and the entire space suit before he donned it. Securing his helmet, he flipped on the power unit and said, "Sully, comm check."

"Comm check. Affirmative, Captain. I read you loud and clear. Comm check is complete."

Thank God the computer isn't a talker. It'd drive me nuts to have it droning on while I work. Bennett secured the tether to his suit, adding an additional set of tools to the outside of his suit—better safe than sorry. Then he secured another tether to the laser-array box and the second set of tools. He opened the door. Kicking the spider into space was satisfying, but tromping Kess's final wish to destroy him was even better.

Karma is a bitch, and so is payback.

He cleared his mind and stepped forward. His body tumbled forward and he opened his arm's wide to slow his movement. Drifting in space was humbling, in a way that nothing in his life had ever been before. Stepping into this nothingness was probably the oddest feeling he'd ever experienced, even trumping his first high-altitude jump.

He could imagine how small he must seem in comparison to the vastness of space, or even in relation to the shuttle. Turning his attention back to his task, he cleared the door.

Bennett used short bursts from his jet pack to move forty feet from the shuttle. The line would reach fifty, but he needed room to implement. Figuring this spot would work, he pulled the box toward himself hand over hand. When it reached him, he pushed a button that folded the box lips back and revealed the device. It was pretty handy having a box that became part of the actual array. Now that was innovation at its best.

When he touched a yellow button on the top of the device, a flap slid back and one thousand small orbs, half the size of the smallest known microsatellites and capable of producing a lot more than small electromagnetic pulses, disconnected from all around the device and moved away. They began their journey into place. He could see them come online, one by one, as they reached their position. He watched until they were lost from sight, hidden behind the earth herself, like a well-formed army encircling the planet. It was fascinating to watch them go.

Bennett didn't allow himself to dither too much— there was enough redundancy built into the orbs that if one were destroyed, another would pick up the slack, at least until there were only two left.

Using the screwdriver on his belt, he opened the main device and accessed the viewing panel, which would allow him to manually destroy the space junk by turning on the laser function for a short-range burst. He pointed the array at Earth and determined which objects were live, transmitting satellites or useful space tech. He distinguished them from the wads of metal, screws, etc., that created a pileup of junk and were dangerous to vehicles moving through the area.

Bennett activated the array and watched the computer double-check the objects that were tagged as trash and ask for his confirmation for destruction. Sighting each one down for a final time, he assessed that the target was indeed trash—including the broken spider. He hit the short-range button, firing the array in a giant singular burst of light. The junk was instantly vaporized.

Good riddance! From items as small as a screw to

larger pieces of solar panels, the array took it all out. The best part was there was no residue from it.

Damn, it was that easy. Was it a wonder that they needed so much security to protect the laser array from falling into the wrong hands? This was a weapon of significance, and it was a protection that would hopefully keep the Earth and its inhabitants safe now and in the years to come.

"Captain, you've received a message from Command Control. Can I patch it through?" asked Sully.

"Go ahead," replied Bennett.

"Captain Sheraton, hold for Dr. Warren," said Jarvis. The liaison's voice was very tense.

"Bennett…" said Kimberly.

"I'm almost done, Kimberly. Can it wait?" Bennett was pleased, but there was more work to do. He didn't want to get distracted by anything until he finished.

"No! That mass we talked about that was going in another direction—it's coming toward you."

"Roger. Now if I can just…"

"Don't you understand, Bennett? A comet is almost on top of you. Get out of there." Kimberly's voice was frantic.

"I get it. Not just yet. I need to complete this next task first. What's the point of being here if I don't finish?" His voice was calm.

"What's the point of losing your life?"

"Kimberly, I understand. I love you more than my own life. I have to go…" Bennett reached up to turn his comm off.

"Wait. Bennett, I love you too. Come home to me." Her voice was wavering. He knew she was crying.

He clicked off the comm, thrusting away his emotion.

Now came the toughest job: turning the array and setting it into its final resting place, so that it couldn't be turned back toward the Earth or used against its inhabitants. If he screwed this up, there was going to be a world of hurt left behind, and he didn't want to be responsible for that.

———〜〜〜———

The Command Control Center at the Lester Facility was full of noise. Worry had everyone chattering at once, and Kimberly covered her ears so that she could concentrate.

According to the live feed from the Warren Shuttle, Bennett had successfully launched the new communications satellite and then arrived at geosynchronous orbit and implemented the array. The space junk was blown up, and thankfully, none of the communications equipment had been caught in the crossfire. Though that stuff wasn't her technology, Kimberly still wanted the mission to be a success. These people were acting as if everything was done. It wasn't. Nothing was complete until the array was turned and locked into place, and Bennett was safely on the ground.

"Kimberly, you asked me to alert you," Sally said. "I'm receiving additional readings from Sully that affect Captain Sheraton's safety and mission." The computer displayed a number of windows on the screen. The large mass had changed course and was moving faster in the direction of the shuttle, like the *Titanic* heading for the iceberg. By her calculation, Bennett did not have very long before the comet made impact with him, the array, and the shuttle. The array would right itself and continue to work as long as it was turned, but the shuttle and Bennett…

She swallowed the knot in her throat, but it wouldn't go down. She could barely breathe.

Pushing the button on her phone, she said, "Sally, get me Sully. Tell Bennett that Control needs to speak to him, or tell Sully that he needs to communicate a message to Bennett immediately."

Sally said, "Working."

Several seconds passed.

"Sally? What's happening?" Kimberly's voice was strained.

"Sully said Bennett's comm is off."

Her voice was frantic. "Try again. Tell Sully about the comet. Make Sully turn Bennett's comm on. Force it, if he has to. Please, Sally. Please. Have Sully help him."

Bennett used his jet pack to maneuver to the other side of the array. He was able to manually get the array halfway turned. Sweat trickled down his back, and he wished he could pause for a few seconds, but being vulnerable out here gave him a sense of urgency and a serious need for completion.

A burst of light out of the corner of his eye drew his attention. He looked briefly at the sun, his visor protecting him from the damaging rays. A panel of information scrolled across the left-hand side of his visor. There was an increase in solar-flare activity. According to his readings, they were in the X-class range—some of the sun's strongest flares. They often messed with the ionosphere, and Bennett knew before he even tried it that the radio would be knocked out.

It was captivating. At 10,000 degrees Fahrenheit,

this mainly-hydrogen ball, with a small percentage of helium added in, was fascinating. Over 90 million miles away from the Earth, Bennett couldn't resist taking a moment. For a brief second, he stole a glance at the sun. The bright orb had bursts of intensity that weren't even visible to his naked eyesight. Though his instruments recorded it, due in large part to the genius of the individuals who designed and constructed the shuttle panels, he was aware that being this close was a rare experience.

"Sully, are you there?"

"Yes, Captain. Command Control has been attempting to reach you. The comet's speed has increased," said Sully.

"Can you access Command Control?" asked Bennett.

"Working…" said Sully.

Bennett closed his eyes, and spots appeared before them. The sun was so much brighter than he had ever considered. As he turned away from it to get back to the task at hand, he saw something troubling. A small piece of debris hit the side of the shuttle, hard enough to dent it.

"Control, are you there? Control?" Bennett asked. No response. Right, he remembered—there was no radio because of the flares.

He was alone in space.

Looking around him, it was hard not to fathom both the beauty and danger of his present environment. "Sully, talk to me," he said.

"I am here, Captain. What can I do for you?" the voice of Sully echoed over his comm. "The Barstow Comet has changed direction. The heat of the sun has forced sublimation—changing solid to gas. Although the comet will not collide with the shuttle, the coma formed by the gases resulting from its sublimation will. As those massive flares of gas ignite and spew, they form the early stages of a cocoon-like cloud around the comet—or to be more specific, a coma. Please note the coma is heading toward you at over eight hundred meters per second. I project the first wave of gaseous force and debris will arrive in approximately eight minutes and forty-three, forty-two, forty-one seconds…"

The muscle in Bennett's jaw tightened. No one knew what kind of volatile environment the comet would create for the shuttle or, more to the point, his space suit. Bennett wasn't interested in sticking around to find out. He moved his arm, attempting to reposition his body. The movement was tedious and seemed to take forever.

"Sully, warn me at the five-minute mark. Until then, silence." Bennett gritted his teeth. Beads of sweat formed on his brow and poured down his face, neck, and back—which was quite a feat in space, given that one of the purposes of the suit was to monitor and maintain a steady body temperature.

Bennett pulled an automatic screwdriver from his belt, and it tumbled from his hand. Turning over and over, it traveled farther away from him, heading toward the sun. Frustration slid through his body, accompanied by an icy-cold sliver of fear.

"Easy, Sheraton. Slow and steady wins the race." He brought his breathing under control, putting his mind in single-task mode. Having planned for such a possibility, he took a second screwdriver from his belt. This one stayed in hand as he readjusted the angle of the hub.

Methodically, he moved the controls for the singular

array devices, shifting them into a steady and sedentary position directed away from the Earth, so no one could use the laser function on the residents of planet Earth. It assured that no one nation could take control of such a powerful weapon. Bennett was pleased with how well the tool worked. Melo would be pleased with his chips. His automatic screwdriver had a DNA coder that worked only on this device with Melo's blood, and it would stop functioning after the laser array was completely online. This was the big idea Melo had provided the engineers: chips with a DNA component. They'd used Melo's blood for the brain chip component and paired it to the related tools. It was a great way to honor the big guy. His brother had made it to space after all.

Additional safeguards had been placed in the software to protect life below from comets and meteors and whatever other alien threat might approach from space. Whether or not the array was big enough to handle such problems, at least it was a start. Finally, the Earth would have some kind of planetary defense system in place.

He activated the array again and watched it shift the orb hardware above his location. With the chips in place, it was like putting an analog system in space, but without actual cords. Without a digital hookup, it meant a serviceperson had to come up here and handle the array with tools that contained the DNA-indexed chip. So, several safeguards were in place.

He secured the screwdriver onto his belt. When he pushed off from the hub, he was tugged back into place: the tether had wrapped itself around the array. There wasn't time to turn everything off, move around it, and get the array back online. Doing the one thing an astronaut never wants to do in space, Bennett unclipped the tether. He guided the line around the edge of the device and dove off the side, pushing with his feet to provide momentum. It was impossible to grasp the line with his massive gloves, so he wound his arm around as much of it as he could.

"Warning. Incoming," said Sully.

A wave of gas blasted Bennett toward the Earth, moving him farther and farther away from the safety of the shuttle. The tether bit into the space suit. Luckily, it didn't rip a hole that would suck away his precious oxygen. Bennett dangled in the heavy, gaseous winds for what seemed like ages. They pulled at him and the precarious tether. *This is what a fish feels like*, he imagined. *Dangling helplessly, waiting to be reeled in or freed*.

"Five minutes, Captain," said Sully.

Finally, the force eased, and Bennett could pull his way back to the shuttle door. When he reached it, tiny specks of dust batted at him and against the shuttle as he attempted to open the key-code panel to open the air lock. The comet dust, finer than sand, covered his mask quickly. He swiped at his helmet visor to clear the debris, leaving an oddly shaped print on his visor.

That can't be good, he thought.

Glancing over his shoulder, he could see larger chunks coming toward him. Even something as big as a pea could penetrate the suit, and these sharp-edged suckers could cut right through his tether and send him spinning into orbit.

A vision of Kimberly flashed through his mind, of her looking up at the night sky, weeping as she thought of him orbiting the Earth forever, just another piece of space trash. *Not now*, Bennett thought. *Not ever!*

Clearing his brain, he forced his body to obey him and to do the task. Prying open the entry panel, he revealed the keypad. He punched in the code, and the door opened. He pulled himself quickly inside and unwound the tether. Securing a second safety line to the inside wall as the door closed behind him, he shouted an order. "Sully, avoid the comet crap and get us out of here! Rotate the shuttle one hundred and eighty degrees until we're clear of the cloud and then down to orbit at two hundred miles above the Earth."

"Acknowledged, Captain." The shuttle moved on a trajectory perpendicular to the comet, toward an orbit closer to the Earth.

For several seconds, Bennett lay on the floor of the bay, grateful to be inside. His muscles ached from holding so tightly to the tether. Then he punched the button to restore air and gravity to the airlock. He pulled off his suit and secured it in the locker of the bay. With the pressure now equalized to that in the rest of the shuttle, he let himself into the main cargo area and worked his way forward to the pilot controls.

He dropped his sweat-soaked T-shirt on his seat and noticed his feet were cold against the shuttle floor. Bothering with socks, shoes, or additional clothing would have taken valuable time. Besides, if he died, who cared how he dressed? If he made it home, at least he was wearing long johns.

"Good to have you on board again, Captain," said Sully.

"Any word from Command Control?" asked Bennett. Rubbing his hands over his face and scrubbing his fingers over his scalp, he checked the progress of the comet's debris. They still had at least five more minutes before the full thrust of it caught up to them. Moving away from its path had bought them some time.

"N-n-negative." Sully stuttered in an oddly high-pitched voice.

Bennett frowned. That wasn't normal! "Show me where we are in terms of orbit, and map it against our entry point." He watched the screen spring to life. Across the starlit windshield, he could see where they were and how far they needed to travel to make their window back to the ground. Checking the gauges, he noticed the batteries were low. He tapped his finger on the screen, but nothing changed.

"Sully, why are we losing power? Debris. The computers…the structural integrity of one of them has been compromised, hasn't it?" Bennett's eyes darted to the rest of the displays. This was the only one compromised. His mind leaped into action, doing the calculations. "Are you there, Sully?"

"…an entire bank of computers powering down. Duty to preserve your existence, C-C-Captain. All power going to life support." Sully's voice was a low thrum.

"Wait, we have plenty of fuel. I think—yeah, I have an idea." Bennett unstrapped himself and crawled under the right-side control panel. Without the hardware payload on board blocking the copilot's seat, there was tons of room to move around on the shuttle.

Retrieving the pliers and extra wire from the tool kit, he opened the electronics of the fuel panel and split the wire. He rigged a little something extra into the electronics panel, and then brought Sully and the rest of the systems back online. He closed the panel and secured the tool before strapping himself back into the pilot's seat.

"Captain, you will need this f-f-fuel. I disagree with your decision."

"Nonsense," said Bennett, aware of how desperately he needed a functioning electronic system to reach his goal. "We're not orbiting the Earth like I originally planned. We're going down right here." Taking the controls in hand, he guided the shuttle in a manual arc, reaching the exact point at which he wanted to enter Earth's atmosphere.

"This is dangerous," Sully said. "Your speeds will exceed the recommended maximums for this vehicle. The issues you might face upon breaching the atmosphere are structural integrity, heat issues including fire, and—"

"Discontinue discussion, Sully." Bennett knew what he was doing. At least he hoped he did. Entering the atmosphere now was a risk, especially with a comet on his heels, but he couldn't chance orbiting and losing power completely. At least this way, he'd have use of the entire system for his descent. Besides, flying by the seat of his pants had always been a rush. This promised to be the flight of a lifetime, and he'd be damned if he didn't take the time to enjoy it.

Flipping a switch, he burned off the last of his fuel. He didn't use it to propel himself; rather, he slowed the shuttle until there was almost nothing left. Turning the shuttle, he spent the last of his precious resources as he entered the atmosphere.

"Verbal account, Sully," Bennett ordered.

"Descent within normal safety parameters. Targeting splashdown off the coast of San Diego."

He knew Kimberly would be watching. His splashdown was originally set for Florida, but at least a thousand eyes were on him, and they'd be able to handle San Diego. Hell, they could send his Teammates out there. Frogmen had been first responders to the original U.S. astronauts for many of their space missions. Those space flyers, the ones from Shepard's day, were used to working with the Navy as their capsules splashed down in water. They could easily do it again. Of course, his shuttle was designed for a runway landing. Would the North Island one be long enough? God, he hoped so!

He grinned. Now that would be an awesome duty station: opening a shuttle door and helping an astronaut out. Maybe he'd talk to Ouster about it when he landed. His hands tightened on the shuttle yoke as he fought to maintain control.

"I'm coming home, baby!" he shouted. "Believe in me."

—~~~—

Kimberly freaked out in the Command Control Center of the Lester Facility. She'd tried to be calm and aloof as she listened to Bennett's progress. All through the preflight check, the launch, and the journey to geosynchronous orbit, she'd remained steady. While Bennett unloaded the array, blew up debris, and sat at the hub, she hadn't uttered a single word. No one stared at her white-knuckled fists or saw the stiffness of her body, which would have given away the fact that she was vibrating with emotion.

The comet had changed everything for her. She'd

been unable to speak, to point out the danger. She'd merely touched Henry's shoulder as he monitored the overall mission time, and he'd been the one to shout out the news. When she'd finally found her voice, she knew her body was in trouble. Her heart beat arrhythmically, and her breath came in tiny pants.

"Anything?" she whispered for the third time.

"Negative," said Sally. The computer's voice was comforting, even if the answer was not.

Kimberly didn't want to pull focus away from the personnel monitoring Bennett and the shuttle systems, but the minute they'd seen the comet turn, and the communication between the ground and space ceased completely, her heart had practically thudded through her chest. It felt as if she were having a heart attack.

Her left hand settled over her heart. It didn't ease the pain.

Crap! Was she having a heart attack? A strange flutter moved up her spine and settled in her jaw. Having one hand over her heart comforted her slightly as she pulled out a pill case with her right hand. Thank God she'd remembered to stuff it into her lab-coat pocket. Picking up a small pill, she placed the nitroglycerin under her tongue.

Liaison Jarvis noticed Kimberly's state and rushed over. "Are you okay? Should I call the medics?"

"No. No. Watch the shuttle. Take care of Bennett— Captain Sheraton. Promise me." Kimberly was adamant.

"Yes, of course." Jarvis moved off reluctantly, though her eyes strayed to Kimberly.

The pain eased as Kimberly eyed an empty computer console farther from anyone's watchful stares and moved slowly to it. It was a relief to sit down. "Sally," she murmured, "monitor my vitals, please."

"Your blood pressure and heart rate have increased drastically. It could be angina or a heart attack. Your vitals are returning to normal, but I can have Dr. Timmox come up to the control room." Sally's voice was imploring, urging her to talk to the doctor.

"Thank you, Sally. Not right now. But if you sense a change, please contact me privately via text. You don't need to acknowledge that order. I know you're listening to me." She tapped the toe of her right foot against the floor. "Sally, is there any way... Can you talk to Sully?"

"I'm receiving a garbled response. I will try again."

"No, Sally. Wait. Before you do, where was the shuttle when you received the response? Can you trace it using that last connection?" If this worked, it would be a miracle. But that was oftentimes the answer to puzzling questions: breaking down, analyzing, and understanding the mystery.

Kimberly looked over her shoulder. The Command team busily reviewed their computer screens, all of them ignoring her. The new project director, Fraz Gorsk, appointed by the Joint Chiefs, came into the room. Of course, they'd completely bypassed her in appointing him. Coming in at the last minute, just as the comet was spotted and so far after Bennett launched, was insane, and she had to deal with the fact that she once again had no control of the situation.

Hell, those loyal to Kess who didn't believe he'd been a treacherous jerk ran to Gorsk, ready to fulfill his every order. Kimberly was so horrified she could barely speak, and now here she was, trying to solve problems in space from down on the ground. The stress was unbearable.

Standing there among her peers with a bright red face and the inability to spit out her message frustrated her to no end. Right now, she didn't give a damn about them. Bennett filled her mind practically to bursting, and she had to protect him.

"Calculating, Kimberly," Sally said.

Kimberly's nostrils flared. The smell of panic made the room ripe. She couldn't wait to get out of here.

"Eureka," said Sally.

Kimberly hid her grin behind her hand. Could it really be this easy? Sally always came through when shit hit the fan. *C'mon, Sally. You can help.*

"Done. The results are on the screen in front of you and your phone. I've pinpointed the two most probable locations," Sally replied, a lilt to her voice as if she were happy.

Kimberly knew it! The screen that had sprung to life in front of her was full of information. She could see a tiny dot, representing the shuttle, and two projected entry points were highlighted. Agreeing with the information she read, she almost wanted to bounce in her seat.

Sally spoke succinctly. "I cannot reach Sully. I've concluded they are currently in the atmosphere. Should I share these details with the group?"

"No. Delete info, Sally."

The screen went blank.

Just then, a hand landed on her shoulder. Looking up, she saw it was Roberts, the liaison with Stratcom—the Joint Space Operations Center, which tracks all space events. He was a fairly decent molecular biologist.

"They can't find him," Roberts said. "If you think he's on his way down…share now."

Counting to ten, she blew out her breath and stood. Clapping her hands together loudly, she shouted, "Can I have your attention, everyone? I believe Captain Sheraton is planning to either touchdown or splashdown near San Diego, specifically, close to Coronado, California."

Rogers shook his head. "That's not protocol. He'd follow his set plan."

"No, he wouldn't. Sally cannot communicate clearly with Sully. They are designed to link up perfectly, regardless of proximity. Given the comet and a multitude of possibilities that we may not even consider, Captain Sheraton is most likely coming in hot." Kimberly's voice was strong and definitive.

"I'll have to discuss this with department heads, and then we'll decide."

Kimberly shook her head. "You don't have that kind of time." If she waited for them to decide, she feared the worst would happen—that Bennett would need to land in the ocean and be trapped without help.

As the scientists gathered in the center of Command to discuss it, she said softly, "Sally, call Jonah Melo's wife on her cell phone."

"Dialing."

Kimberly turned away from the men. The call connected. "Alisha, this is Kimberly Warren. I don't have a lot of time, but I need your help."

"Of course! Wait, I'm putting you on speaker." The sound on the other end of Alisha's phone amplified. "You have us both now."

"Melo, there's a problem. There's a comet, and I

think the ice chunks from it damaged the communication system. Bennett is in the atmosphere now. There's no way the shuttle can make it to its prearranged landing point. Do you know where he'd go?"

"The west coast, from the Silver Strand Training Complex to the Amphibious Base to NAS—that's Naval Air Station North Island, off Coronado, California—or somewhere in that vicinity," Melo said. "We know that water like the back of our hands."

"I think so too," she whispered. "I can't get them to listen to me here. Can you do something to help him?"

Melo was silent for a moment. "Yes. I'm actually on base, visiting SEAL Team ONE. I'll put a plan into action. Can you get a helicopter here?"

She smiled. "Why take a helo when I fly CarP? Can you let the tower know I'm coming?"

He laughed. "Yes, I'll let Command know that you'll be landing at NAS or somewhere around there." The phone went dead.

Silently, she slipped out of the room, closing the door behind her. The men could bicker all night long. There were people from Melo and Sheraton's SEAL community willing to help, and she could get to the man she loved. The weight of how deeply she loved him settled on her shoulders, and she stumbled.

Steadying herself against the wall, she took several breaths to regain her equilibrium. "Sally, I need you to keep tracking Captain Sheraton and show his progress on my phone. This data will travel with me outside of the Lester Facility."

"This is forbidden. It is against standard protocols, Kimberly. *Your* protocols."

"I know, Sally, but they are *my* rules, and I command this action with master key 60LKH4327J. Confirm." Kimberly made her way down the main hallway, turning at the far hallway for the flight hangar. She had a date with CarP.

"Acknowledged. The requested information is on your phone, Kimberly. Fly safely. I will be monitoring you." The computer's voice was soothing, something she herself had programmed in. It was oddly comforting right now.

"Thank you, Sally," said Kimberly. If she didn't know better, she'd wonder if the computer was worried about her. Of course, that was a question of sentience. Computers being aware…well, that was best suited for another discussion at a different, less life-threatening moment.

—∞—

Inside the Warren Shuttle, the temperature was increasing. There was no way to lower the heat, and Bennett was burning up. Sweat dripped into his eyes, and he blinked rapidly to clear them.

Wires hung out of the lower console, and stuff slid around the floor. No matter how much one attempted to secure items, coming through the atmosphere had to be like giving birth…messy.

Remaining alive was the primary objective. Bennett gritted his teeth. The pressure in the cabin had already popped one eardrum, and that was his "good" ear—the one that hadn't been somewhat affected by the constant drone of gunfire over the years.

Warm fluid trickled from his ear down his neck and

onto his shoulder. Most likely it was blood. He couldn't let go of the yoke to wipe it away. It didn't matter. There was nothing to be done about it anyhow. Either it would heal, or it wouldn't.

The priority was getting the shuttle safely on the ground and surviving the journey.

The windshield finally cleared of dust as the shuttle hurtled toward the Earth. He needed to slow down before he reached a critical-mass point where the structural integrity gave away. His mind flashed on Kimberly, and he remembered a few fascinating design features that she'd added, despite her peers' objections.

"Sully, are you still there?" Bennett asked.

"Affirmative."

"Calculate the sequence that will slow us the most using the air-brake flaps, and then use it. Most likely those flaps will snap off, but it's possible it will help us slow down." Bennett's arm muscles shook as he fought the force of the juddering yoke to hold it steady.

Sully counted down. "I've calculated that releasing them in bursts of two flaps will be most effective."

"Understood. Implement." Bennett's heart raced, and his pulse thudded hard.

"Set One. Set Two. Set Three. Set Four," Sully said.

As the flaps lifted, the shuttle did indeed slow its speed. Several of the metal panels ripped off, but it gave Bennett enough wiggle room to ease off the yoke and direct the shuttle into a more gentle descent. Relief flooded him as this took the pressure off.

Mountains came into view as the shuttle hit waves of turbulence.

Sully said, "Extreme turbulence increasing."

"Expand and elongate the wings," commanded Bennett. When Sully didn't answer, he flipped a switch to lower the air brakes. He pulled a lever next to his seat that manually set the wing-extension mechanisms into action. They snapped into place exactly as they were designed to do. The giant wings caught a thermal, and it lifted the shuttle high above the turbulence before releasing it back to the wind. They hit several more pockets of thermal air before reaching San Diego. By this point, all of the systems were off-line. He glided over Coronado. It was an eerie and oddly exciting feeling. Without enough power to stop the shuttle, it would crash into whatever was on the runway and probably keep going.

SEALS trained off these waters, diving and prepping, and there would be a BUD/S class seeing him crash-land. That would get someone's attention. Bringing his focus back to his flying—or gliding, rather—he caught a great wind and soared upward.

A thought flashed through Bennett's mind. He knew why Kimberly had named the onboard computer Sully. She did it in honor of one of her favorite Air Force pilots, an honest-to-goodness hero: Chesley "Sully" Sullenberger III. He laughed aloud, releasing some of the tension that had built up inside of him. Man, why had that revelation taken so long? Looking forward to teasing her about it gave him another reason to come back to Earth safely.

Circling over the Amphibious Base, he thought of his life as a Navy SEAL. It had been the best experience of his life, unquantifiable and indefinable. His eyes widened as he spotted Kimberly's contraption, the CarP, and intense pleasure surged through his body. "That's my girl! I knew you'd come through."

Melo waved one arm as he leaned on a crutch with the other. He was right there beside her. "Good on you, Melo, a decent swim buddy to the end," Bennett said.

Just as he'd expected, on the shore were several Basic Underwater Demolition/SEAL classes with their helmets stacked on the sand behind them, as well as half of the SEALs on the base. They'd all come out on the beach to help. They launched RIBs, or Reinforced Inflatable Boats, into the water and crawled on board. One SEAL directed the action in each boat, most likely an instructor, and several SWCC—Special Warfare Combatant-Craft Crewmember—boats, which were larger crafts, already waited for a cue to join in the rescue.

"Here goes," Bennett said. Using the manual lever, he lowered the flaps and did his utmost to land the shuttle on the water. Unfortunately, the vehicle sank like the two tons of metal it was, and he unclipped his harness and rushed to the escape hatch.

Pressure from the water above prevented the hatch from releasing. Bennett made his way back to his seat. Underneath was a bottle of oxygen and a mask. This was why it was always important to read the instruction manual. If he hadn't known all the specs of this bucket of bolts, he might have begun to panic. The oxygen, along with his training, made him fairly calm. They knew where he was and what would happen when the shuttle sank.

The only personal items he had brought on this mission were the two knives strapped to his legs and the Ka-Bar knife. Ka-Bars were from the time of the Frogman, but SEALs still used them today. Pulling it from the small compartment on the other side of his chair, he withdrew duct tape and stuck the stuff around the mask, creating a solid seal.

The oxygen was cool and relaxing as it pumped slowly into his lungs with each breath. Bennett realized his mistake almost instantly: there was no way to vent the carbon dioxide.

But seeing his Teammates appear on the other side of the shuttle's glass made him grin. He'd be out of the shuttle momentarily. They motioned to him and he got the gist of what they were going to do.

Holding on to a safety bar, he watched them break the glass with several gunshots. Water gushed inside, filling the shuttle quickly and completely. Bennett allowed a few seconds for the water pressure to stabilize before he swam out to them. When he scraped his leg along the glass, he felt the sting and welcomed it. He was alive, and pretty soon he was going to have Kimberly in his arms.

Nothing prepared him for his body's reaction as he left the shuttle. Spasms rocked his torso, and if the mask hadn't been taped on, he'd have lost it. Hands grabbed him and directed him slowly to the surface.

Bennett knew he needed a hyperbaric chamber. Its purpose was to over-oxygenate the blood and reduce the build-up of gas bubbles in arteries and veins, allowing deprived tissue to heal. He knew the Amphibious Base had one. More than a few diving accidents had happened over the years, and having a portable chamber to treat decompression sickness, or the bends, as quickly as possible had saved many lives.

An invisible weight crushed the air from his chest. He couldn't see what was making it happen, but he knew that it was gravity, the change in pressure brought on by his time in space, and the swift descent to Earth. All of it had screwed with his body's equilibrium. Pain racked his body as waves of dizziness overtook him.

Someone ripped the tape away from the mask and his body. He took tiny breaths, and each one hurt worse than the previous one. But the smell of the salty, sweet air was nirvana to his psyche. The Pacific Ocean, the sand, and something else—rather, someone else—made his nostrils flare. It was her.

He opened his eyes to see Kimberly looking down at him. Her worried expression made him smile. Nothing came out when he tried to speak. He wanted to reassure her, let her know he would be okay. She kissed his lips. It was brief peck, yet oh, so tender.

His throat closed as he coughed and choked. This was a crappy way to die: survive a peril-filled mission and the harrowing descent back to Earth, only to croak on the beach where he'd started his whole Navy SEAL journey.

Hands lifted him, moving him at a swift run toward… something. A cloudless blue sky sped by above him as the sun warmed his skin. His eyes blinked like a slow motion camera until they were too heavy to keep open, and then all sensory information ceased. The world faded to black.

Chapter 14

THE SOUND OF AN AIR COMPRESSOR WOKE BENNETT. IT was loud as air hissed around him. Damn, was he back in the Lester Facility? That place needed a heater—and a splash of paint color.

He tried to speak and nothing came out. His body hurt, and he could taste salt water on his lips. *Think. What happened last?* Images filled his mind: the shuttle flying through the air, the ocean, and his brethren outside the window as they swam in the water surrounding the shuttle. Had he crashed it? Was he alive or was he in hell?

Prying his eyes open was no small feat, as they were caked with gunk. Through the glass he saw a man in a lab coat and Kimberly. He was encased in some kind of tube. Hell, it felt like a coffin, and he resisted the urge to struggle. This was the reason SEALs were put in uncontrollable situations like waterboarding: so they could think clearly when the shit hit the fan.

Bennett calmed his nerves. He focused his gaze upward. By the way Kimberly gestured, he could tell that she was angry. As her hands settled on her hips and the doctor stopped talking, they appeared to be at a stalemate.

Kimberly, his lady, was a fighter. Her jaw stretched wide as she yelled. He wanted to remind her to watch her blood pressure, to remember her heart. Protecting it—and her—was a priority.

Rubbing at his face, Bennett remembered more aspects of the landing. He took a tentative breath and was relieved to realize that it didn't hurt as much as he thought it would. He performed a swift physical inventory, and he decided that with the exception of the giant gash on his leg, he was in relatively good shape. He tapped on the glass in an attempt to gain their attention.

Two pairs of eyes that had been staring daggers at each other turned toward him. Kimberly's hand lay flat on the glass. She smiled at him. Worry was still etched on her features, but there was relief there too.

Placing his hand below hers, he smiled up into those beautiful eyes. The love he saw there made his heart skip a beat. He knew that she was one of the individuals responsible for making sure that a crew was there to meet the shuttle. What an incredible lady! She was a fighter that wouldn't let him down.

Despite the past, he made a promise to himself…that not only would he cherish her and enjoy making love to her for the rest of his life, but he would ask her to be his wife. That was the only kind of forever that would make her into his life partner, his swim buddy, and an integral part of his world.

Her mouth moved, but he couldn't hear what she was saying. A speaker squawked, and he flinched. Kimberly was back to yelling at the doctor.

"Hello?" The doctor moved into view. "I'm Dr. Naisse. How are you feeling?"

"Better." His throat was raw. "Water?"

"Next to you." Pointing to Bennett's left side, Dr. Naisse urged him to drink. "In addition to your current need for the chamber, you have four crushed disks in your neck and back."

Bennett grabbed the water and had swallowed two bottles before the doctor warned him to slow down. His body momentarily considered heaving the liquid back up, but his need for hydration was too great, and happily, it stayed down. "Uh-huh."

When he tried to move his body to the side, his whole being hurt. Perhaps his body was more damaged than he realized. He had hit the ocean like a ton of bricks.

"As you can probably guess, you have whiplash too. Don't try to move too much for the next few hours. When you're in a larger environment, we'll get a physical therapist to put you through your paces," Dr. Naisse said. "Most of the bruises on your body are from the safety straps. Three of your ribs are bruised on each side, along the axis of the straps. You might end up with a giant *X* over your chest, like a superhero, for a while." The doctor smiled. "That was a joke. I guess you're not in the mood to laugh."

"Not really," stated Bennett flatly.

"Well, Captain, let's get down to additional immediate matters," Dr. Naisse continued. "*Your* Dr. Warren would like to have you moved to the Lester Facility. Because you're an operational sailor in the Navy, I've explained to her several times that this is impossible." With a pointed look at Kimberly, the doctor continued. "You will be moved to a facility of our choosing. In the meantime, I would appreciate you having a discussion with"—the doctor coughed—"*her* about the necessity of following these steps. The Navy has rules we must all abide by."

Kimberly took the doctor's place. She checked over

her shoulder and then gave Bennett her full attention. "I spoke with Ouster," she said. "He's speaking with SECNAV for me."

Bennett coughed. "Oh, man! I'm sure that's going over well."

Kimberly frowned. "Listen, you, I want you where I can see you and help you. I'm not letting you out of my sight for a very long time."

"I get it." He smiled up at her. "I feel the same way about you. But SECNAV doesn't handle this kind of stuff. Proper channels, and all that."

She leaned over the glass, her face very close. "You just risked your life to blast away tons of space debris orbiting the Earth, cleaning up mistakes that mankind needed to erase before it became a junkyard too cluttered to allow us to reach the stars. Then you risked it all to move a laser array into position to protect the Earth from incoming threats, all while a giant comet pelted you with God knows what! SECNAV can take five minutes out of his precious damned schedule to see to your well-being."

A chuckle escaped Bennett's lips. "When you put it like that—"

The tension in her face relaxed. "I do." She looked away for the space of several heartbeats, and when she looked back, her eyes were filled with tears. "I…I never gave up hope."

"I didn't either."

As tears fell on the glass, he touched his finger to each fat, wet drop, wishing he could touch it, to hold her and comfort her. His eyes sought hers. "I love you, Kimberly."

He didn't like the dark circles under her eyes or the

tension around her mouth. "You need to rest, my love," he said.

"I know. It's just, I love you too. I wouldn't let them give up on you." She sniffed and mopped her face. She kissed the glass and then wiped away the mark. "Enough of that. Who wants to see a weeping woman when they wake up?" She smiled weakly at him, forcing her face to morph into a brightness she didn't feel.

Bennett attempted to comfort her. "Soon I'll have you in my arms."

She merely nodded. Her fingers pulled at the edges of the semi-wet tissue. "Until then, I've made all the arrangements," she said. "When SECNAV signs off on your transfer, we'll go to the Lester Facility, and you'll enter our hyperbaric chamber. It's fully equipped to handle your decompression, and the best part is that we have a glass chamber next to it for husbands or wives, so they can keep their loved ones company. That was my idea, though I never realized I would be the first person to use it."

"Looking forward to it," Bennett said. He listened to her ramble on. It was the sweetest sound he could remember. His eyelids were heavy, and he drifted to sleep with her almost close enough to touch, the sound and vibration of her voice already working its magic deep inside his heart and soul.

His lady could move mountains. Kimberly was some kind of miracle worker, to have kept her promise as she had. Within two hours of Bennett waking up, SECNAV had signed off on the transfer and the portable chamber was loaded onto a truck with several armed guards, a medical team from the Lester Facility, and her.

At first, the place had really worked for him. But six days trapped in the Lester Facility's hyperbaric chamber frayed his remaining nerves. Pacing was not an easy task. In the main room were a table and chair and several monitoring devices. He spent most of his time on the treadmill or the stationary bike, and he made use of the full set of weights.

True, it was better than the cramped, portable version, the one Amphibious Base had, but being trapped was like caging the human spirit and expecting it to thrive. He spent two hours in the morning and two hours in the evening running, just to pass the time. His bones ached now and then. According to the osteopath, he hadn't been up there long enough to lose bone density, but, he still felt weird, as if his body were still adjusting to normal gravity. Her prescription was to walk five miles a day and keep increasing it.

Running was his preference. With his eyes closed, he pictured his feet sinking into the sand as he ran down the beach from the Amphibious Base to the edge of Naval Air Station North Island. As he passed the Hotel Del Coronado, he saw workers cleaning the chairs and straightening up from the night before. At 0400, the beaches were mostly deserted, and he enjoyed the sparsity of humanity and the peacefulness.

He splashed into the foamy tide on his way home, the spray bouncing up, hitting his body and dotting his shorts and shirt with salt water. As he looked across the waves, he saw dolphins surfing and birds screeching as they flew in circles above them. The birds waited for the dolphins to halt their nonsensical playtime antics and then got to work, driving the fish to the surface of the water.

A noise alerted Bennett, and his eyelids fluttered.

"Your heart rate and blood pressure are optimal, Captain Sheraton," said Nurse Francesca Bixby over the intercom. Her husband was a nurse too, and he recorded the readings into a chart. The chemistry between the married couple was obvious, and Bennett envied their stolen caresses and kisses.

Right! Reality. He nodded his head. "Thank you."

Hearing a voice piping into the middle of his mental mechanisms kind of ruined the fantasy, but hell, there was a staff of twenty watching him during the day and a staff of ten at night. Seemed like overkill to him, but Kimberly said it was a necessary precaution.

If he'd had to put his finger on the three things he hated most about being in the chamber, in order of importance, it would be being unable to hold Kimberly, loss of freedom to run outside, and smells. Other than his own scent, there was no smell to this place. Barren of anything, it made him crave foods that had odors. Not that the doctors would allow anything but very bland, digestible meals.

Of course, being in the Lester Facility with Kimberly was significantly better than hanging out in the other hyperbaric option, a tiny one-window chamber at Balboa Naval Hospital. He'd visited Teammates there who had gotten the bends while on deep dives. It wasn't a pretty place. No soft bed, workout equipment, or luxuries of any kind. The bathroom consisted of a corner unit that was open to the entire room. The Lester Facility, on the other hand, was incredible. He shouldn't complain, or even get frustrated. He was a very blessed soul!

His lady dictated most of his care, and she made sure
that his meals were loaded with his favorite items. She
even slipped him several research projects to keep his
mind engaged. In the evenings, when the main medical
group left for the night, the on-site evening staff were
present. They were mindful of his privacy and allowed
night mode—darkened windows, intercoms and monitoring cameras off, and physical monitors disengaged—so
he and Kimberly could "talk." With a thin piece of glass
between them, it forced their intimacy to be…creative.

Stretching out on the bed, he tucked his hands behind
his neck and waited for her to arrive. From this angle,
he could see the other glassed-in room. It mirrored his
own space, except hers had a door that she could leave
through at any time.

"Sally, can you give me the highlights of the day?"
Bennett waited. When she didn't respond immediately,
he called out for her again. "Sally?"

"Sorry for the delay, Bennett. Kimberly wishes to tell
you the main news of the day. She will arrive in 4.329
minutes." The computer clicked off.

He counted to himself until he saw movement out of
the corner of his eye. There she was! His lady.

She bounded onto the bed. Pressing her face against
the glass, she kissed it, and then wiped off her lip print.
She pushed the intercom button to On and lay down next
to him.

"What's cooking?" he asked. Her face was lit with
joy. Her eyes sparked with mischief, and he knew she
was up to something. "Give it up…"

Tucking her hair behind her ears, she said, "I found
a new planet. My mother had spotted something she

thought was a new planet over twenty-five years ago, but after a few weeks it disappeared. The other day, I had this hunch, so I checked the coordinates she used, and there it was. My calculations show that the planet reveals itself every twenty-five-point-seven years. Since it's orbiting something up there, I hypothesized that it's moving around something big."

He sat up, leaning against the glass that separated them. "Congratulations! That's astounding."

"I know, right?" She took a deep breath and on the exhale, spoke very quickly. "Well, as you know, I have the privilege of naming it, so I chose Sheraton Warren, for you and for my mom. I'm in there too, if they need the name of the person who identified it. I just…needed the two people who have changed my life to go down in astronomy history with me."

His fingertips brushed the glass along the place where her cheek touched. "I'm honored, my love."

Her smile was warm, inviting. "I'm glad you like my surprise. And I have another for you too." Standing up on the bed, she slowly unbuttoned her lab coat to reveal a cherry-red negligee made of lace.

Blood rushed from his head to places lower on his body as he grinned at her. "I hope you're keeping all of these beautiful nighties, because I want a rematch with them. I'm going to remove several of them with my teeth. This one is special. I'm taking it off you with my tongue."

She laughed. "How on earth are you going to do that?"

"I'm creative." He winked at her, and then he stood and removed his running shorts. He turned on the radio, and a light jazz song filled the room. His delight

brimmed as he watched her dance to music, performing for him—making him laugh and ache with desire.
Then she lay on the bed as close to him as she could
get. Her fingertips traced the outline of the nightie over
her body before she wet two fingers. She rubbed them
over her lips, down her neck, between her breasts, and
over her nipples.

His cock was ramrod straight, and he cupped it in the
palm of his hand.

The sexiness of her teasing her nipples with the edge
of her pink, polished, and glittery fingernails made his
hips involuntarily thrust in the air. She knew exactly
how to push his seduction buttons, and this show was
tailor-made to bring satisfaction.

"If only I could touch you..." His voice trailed off.
Need beat at his psyche. It had been too long since he
held her, stroked her, made her utter those sweet sexy
noises, and smelled the glory of her skin and hair.
Thinking of it made his mind conjure up the combined
scents of lavender and jasmine.

"Uh-huh. I know. Me too," she replied in a breathy
voice. Her eyes were locked to his, her eyelashes sweeping down in lazy arcs now and then as her fingers found a
sweet spot. Continuing her seduction, she slowly lowered
one shoulder strap and then the other one. Her nipples
shone through the lace, the rosy tips thrusting firmly
between the patterns of the flower design of the lingerie.

He groaned.

When she finally pulled the nightie down over her
breasts, Bennett wondered how long it would take to
put his chair through the glass partition. If it had been
normal glass, that would have been one thing, but as a

wall in the chamber, there were many other elements and design structures involved to create a pressure seal.

"Uh-uh-uh. Easy, SEAL. I'm yours, now and forever." She pushed the red lace past her waist and over her hips. She dropped it on the end of the bed, and the fabric seemed empty and uninteresting. The woman definitely made the garment breathtaking.

"Eyes here," she said, directing his gaze back to her own. Opening her mouth, she placed two fingers inside and laved them with her tongue until they glistened with wetness. Then she trailed a line down her stomach, over muscles that twitched with delight at the attention, until she reached the heavenly patch he wanted to settle his head against.

His voice was husky with desire as he watched her rub her fingers against the tiny nub. "With my lips and tongue, I'd part those lush lips and tease my way to your clit," he said.

Her hips lifted, responding to him, and gave him a glorious view of her most sacred place. Her fingers toyed with the plump flesh of her thighs and labia until his breathing became ragged.

"Gorgeous," he sighed.

"So handsome," she returned. "My sexy astronaut who's traveled to places high in the heavens."

"I know what heaven means with you in my life, Kimberly."

A smile lit up her eyes, and her face was such a thing of beauty, she had to knock on the glass to get his attention. "Bennett. Watch me..." Her fingers moved between her thighs, sinking into her sheath. Her throat constricted, issuing a series of moans. In and out her fingers moved until her body shook with the need for release.

His hand kept time with her with a rapid up-and-down motion as he rubbed his shaft. He wanted to bring himself at the same time she came. "Yes, my love, that's it. Now, come with me. Come for me. Show me how you can glisten and shine."

"Bennett!" she cried out as her body shook with a climax, spasms making her body shake with the enormous release.

"Kimberly," he sighed as his body drove over the edge, all due to her boldness, beauty, and bravery. It was a rare woman that could come while someone else stood mere feet away. Granted, they had privacy with the darkened chamber windows, and the intercoms and monitors were off, but still… They knew. And his Kimberly didn't give a flip about it.

Side by side, they lay naked. His hand was on the glass, and hers was on the same spot on the other side. Her hand looked small against his. Picturing it wrapped around his cock made him partially hard again. He dropped his hand. Rolling onto his side, he looked her up and down. "How did I land such a stunning lady?" he asked.

"Brains and brawn, Bennett: two attributes that are often-times lacking in this world." She shifted her position until she was lying on her stomach, her knees bent and her feet kicking at the air. "I have more good news. I spoke with Dr. Timmox, and as you know, they've been adjusting the pressure. You've been at a normal setting for two days now without any ill effects. Tomorrow, you're being released."

"Thank God!" he shouted. He whooped with delight. "Hooyah!"

She pointed her index finger at him and then tapped

the glass with her fingernails to get his attention. "Bennett. Don't get any silly ideas. You are still required to stay within the Lester Facility through the rest of the week, and you have to wear a monitoring harness for two more days. After that, you can go anywhere you want—within reason, of course."

He touched his ear. "Did they mention anything about my eardrum?" It had burst while he descended to Earth in the space shuttle. The rapid speed had really done a number on him, not that he'd had any choice in the matter. At the time, it was a life-or-death decision. Given that he was back on Earth safely—and had recovered enough to fool around with his lady—it had been the optimal choice. Sacrificing his hearing was probably a small price to pay. His other eardrum had been damaged by routine gunfire, but hey, there were amazing hearing devices and innovative surgeries out there. He'd meet this challenge the same way he did all the others: one step at a time.

Kimberly leaned her whole body against the glass. His fingers traced the outline of her body. The cool glass barrier did little to ease his desire. He wanted to feel her skin against his and drink from those gorgeous red lips until he was drunk on her kisses.

"Soon," he sighed. "Holding you cannot come soon enough."

—◆◆◆—

The day of release did more for his sanity than anything else.

Kimberly stood on the other side of the door, and she rushed into his arms and held him tight before he was even out of the chamber. He didn't mind it one bit. He enfolded her and relished the scent of her hair and the softness of her skin.

"Captain Sheraton, we will need to take your vitals before you go back to your quarters, and you'll need to wear this monitor so we can keep an eye on your heart rate," said a voice from behind them.

Slowly, Bennett loosened his embrace and faced the voice. He looked the eager doctors up and down, and said, "No offense, but I don't want anyone monitoring me for the next seventy hours except her." With that, he took Kimberly's hand, and they walked out of the room and down one of the long facility hallways. As they came to a fork, he said, "I don't know where I'm going…"

"We're underground, that's why. Follow me." She tugged him toward the left side of the hallway, and then they hitched a ride on a small tram that dropped them at Kimberly's door. She swiped her badge over the sensor and pulled him in behind her. "My quarters are more comfortable."

The door closed, and they were finally, truly alone—not just being ignored or given privacy by the medical staff. This room was completely unmonitored, except for… "Sally, can you log off or turn off?" asked Bennett.

"Yes, Captain. Good day." The computer logged off.

A weight lifted from him, even as his body thrummed with exhaustion. "How could a walk and a ride tire me out?"

"Gravity." She pulled her sweater over her head and took off her pink lace bra. His eyes followed her every movement as she released the snap on her pants. She wiggled out of them and her lacy pink underwear. "We don't have to make love. I just want to hold you."

"Hell with that!" he said, practically ripping off his clothes. He scooted back on the bed and opened his arms to her. The minute her naked body lay against his, part of his soul released the tension that had been inside of him. He remembered the moment in space, when he wasn't sure whether or not he was going to make it. He hadn't wanted to be another piece of space junk floating around the Earth, making her hate the stars because they were separated forever. His eyes filled with tears as emotion squeezed his chest.

She hugged him tightly. She didn't say a word as his tears fell on her. Kimberly just held on to him.

When the feelings were spent, he wiped his eyes with the back of his hand and then pulled her up so her face was even with his. He kissed her, and her response reached into his soul, touching him, filling him up, until the place that had once been empty brimmed with her and their love for each other.

Her hands stroked him, scratching fingernails over his scalp and then down his neck and shoulders. Like a cat, he moved into the touch until her fingers caressed his muscles and moved lower on his chest, tracing the hair line until it reached his shaft. Wrapping around, she held him tenderly and reverently.

His lips sought hers, getting lost in her soft kisses as she stroked him, the firm hold driving him closer to the edge as she stroked from base to top, over and over. When he was close to coming, he broke the kiss, his hands seeking to pleasure her.

One touch showed him that she was wet, ready, and aching for him. He couldn't resist pleasuring her, bringing her to the brink and watching her come. The sounds of her pleasure made him harder, and his body ached with the need to be inside her.

With his hands on her hips, he guided her onto his waiting cock. She sighed as she sank onto him. His body was encased in the most exquisite place, and he never wanted to leave.

Her hands braced on his chest, and she slowly moved, scooting her hips back and forth as she changed her rhythm, pulsing up and down. His hands sought hers. Entwining their fingers, they locked their eyes together as their bodies moved as one. The connection was intense, as if they were inside each other's soul. They climbed the peaks of their excitement until there was nothing left of their desire except pure bliss.

Sated, she laid her body on top of him. Sweat beaded on her back.

He wiped it away with the tips of his fingers, gently, and then pulled a blanket over them.

Will his tenderness ever cease to amaze me? She hoped not as she snuggled against him.

He held her tenderly. This was the woman of his dreams, the one he wanted to be his other half. His gratitude at having found her was boundless. Never, ever was he going to let her go. Kimberly was the only woman he wanted to be with…for the rest of his existence. If they made babies together, they would be beautiful. If not, that was fine too. She was his, and soon, he was going to put a ring on that gorgeous finger of hers.

Closing his eyes, he lost himself in her, in them, and the possibilities of a life together.

He slept for seventeen hours straight. After that, he couldn't wait to be on his feet. Kimberly must have been out working. She wasn't in the room, and a trail of towels led to the bathroom.

Wandering around the room wasn't very thrilling for him, so he showered, dressed, and grabbed a protein bar before making his way to the R & D Center. The hallways were fairly empty, since the mission was complete and the facility had gone back to business as usual. He wasn't sure what that was precisely, though it obviously involved space, but he looked forward to finding out more about their daily workings.

Using his ID, he let himself in a large door. It was the R & D Center, and blissfully, it was empty. He explored the room, discovered some great hardware and tools in the supply corner, and put himself to work building something special. Not being an engineer wasn't hampering him too much as he put the finishing touches on his special gift. In his opinion, he had done a fairly decent design job, and he could hardly wait to surprise Kimberly with it.

"Captain, Dr. Warren is paging you," Sally said.

"Tell her to meet me on the roof. I'm on my way."

"Affirmative."

Bennett took his invention and headed out the door. He made his way down the hallway and up to the roof. His feet crunched on small pieces of gravel strewn here and there.

He could see her standing in the distance and framed by the view. She looked like a painting, a cross between a Renoir and a Kinkade. The image would be burned in his brain for eternity.

The sky was pink and blue with white-hot outlines surrounding some of the clouds, and he knew the colors came from the sun setting over the Pacific Ocean. This moment would be even better if he could stand on his favorite beach, just below the new Silver Strand Training Center. With the waves crashing and the scent of the salt water—well, he would remember this moment too.

He picked up his pace, rushing to her. He needed to hold her, touch her, and fill his senses with her. He gathered her up in his arms and kissed her.

"Bennett. Isn't the sunset beautiful?"

"You are more gorgeous than anything," he said. She smiled up at him.

With the puffy clouds of blue and pink sweeping the sky and the smell of aviation fuel and pine trees perfuming the breeze, he smiled back at her and got down on one knee. He took her hand in his and swallowed the lump of emotion rising in his throat. Withdrawing a thick metal ring from his pocket, he said, "Will you marry me, Kimberly?"

Her mouth dropped open, and her face was a mask of shock. "Yes," she said as her body shook with excitement. "Yes. I will. Oh, my God, yes."

Pushing the ring—comprising platinum, twenty-four-karat gold, copper, and silver wires wound together in an intricate pattern—onto her finger, he kissed her finger and the palm of her hand. He stood, pulling her into his arms. "I love you, Kimberly. Each wire represents something different that we share—our respect for one another's lives and dreams, our enduring love, our dedication to happiness, and finally, our future entwined with whatever that will hold."

"It's wonderful! Did you make it?"

"Yes, in the R & D Center."

"I love it, Bennett, and I love you." Her voice was filled with emotion, and he kissed away the tears that dotted her cheeks. "Thank you," she said. Her fingers played with the ring as she spun it, traced the patterns, and held it tight. He loved watching her do it.

They lay down on the roof and gazed up at the sky. He held her close, and they were both finally still as they watched the darkness descend. They pointed at the first few stars as they appeared, and then—as if someone had turned on a switch—the sky was bright and full of them.

The sounds of nighttime surrounded them…crickets and frogs and the occasional hoot of an owl. The wind rustled the pine trees, releasing their scent in greater waves as the night air grew colder. He wrapped her even tighter against him, shifting his body to the side so he blocked the wind and their shared body warmth grew.

"Well, my love," he said. "Do you want to hear a story…the one I will tell our children one day? That is, if you want them?"

"Yes." She sighed. "As many as we can."

"Good, because I think I forgot a condom earlier this morning."

She smiled and then waved her hand in front of him. "Tell me the story."

"Fine," said Bennett. "One day, I received a call from Admiral Ouster. Now, I didn't pick up on the first ring, because I was dozing on the beach after a strenuous event. Well, that phone call brought me to the Lester Facility, where I met you…"

Chapter 15

Visiting the Commander-in-Chief at the White House was an occasion that had several surreal qualities to it, beginning with an embossed invitation and ending with a flight on a private jet from San Diego to Washington, DC. They went through the giant gate, took a walking tour of the gorgeous gardens, and then passed through the building's many metal detectors before they even made it inside.

This would be an overwhelming experience for anyone, let alone a sailor who had played astronaut and crashed a shuttle in the ocean. It might have been easier in a Tommy Bahama silk shirt, pair of shorts, and running shoes rather than in his dress whites.

He fingered the new platinum band on his ring finger. They'd visited the Justice of the Peace the day after the proposal and tied the knot, just the two of them. It was perfect. They were planning a party a couple of months from now—nothing garish, just a few kegs, a bunch of SEALs and Frogmen, and some scientists. It was destined to be a helluva party.

Of course it didn't stop his lady from being the belle of the ball. She wore a long, blue silk dress, and as usual she was perfect. She was as calm as a cucumber during this White House visit, as if this were something she did every day, providing pleasantries and appreciative comments about the decor, the tour, the dishes, and the kindness of the staff.

Who needs a whole room for dishes? He supposed if he had that many historical ones, he'd probably have a dedicated room too. Maybe he'd do that with his favorite weapons. Boy, Bennett loved those. He had collected a ton of them from his travels over the years. He could dedicate a whole room to just knives and another to swords.

He had to admit he was a little unnerved by the visit. The day sped by at lightning speed, halting at a point where the exhaustion from his injuries threatened to overtake him. That was another first for him. He had hiked his way out of Syria on an Op that had gone sideways—almost two weeks humping with his Team until they could safely get a hop—and still he had never been this tired. The Lester Facility Medical Group had told him that his body would need a few more weeks, or even possibly a month, before it was back to its normal energy level.

"Are you okay?" Kimberly whispered. There was a three-carat diamond ring set in platinum next to the wire ring that he had made. Kimberly had insisted she keep the wedding ring. The materials from R & D were top grade. He was flattered, and he had to admit the rings looked pretty snazzy together.

"Sure," Bennett replied. He was unwilling to give in to exhaustion, but he did lean heavily on Kimberly for a few seconds. He needed a break. To onlookers, it appeared to be a private moment, a shared intimacy between lovers. No one else knew that waves of dizziness might bring him to his knees at any second, an embarrassment that he would *not* allow to happen. Seriously, he told himself, that wouldn't do when one was standing in the White House surrounded by Secret

Service and the top echelon of government, as well as the Leader of the Free World. *Stand tall and smile*.

Kimberly squeezed his arm. She smiled encouragingly at him.

The starch in his dress whites scratched his neck. Of course Kimberly was over the moon about his duds, but what lady didn't like a man in uniform? On the other hand, what he was always thinking was how fast they could both get naked! Of course, they'd both have to wait until their White House visit was over.

He gently touched his earlobe. The bursting of his eardrum hadn't quite healed properly, and the ambient sounds were like a radio tuner set to static. His balance was often affected, and he had four crushed disks in his neck and back. Neither of them would admit his fatigue in public, but after a full day of shaking hands and playing nice with everyone and their brother, mother, and wife, all Bennett wanted to do was to crawl into bed beside Kimberly and make gentle love. His appreciation for her went far beyond the physical connection, though. It had begun with interest and intrigue and morphed in friendship and joy, and from there he had fallen hopelessly and completely in love with her.

In the past, he'd thought a relationship with the opposite sex had to do with time in the sack and tolerating each other's idiosyncrasies. Kimberly had opened his eyes to the truth. A real connection grows out of similar interests, goals, and the enjoyment of friendship with someone you just can't wait to spend time with, with whom you have a mental and emotional link that far outweighs any other consideration. Making love to your best friend, a woman to whom you are committed as a lifelong swim buddy, is frosting on the cake.

He had to admit it was a plus that her body fit perfectly under the crook of his arm, melding to his as though they had been made for each other. Perhaps there was something to the concept of one fitting perfectly with another, like a hand in a glove. His past beliefs had dictated that a person makes their own luck and success in life, and now he knew that sometimes life itself throws you wondrous curve balls. He looked at the lady next to him. Damn, he looked forward to spending a lifetime with her and to fielding more of those, ah, curves.

"Husband, that Agent is signaling you," she whispered.

His head snapped up, sending pain through his shoulders and arms. He focused on the Director of the Secret Service. He nodded at the man and watched him approach.

"Captain Sheraton, before you and your wife depart, there's a visitor who would like a word. If you'll follow me." It wasn't a request. As the highest law-enforcement group in the country, which reports directly to the Commander-in-Chief, this was an order an active duty Navy man could *not* refuse.

Bennett took Kimberly's hand, and they followed the man into a small parlor. He smelled wood polish and the fresh roses that decorated the room in small vases along the windowsill, and his nose wrinkled as he held back a sneeze.

Left together, just the two them alone inside the small, pink-and-cream room that contained only four ladies' parlor chairs and several paintings by Turner, Bennett couldn't resist taking advantage of the present opportunity. Sneaking a kiss right here, where the nation's action began, was a romantic fantasy of his. Tugging Kimberly close, he lifted his eyebrow and kissed her with the pent-up energy he'd held in all day. What could he say? He was a red-blooded man.

"Bennett, here?" she teased, blushing.

"I like how your cheeks turn such a becoming shade of red when you're embarrassed." His hands swept down her back and hugged her waist. Being alone had its advantages.

She squirmed against him, not to escape, but rather to fit herself closer to him. "What an incredible day. We met the Commander-in-Chief and the First Lady— very cool. And the tea cakes were so yummy. It's just been…a whirlwind."

"Yes, it has. You've done beautifully. Not that I would expect any less from my lady," he murmured against her lips. "As you would expect your man to per- form well." Brushing tender kisses across her lips, he savored the moment. This was a day he'd keep tucked in his memories.

The door opened abruptly behind them. Someone cleared his throat. "Excuse me."

Bennett dropped his hand as his eyes widened, and he thrust Kimberly an arm's length away from him. He was greeted by not only Admiral Ouster, but also the Secretary of the Navy, Samuel King. It was his turn to be embar- rassed. Here in person—*the* Navy Sailor—King was a legend for his decisive strategies and absolute loyalty to his sailors and the rest of the troops. He proved he cared about the Armed Forces every day he served in this office. Quite frankly, Bennett would follow the legend anywhere.

Bennett saluted SECNAV, standing at extreme and

absolute attention. This man was the person in charge of
the whole fucking Navy. In his opinion, SECNAV, as a
Medal of Honor recipient, ranked even higher than the
Commander-in-Chief, regardless of who was in office
or what party ruled. It was SECNAV's war record that
blew Bennett's mind.

"At ease, sailor," replied SECNAV with an amused
expression on his face. He shook hands with Kimberly
next and then kissed her cheek. He gestured at the chairs.
"Please have a seat."

The four of them sat in matching pink floral chairs. It
was somewhat comical that they were all sitting in the
dainty and tiny chairs. It made Bennett want to crack a
joke as the big men across from them searched for a way
to get comfortable on the small cushion. He decided to
refrain from opening his mouth, wanting to be respectful
and waiting instead to hear what SECNAV had to say.

SECNAV finally found a comfortable position and
gave his attention to Kimberly. "Dr. Warren—or should
I say Mrs. Sheraton—good to see you again." His smile
was warm and inviting as he reached across the expanse
to squeeze her hand briefly. "How's it going, Kimberly?"

"Richard, it's a pleasure. How are Christy and the
kids?" Kimberly smiled, obviously more familiar with
SECNAV and his family than Bennett ever knew. "And
my namesake, how is she faring?"

"Everyone's good. Thanks. I just can't believe we're
parents again at our age. She's a pistol, our Kimberly—
just like you. What a set of lungs on her!"

"Well, I look forward to a visit. Why not hop over to
the Lester Facility with the whole family? You can get
a hands-on experience. I'm sure everyone would love

it." Kimberly laughed. "I'll put Quincy through some astronaut training."

"He'd be over the moon for training and a visit. That reminds me. Quincy said that he would like to contact you about his report on futuristic vehicles designed for daily use. Do you have time next week for a chat via Skype or FaceTime?" SECNAV leaned forward, his elbows on his knees and his face relaxed. "Christy would yell from here to Texas if I didn't ask for your assistance. I'll get her to check the schedules and set up a time to visit the Lester Facility. Boy, does she have a lot to say about babies and teens right now! She's been holding off on phone calls until your schedule, uh, settles down. Personally, I'd like to send her on a two-week vacation, but our kids might eat me alive without her."

Kimberly laughed. "Great. I look forward to it."

When had his honey become so familiar with SECNAV? Obviously they had been friends for a long time. Bennett had never seen the man act like this. It was good to know he was human and normal, having real relationships and issues like everyone else. He was proud of Kimberly too. How could he not appreciate a brainy, beautiful, and vivacious woman like her? Honestly, she blew his mind, and he was grateful to be spending the rest of his life right beside her.

"Of course! Any time is great with us. Just give me some warning, in case I'm out flying my CarP." She smiled. "I'm sorry, I'm hogging the conversation. We're here for Bennett."

All eyes shifted to him. Bennett stilled. Being in the hot seat was never a comfortable position for him. The shadows were much more to his liking. It was one of the many reasons he was a SEAL, because he enjoyed serving on a Team and being out of the limelight. Every action was for his country—well, except for loving Kimberly. That was definitely *all* for him. "Sir," he said.

"Thank you for taking the time to meet with me and Admiral Ouster," began SECNAV, his tone more formal. "As you know, we are very grateful for the positive outcome of your mission, and I'm sure you understand the need to continue to keep the entire event covert. I don't know if you were aware at the time, but the hub you placed in geosynchronous orbit also collects data. At the poles, the ozone layer has cleared significantly since the debris was removed. Seems the trash was reflecting light and eroding our atmosphere, which is now resolving quite well. You did a lot of good up there."

SECNAV glanced at Ouster. "I know you have places to go and things to do, so to the bottom line. I know you have a year and half left on your current contract with the Navy. In truth, you could probably spend it all getting your body back up to speed."

The muscle in Bennett's jaw ticked. What was SECNAV getting at? They weren't kicking him out for medical after this last mission. Damn, that would be a shame.

"We know your dedication has been stalwart, and we would like to honor your service with either full retirement benefits now, or you can spend the rest of your allotted time assigned to Dr. Warren's space-shuttle project at the rank of Rear Admiral. That's a one-star, as you'll have to earn the two, and you can help her develop the next generation of returnable shuttles like the X-37B space plane." SECNAV shifted in his small floral chair. "If you decide to take us up on the offer of working with Dr. Warren, we'd like to sign you up through the thirty-year mark. Do you need time to consider your options, Sheraton?"

"No, sir." Bennett was thrilled. He was going to make rank, from Captain to Rear Admiral. He glanced at Kimberly. Her hands were folded in her lap as if she were saying a prayer. "Count me in for thirty."

Ouster piped in. "I'll handle the details." The happiness on his face was evident as he looked at Bennett, sort of like a father looking at his child. He beamed that same way at Kimberly.

"Good man. Good, good." SECNAV stood, and everyone mirrored his action. "I will add another medal to your already outstanding record, Sheraton, but none of the, uh, current details of this mission will be listed." He held out his hand.

Bennett took it, and with a firm hold he shook it. "I understand, sir. Thank you."

"You have our eternal gratitude for your service and sacrifice, and if there's anything I can do to assist you in the future, please let me know. I believe Dr. Warren has me on speed dial, and my wife too." SECNAV released Bennett's hand, smiled at Kimberly, and departed with Ouster.

As the door closed behind them, Bennett pulled Kimberly back into his arms. "How well do you know them?" asked Bennett, curious.

"I helped Christy with her thesis. We're very good friends." She wrapped her arms around his neck. "Jealous?"

"Nope. I'm in awe of you. It's a good thing. Keeps me on my toes. Now, where were we?" He snuck one more quick kiss and then a long tender one before they left the room. All in all, the day had been incredible. How could anyone have had a more inspiring experience? He linked his hand with hers, and they walked through the iconic and historic halls. As they made their way toward the exit, he knew that this day was one that would live on as epic.

Absolute silence, peace, and harmony awaited them. Kimberly was ready for some downtime. Her cheeks hurt from smiling so much, and she rubbed her cheekbones as Bennett keyed open their hotel-room door.

With the Secret Service's assistance, they'd arrived here in record time. Both she and Bennett were prepared to do precisely what both of them had been fantasizing about—getting naked and being alone with each other.

A pale glow came from the lamp beside the couch. She could see directly into the bedroom, and the turndown service had left chocolate mints on their pillows. Bennett locked the door as she took a complimentary bottle of water and drank half of it. She lowered it to the coffee table, and he snagged the bottle. He finished it and tossed the empty container into the recycle bin.

"I can tell that nothing will go to waste around you. Every meal will be finished…" she began.

"…and every drink consumed." He paused and kissed her shoulder.

She smiled. She liked it. With Bennett in her life, her world felt complete now, as if this was how things were meant to be.

Kimberly scanned the room: it was plush, a large suite with a living room. The green floral pattern on the walls and matching cream furniture with pops of bright color were busy and overdone, but as she snapped on a light, she noticed the soft warmth the overall color scheme provided for the room. It inspired comfort.

Much better at night, she thought.

She took off her shoes, grateful to be out of her heels, and wiggled her toes in the thick cream carpet. No one woman should be asked to wear those torture devices for more than two hours at a time, and after eight on her feet, she was past due for a foot rub. Looking at Bennett, she was pretty sure she could talk her way into one. She dropped her purse on the overstuffed chair nearest the bedroom and guided him to the identical chair to the right of hers and eased him into it.

Without a word, she untied his shoes and pulled off his socks. She had been playing nursemaid and loved it. Also, the best way to communicate was by doing to him what she loved herself, so she rubbed his feet and watched his eyes drift shut. His breathing relaxed and she smiled to herself.

As her fingers tired, she moved away, unwilling to disturb him. His hand snaked out, secured her forearm, and hauled her onto his lap. She shrieked. "Damn those SEAL reflexes."

He smiled as his eyes opened and he kissed her. "Yep. I'm tricky. You better watch me."

"Fine." She laughed, pulling him to his feet. "I'll watch you like a hawk, and I'll have my way with you too."

"I'm yours. Do with me what you will." He spread his arms wide.

Kimberly liked the control. She pushed the buttons slowly through the holes, releasing him from his jacket.

She pulled off his cotton T-shirt, running her hands over his muscled torso and avoiding the many bruises. She slowly kissed her way down the center of his body until she reached his belt. Her fingers worked quickly, releasing it and pulling his pants off. "Tighty-whities. I'll never get used to you wearing them," she said.

"Me neither. Only in uniform. Don't want to share the family jewels with the whole world." He chuckled.

"Shall I proceed, husband?" she asked, cupping his buttocks and giving the muscled orbs a squeeze.

"Aye, aye, wife. Though in Navy life, the significant other always outranks her husband. So let's just put it this way." His eyes held hers, the emotion weighty and dark in them. "I trust you…with my heart, my body, and my life."

Her eyes filled with happy tears. Never in a million years would she have imagined she'd find a man like Bennett. His tenderness was incredible, and the way he honored her with his actions and his attention had made indelible marks on her heart and soul. She kissed him with the wealth of her adoration. "I love you, Bennett."

"I love you," he replied, holding her close. His scent enveloped her, and she had never felt safer, happier, or more at peace in her entire life. Maybe this is what her mother had meant when she said, "Reach for the stars." In other words, "Go for all those dreams you have, and never stop until you attain them."

"Thank you for helping me…make my goals into a reality. I never got to say that to you before." Her gaze held his. She loved him more than she had words to express. In large part, he had been responsible for saving not only the world, but also her own dreams. If he hadn't been so dedicated, she didn't know if the mission would have happened.

"It's been an honor," Bennett said, "and thanks for choosing me for the flight."

She kissed the corners of those beautiful thick lips before she placed one in the center. "Was there ever a doubt? Please!"

"Nope." Despite his injuries, he lifted her into his arms. Well, at least his ego was intact, among other things. She laughed.

"Bennett! You're hurt! Put me down," she protested.

"Kimberly," he said. "I'm healing, and you're the one saving me, Doc." He laid her gently on the bed and lowered himself beside her. "I look forward to spending eternity with you, one moment at a time."

Her hands stroked his cheek, his chin, and then settled on his chest. "Forever, Bennett."

He kissed her, and she was lost in their world. Their bodies twined together, fitting as if Rodin had carved them from stone. As her nails gently scraped down his back and he hummed delightedly in her ear, he added, "Never, never, never quit. For SEALs, it's all about... love, courage, and innovation."

"It's in your spirit, this warrior's heart. You, with your soul of a SEAL, have changed my life. I love you."

He said, "And I love you. With all my heart, and in ways I never believed possible. It humbles me."

"I trust you with my head, my heart, and, well, all of me." She smiled, her eyebrows framing the naughty glint in her eyes. "So let me share my wildest fantasy." With that, she pushed him onto his back, ready to have her very wicked way with him. Bennett "Boss" Sheraton was hers—her beau, her love, and always, her star man—and they would be linked together forever.

Author's Note

Research for this book was an absolute delight! My husband and I have always been fascinated by the stars, so when it came time to write another book for the West Coast Navy SEAL series, I approached my editor with the idea of honoring both the space program and our Frogmen/SEALs. I revealed the history of Navy Frogmen (UDT—Underwater Demolition Teams) and SEAL Team and their unique relationship with the space program. This was a captivating and effective union that saved many lives and served many functions. Listed below are some of my favorite notes and reference materials.

1. History of Navy Frogman and SEALs in reference to the astronaut program—from the National Navy UDT-SEAL Museum website:

> Underwater Demolition Team (UDT) frogmen, precursors to the Navy SEALs, played a key role in the Gemini and Apollo space missions. It was the job of the Navy frogmen to leap into the water from a helicopter to recover space capsules that had just ended a fiery thousand-mile-an-hour drop from space to splashdown in the ocean. The frogmen have reported the capsules were still steaming when they swam up to them. https://www.navysealmuseum.org/home-to-artifacts

-from-the-secret-world-of-naval-special-warfare/
navy-seals-udt-frogmen-and-the-space-program

Among those brave men were some good friends
of ours: Navy SEAL Jerry Todd and Corpsman Greg
McPartlin.

2. The pool scene in my book is a nod to Navy SEAL
Chris Cassidy, who truly did rescue another astronaut.
(I used a rescue diver instead, because I didn't want to
overshadow what an amazing thing Cassidy had done.)
You can read about it in more detail on NavySEAL.com.
Cassidy also did two space walks, was in space for over
180 days, and was the second SEAL to visit space, the
first being William Shepherd.

3. William Shepherd was a Frogman and SEAL,
having served in UDT 11 and SEAL Teams ONE and
TWO, and spent more than 159 days in space. He was
part of the first crew on the International Space Station
and served as the first adviser (in science) to the U.S.
Special Operations Command.

For more information, check out NavySEAL.com and
Michael P. Wood's book *U.S. Navy SEALs in San Diego*,
and visit the National Navy UDT-SEAL Museum in
Fort Pierce, Florida.

Additional Resources (and Fascinating Information on the Topic)

Arstechnica.com, August 3, 2015. "NASA Is Crash-Testing Cessnas So We Can Find More Planes When They Do Crash." http://arstechnica.com/science/2015/08/nasa-is-crash-testing-cessnas-so-we-can-find-more-planes-when-they-do-crash/.

Astronomy Magazine, April 29, 2015. "Astronomers Discover Three Super-Earths Orbiting Nearby Star."

CBSNews.com, July 30, 2015. "NASA Crashes Planes to Save Lives." www.cbsnews.com/news/nasa-tests-emergency-locator-transmitters-small-plane-crashes/.

NASA.gov, release 09-239. "NASA Portable Hyperbaric Chamber Technology Finds Home on Earth."

News.com.au, April 05, 2012. "Orfield Laboratories' Anechoic Chamber Is the World's Quietest Place."

Phys.org, July 30, 2015. "Astronomers Find Star with Three Super-Earths." http://phys.org/news/2015-07-astronomers-star-super-earths.html.

Spaceline.org: Dedicated to Covering the Past, Present, and Future of Cape Canaveral.

United Nations Office for Outer Space Affairs, "Outer Space Treaty." www.unoosa.org/oosa/en/ourwork/spacelaw/treaties/introouterspacetreaty.html.

United States Strategic Command. www.stratcom.mil.

Acknowledgments

With great thanks to:

My cherished husband—retired Navy SEAL, EOD, and PRU Adviser—Carl Swepston; the outstanding retired Navy SEAL Thomas Rancich and his remarkable Liz; the incredible Rear Admiral and #1 Bullfrog Dick Lyon and his fabulous wife Cindy; old goat roper John T. Curtis and his marvelous Miranda; inspiring retired Navy SEAL Moki Martin and his family; Greg McPartlin, Navy Corpsman and the owner of McP's and his family; former Navy SEAL Hal Kuykendall and his lovely wife Denise; retired Navy SEAL Jerry Todd and his terrific Pete; Frank Toms (UDT 11/ST1) and his wonderful family; our dear friend Medal of Honor Recipient John Baca; Medal of Honor Recipient Mike Thornton; the Vietnam Era "Old Frogs & SEALs" who contributed comments and stories; and *HOOYAH!* to all of our operational friends.

To D. C. and Charles DeVane, for the rocket scientist and his lady love—thank you for everything, especially for being such outstanding friends!

To Suzanne Brockmann and Christine Feehan—thank you for being such great inspirations!

To Marjorie Liu—for brilliant insights!

To Joanne Fluke and John Fluke—wonderfully talented souls!

To Cathy Maxwell and Kim Adams Lowe—*HOOYAH!*